BROWN SUGAR THIS CHRISTMAS

BOOK 1 OF SAG HARBOR BLACK ROMANCES

LULA WHITE

A huge thanks to my writing partners and mentors, who kept me going, gave honest feedback, and encouraged me:

Sable Jordan
Merri Mayweather
Annette Noble
Rosie Meleady

And of course, my crazy and incredible husband.

THE SAG HARBOR COMMUNITY OF BLACK HAMPTONS

Books In The *Sag Harbor Black Romances*

Brown Sugar This Christmas - Maddy & Jerrell

Hot Chocolate This Winter - Chrissy & Sheldon Part 1

Flinging All Spring - Adella & Desmond

Overheated for Summer - Chrissy & Sheldon Part 2

Rouse Family Christmas - All Couples

Books in the Sag Harbor spin-off *Explore Men of the Hamptons* series

Explore You - Kevin & Cher

One Tasty Night - Solomon & Chaitra

Taste You - Solomon & Chaitra

Drink You - Lion & Kamila

See Through You - Keenan & Eugenia

Find You - Roland & Neeraja

The Sag Harbor world includes two book series- nine books and three novellas.

The events do not occur based on order of the books. Here's the order in which to get acquainted with this world:

Brown Sugar This Christmas

Hot Chocolate This Winter

Flinging All Spring

Overheated for Summer

One Tasty Night

Explore You

Rouse Family Christmas

Christmas Down Under (Newsletter only)

Taste You

Drink You

See Through You

Find You

It all started with 3 childhood friends
Books 1-4

Maddy

Chrissy

Adella

The Old Hamptons Money

ELLIS/PAGE BLOODLINE

Maddy marries Jerrell
William
Marguerite

TOWNSEND COUSINS

Chrissy marries Sheldon
Cher marries Kevin
Neeraja marries Roland

ENGLISH FAMILY

Solomon marries Chaitra
Lonnie
Constance
Rachel
Martin
Adella marries Desmond
Ilyana

MIDDLETON SONS

Lion marries Kamila
Brendan
Kevin marries Cher

These Black families have thrived in New York since 1700s & 1800s.

The English family arrived in the 1970s & 80s during the real estate boom.

Explore Adventures is created by Keenan, Solomon, & Kevin

New Hamptons Money, Books 5-12

ROUSE FAMILY

Roland marries Neeraja
Sheldon married Chrissy
(ex-wife is Eugenia)
Etta
Kamila marries Lion
Jerrell marries Maddy

These Black families arrived in New York after 2000.

MCLAIN FAMILY

Chaitra marries Solomon
Desmond married Adella
Keenan loves Eugenia

www.lulawhitebooks.com

email: lula@lulawhitebooks.com

www.blackluxuryromances.com

Hey Loves, I have a playlist for all books in the series. These are the songs I listened to while writing this story, and am sharing with you if you want some feels with that holiday warmth. In my Loves Letter and on my web site, I'll share which songs go with which scene.

On Spotify it's free to set up an account and listen. If you're reading the paperback version of this, you can just go to Spotify and search by the book's name.

Brown Sugar This Christmas on Spotify

NOT SORRY

MADDY

A frustrated Maddy pressed her eyes closed, cupping her cell phone to her ear.

"No, Mama, I mean it. Promise. Or I'll go to Jackson Hole instead," Maddy whispered while hovering in a corridor of the Dirksen Senate Office Building on Capitol Hill.

"Girl, I'm not promising you anything! You get your butt on that train and get up here. It's been long enough. Stop acting like you're two."

Maddy's dread rolled around in her chest like marbles.

"Mama."

"Maddy."

Madison Page scoffed. As always, they wound up in some kind of standoff.

All she had to do was say, *No, I can't go back to Sag Harbor yet.*

It was still too painful.

"I have to go. I have a meeting in ten."

"You said yesterday that your schedule for today was light.

Now there's a meeting?" her mother asked, calling her on her bullshit.

Maddy rolled her eyes, thinking fast to worm her way off the phone.

"The Senator took a last-minute constituent meeting. I need to make sure he's ready."

Okay, so it was a lie. Maddy's Senator and boss had already left Capitol Hill for Christmas with his family.

The thought of returning to the Hamptons squeezed her chest like a rope tying up her lungs. This time, her GeeGee wouldn't be there.

She could be in Wyoming with her sorority sisters by morning—gorgeous snow, tranquil sunrises, and none of her grandmother's scents or trinkets. She had already spent thirty-one Christmases with her family. What difference did it make to miss one?

Her mother continued, "The Madames want you to judge the debutante competition, and the debutantes would be excited if you came back. I'm bringing your old debutante dress and crown. With your figure, you can still wear anything. A few of your running buddies are coming. Adella, Chriselle. It'll be just like old times. Hayrides, horses—"

Maddy held firm.

"Mama, promise me. *No* blind dates. No 'incidental' meetings."

She loved her mother dearly, but the woman did not understand how fed-up Maddy was with disastrous fix-ups. And the resulting humiliation when it didn't work out. All because her mom thought her friends' sons looked good on paper.

"Fine. I promise. Now will you please come and be with your poor parents for Christmas?"

"And I am bringing work with me, so I can't attend every activity."

Maddy had too much riding on her next couple of committee hearings. It would mean the difference between being laid off if the Senator didn't win re-election and being elevated to the State Department or even the White House.

Her mother sighed. "Alright. I won't interfere when you need to work."

Maddy finally shut off the phone, hoping she wasn't making a mistake.

"Bossy ass mama, huh, girl?" a familiar voice popped up.

Maddy's fellow staffer Lana Gilley appeared at Maddy's desk, wearing her usual sly smirk as if she had more to say but was kindly holding back.

Maddy laughed. "I was that loud, huh?"

Lana shrugged. "No. I was coming down here to see what you decided for Christmas, caught some of it in the hallway."

"Girl, you don't know the half," Maddy quipped.

"And damn glad I don't." Lana looked around the office at the other staff for the Senate Foreign Relations Committee, and asked in her native Texas accent, "Y'all are still on the clock?"

"This whole trade situation is hitting us hard. I have a memo due to the Senator the Monday after Christmas."

"Oof," Lana said with a painful face. "Hit me up when you get off and we'll grab a drink. You can relax before you go to see Mama."

A light turned on in Maddy's head.

"Come with me," she suggested.

She could use a friend to pull her away from her mother's side in a pinch.

"What?" Lana's face wrinkled. "Country ass me from

Texas? Girl, I'll have all of you big-money Hamptons negroes in there sucking down neckbones, pig ears and fat back. For real though, your mother might not like me. I don't come home by curfew." She sucked her teeth and winked. "I'd find me some Hamptons honeys to wax my boat."

Maddy perked up. "It's perfect. You can steal me away when Mama works my nerves."

What harm could Lana do?

The Texan slid her hands over herself, eyes lighting up, tongue poking through her burgundy matted Mac lipstick. "Sag Harbor, huh? Chocolate men with money? Alrighty then, let me go and… conduct independent research."

Maddy snorted. With feisty Lana around, Maddy might not hear so many awkward remarks of "whatever happened to" or "how come you didn't marry" or "wow, I'm so sorry about that." Lana's sharp-witted comebacks might keep people's noses out of her business.

At five o'clock, the Staff Director finally released them all, issuing a stern warning to have briefs ready, work cell phones on over the weekend, and laptops on hand for remote committee calls if the Senator needed.

"United States affairs never go on holiday, folks," the Staff Director admonished. "Say, Maddy?"

"Yeah?" she asked, her laptop and work phone already shoved in her bag.

"That South America hearing right after New Year's is a big deal. Senator's excited about that last briefing pack you delivered. You'll be running lead for that hearing, so don't let us down. He might email you over the break for briefing materials. I know you're taking a little time off, but stay alert. Bring your A game."

An elated smile lifted the marbles in her chest, at hearing this news. "Of course, Mike. I'm on it."

Within sixty seconds, Maddy's patent leather Christian Louboutin's were flying down the one hundred-and thirteen-year-old marble steps of the Dirksen Senate Office Building when a voice called out for her.

"Maddy! What's happening for this weekend?"

She grimaced. Sherman. Her convenient sex buddy.

He did a jog to catch up to her. "I can come and pick you up for dinner. *McClendon's*? A little dancing after? And then head to my place? I even bought some of those candles you like."

She paused on the gold-rimmed stairs. She should've told him the truth, that there was no way they would ever be serious. But his tongue was too convenient. And she had no other alternative lined up to relieve tension.

"Actually, I'm headed North to my family. Let's do a rain check. Hope you have a fun weekend."

"I can take you to the train. It gives me time to eat up those pretty brown eyes."

Maddy cringed. "I already have a ride. We'll hang out when I get back? Enjoy your Christmas."

Dismissing him with a wave, she pushed through the heavy, gold-embellished glass. She still needed her hands and feet done before the salon closed, to get a hair blowout, go home and pack, and then wake up in the wee hours for Union Station.

Foggy Bottom coastal air splashed her face. Flanked by the United States Supreme Court three blocks away, the U.S. Capitol, and sandstone-brick government buildings, she threw on her shades, tightening her Burberry camel-hair coat against the forty-degree cold. Though she was born in

Virginia Beach, and summered in the Hamptons, it was Capitol Hill's DNA that ran in Maddy's blood.

The next morning, her heart pounded as she and Lana departed Union Station on the 5:15 a.m. train to Grand Central Station in New York City.

Downing her mimosas on the ride, Maddy tried to drown her nervousness about returning to her family's ancestral vacation home. Who would she see? What would be said? Would she run into her old crush? The Christmas lights in her chest tangled around each other at the thought of seeing Kevin Middleton again. She prayed he was overseas somewhere, and nowhere near New York.

That afternoon, she finally drove a rental car onto Eastville Avenue, the Black section of Sag Harbor.

Salty, unforgiving winter air slapped her face immediately, whipping her well-coifed hair out of place. It felt like her grandmother's spirit was admonishing her for taking so long to return.

"Well, ain't this cute," Lana noted.

The Texan's eyes studied the humble clapboard houses situated in quiet, all-American wealth—flags waving outside wooden shingles, on wide porches, next to tall, chocolate Nutcracker statues that flanked regal glass and wrought iron doors. Black Santa Clauses stood watch over sprawling displays, including a manger and a Candy Cane forest.

Maddy's heart opened like the windows of her childhood playmates' houses.

The light blue clapboard house her family had owned for four generations stared back at her. She said a silent prayer that her grandmother would send her the strength to get through these next few days with no drama.

"Girl, you got this. I'm here with the jokes and shenanigans, and plenty of liquor in my bag for you to pour in your 'hot chocolate'," Lana muttered with a snicker.

The front door flung open.

"Maddy Marie, is that you?" A curvaceous, thick-hipped lady came down the front steps.

Maddy strained for a moment. "Chrissy? Oh, my God." She looked a lot different from when they'd last seen each other three years before in L.A.

She rushed to hug her childhood running buddy.

Soon as she moved, Maddy's four-inch heel twisted inside an unexpected snare. While trying to yank away, instead, she slammed onto the concrete sidewalk.

Immediately, the rough fall transported Maddy back to being age eleven again, back on the pavement, blood from her forehead staining the sidewalk. And a boy's ugly laugh cackling in her pubescent memories.

"Oh, shit, girl, that sounded pretty bad. You alright?" Lana asked, cutting into Maddy's flashback.

Oh, damn!" a thick male voice said behind them, "You good? I thought you saw them!"

Still on her hands and knees, Maddy felt wet tongues licking and nipping her face.

Maddy tried to push herself up.

"Dude, get those things off of her!" Chrissy cried.

"I'm trying! They're not..."

A web of long leashes twisted and pulled, wrapping Maddy inside a canine cage. Overwhelmed, she found herself trapped among a pack of high-energy dogs. All several sizes, jumping on her.

The rich male voice fretted.

"You need me to help you up? Hold on. These dogs... I thought I had them under control. They're not mine."

A dog-walker who couldn't walk dogs.

Great.

Chrissy and Lana helped her fend off the pets, and Maddy inspected herself. Her fresh gel job was scuffed up, black marks stretching across three nails she'd used to break her fall. Her jeans had a small hole.

Ugh.

This was definitely a sign.

"Well, apparently, they weren't under control," she snapped, frustrated and silently cursing herself for being here. "I haven't heard you apologize yet."

"Sorry? For what? It was an accident. Not my fault," the stranger retorted.

Maddy still hadn't bothered to give the man the blessing of her eye contact.

"Are you blind?" Maddy shot back as she brushed herself off with Chrissy's help. "You didn't see somebody was standing here? Maybe you should have, I don't know, done something that made sense, like take them around on the street?"

The dog-walker huffed. "Ha! I had just as much right to be on the sidewalk as you did. But I am sorry you weren't paying attention."

The dogs kept jumping on her, dirtying her jeans with wet, soggy sand clumps.

"Can you move somewhere else with them and be on your way?" Chrissy insisted.

But Lana chuckled. "I think they found themselves a new girlfriend."

"It might be your scent. It's kind of fruity," the male noted.

Maddy had asked her grandmother for a smooth holiday, and even from heaven, that snarky old lady had jokes. This trip had disaster written all over it. Maddy could have been on the slopes right now with her sorors.

"Don't worry about it. Maybe you should find another line of work."

"Well, actually, this is not my j—"

"Baby! You're here!" Maddy's mother called in a sing-song voice. "Now the party can get started. Come on in here. I need help with this tree and decorations, and to finish these plates for the crab boil tomorrow night."

Maddy embraced her mom, as Chrissy and Lana started unloading the car.

"You have a nice day and hope your leg is all right, ma'am," came the male voice behind her.

Maddy had already forgotten he stood there. Why hadn't he scurried off? As an afterthought, she finally turned to him.

"Whatever. Forget it. Just get your dogs under…."

At last, she gave him eye contact.

Her tongue froze at the sight of this Christmas ornament —a tall mug of hot cocoa, with a pair of chestnut irises roasting on an open fire of endless syrup-colored skin. Under rolling, jet black waves of hair. The pulse in her chest thumped so rapidly she could no longer feel it.

"Control," she finished.

The Sag Harbor winter breeze froze her hot irritation. Her eyes unwrapped him from head to toe.

He stood embarrassed, somewhat frazzled as the dogs still jumped and lunged. Even under his thick leather jacket, sweater and jeans, she could see his taut arms and delicious physique wrestling with the dogs.

"This was unfortunate," he said while the leashes twisted around him. "Why don't you let me…"

"Let you what?" Maddy inquired, shifting her weight while

she still waited for the apology. She forced her eyes from the smoothness of his lips.

"Buy you a coffee for your… inconvenience," he said, looking at her torn jeans.

But Maddy's jaw dropped. Her Capitol Hill sense of justice wouldn't let this go. "Or you could just say sorry for letting your dogs run out of control."

The handsome stranger's eyes squinted at her, his agitated face throwing hot spice between them. "I'm not sorry for something I didn't mean to do."

She scoffed, rolling her eyes. "Of course. Somebody like you wouldn't be."

"*Somebody like me?* Wh—what is that supposed to—"

Maddy pivoted, turning her back to the dog-walker. She intended to let him know how sorry he *would* be. Walking away, she tried her best to focus, and not trip over herself.

"Merry Christmas and have a nice life, lady," his liquid voice called behind her.

"Just learn how to do your job."

"It's not my j—"

She closed the gate to the fence on him. Her boots kept walking. Thankfully, this jerk didn't look familiar, and she'd never have to see him again.

THE DOG-WALKER

JERRELL

Who does this chick think she is?

Jerrell fumed while wrestling all six of the dogs scurrying around his legs.

What was he even doing out here when he had a business to run? Fulfillments to ensure, deliveries to supervise, and shipments and events to sign off on. His fledgling venture needed him.

Oh, yeah.

He was desperate to make new customers out of these dogs' owners.

"Come on. Let's get you guys back to the firehouse."

Their leashes tripped him as he steered them away from the sidewalks now. Black residents of Sag Harbor looked at him, shaking their heads and chuckling at his predicament while decorating their yards. Meanwhile, his cell phone kept buzzing in his pocket.

Jerrell's eyes dropped to his insistent phone. What could be wrong?

"Diedre, what's up? Deliveries going alright?" he asked, rushing with the leashes and galloping bodies.

As they meandered around fire hydrants, tangled with wrought-iron gates, pulled from four-way intersections, Jerrell still smashed the phone between his shoulder and his ear.

"Rashad is sick," his sympathetic best-friend, who was temping as his store manager, reported from Brooklyn.

Damn. That left Jerrell without someone to deliver throughout the city and drive the freshly baked orders from his shop to Sag Harbor. Another worker had already quit the day before in a refusal to work overtime. "Alright, give me a sec and I'll hit you back."

His finger pressed a single digit for speed dial, as Jerrell called the most reliable person who always came through for him.

"Kami, whew girl, am I glad you picked up!"

Amused laughter rolled into his ear from the other end. "Oh ho ho nooo… don't drag me into it."

"What do you mean? I'm not dragging you into anything," he proclaimed in his most innocent little brother voice, making his way back to the Sag Harbor Firehouse.

"You know exactly what I meant," his older sister said, slurping a drink in his ear. "You, Mama, Daddy. This whole episode where you plan to show them you're Mr. Billy Badass, who doesn't need help, and you'll prove them wrong. Count. Me. Out."

"I wasn't even going to… Kami! How could you?" Jerrell scoffed, faking an insulted tone. "I was just calling to see how your week's been. What are you doing tonight? How's your love life? Has anybody tuned you up lately? Because Rick's been asking."

"Bye, J."

"Okay, alright! I've got a shipment sitting at the store and my delivery driver is sick," he closed his eyes, took a deep breath, praying she didn't make him beg. "Come on, Kam Kam, can you help?"

"You know, you wouldn't need help—and you'd be chilling with your boys courtside at the Knicks right now—if you had just listened to Mama and Daddy. And kept your real job," she said in a sing-song voice.

"Kam, stop tripping. You and me, we are better than that. I really don't need that," he replied, gazing at a Black man entering his driveway with his speedboat in tow.

"What's in it for me?" his sister asked, loudly sucking a beverage in his ear.

"I'll love you forever, and you'll always be my favorite."

"Tickets to the next Beyonce concert, front row."

"Girl, what!" he yelped, wrapping the dogs' leashes around his forearm, and lifting his legs to keep from getting ensnared. "You do know I don't work at Earl Lynch anymore, right? Those corporate hook-ups are gone now, so get real."

"Not my problem. You want your goods or not?" Kami asked. More slurping.

He cut his eyes, quickly assessing other options. Exes to call and butter up. No, not that route. One favor would open a can of worms he didn't have time for now. His boys had left town, or were with families and significant others on holiday. His brother Sheldon and sister Etta were busy working, and there was no way he would call his oldest brother Roland and listen to his fussing. Kami was the only sibling whose schedule allowed her to come and go as she pleased.

"Alright, fine. When can you be here?"

Finally, he entered the Firehouse where bustling senior

women had wrapped up their bridge game, and were standing atop chairs and step ladders, stringing up decorations. Even though he'd only started delivering in Sag Harbor a week earlier, he quickly learned that the Sag Harbor Firehouse was the epicenter of the Hamptons Black community.

"Oh, sonny, how kind of you to help out us gals. I hope our little angels were no problem for you!" Mrs. Emma greeted her collie.

As Jerrell handed each woman their leash, he pasted on what he hoped was his smoothest, most unbothered smile. "No, ma'am. Not at all. Easy as pie."

She tapped his shoulder. "Oh, and speaking of pies. That Pauletta's Sinfully Pecan is sheer heaven. It's already gone!"

Jerrell beamed as the women complimented his grandmother's dessert. The dog-walking fiasco had been worth their smiles. He was almost floating on clouds.

Until he heard three words.

"We want more."

For a moment, he couldn't have been more delirious. His gamble was paying off! But the bright God rays shining on him started to flicker with lightning.

More?

He didn't have enough staff. His grandmother and great aunt were already grinding overtime to bake pies for on-time delivery.

"Um," he stammered, "when do you mean? Next week? On Christmas Day? Christmas Eve? New Year's? What are we talking? And we'll be sure to have it ready for you." He swiped up the app on his phone for processing orders.

Emma's pecan-colored face crinkled into sugary amusement. Her lips spread into a loving grin as if Jerrell belonged to her. It was why he simply couldn't bear telling her he was too busy to walk hers and her friends' dogs. She chuckled and pinched his jaw.

"Tonight, dear. We were hoping you could get us some more of these goodies before the game night tomorrow." She tapped his arm lightly. "That won't be a problem for you, will it?"

Jerrell's oxygen bottomed out of his lungs. "Of course not."

Mrs. Emma was one of the most influential ladies in Black Sag Harbor. The word "no" was not an option.

Never in his wildest dreams had he expected this. Dr. Page, his father's dentist and financial client, had been spot-on in advising him to sell in Sag Harbor. What Jerrell hadn't counted on was getting such a big response so quickly.

So, he called his grandmother, and laid out the situation. They had prepared the weekend pickups and deliveries, but to reserve money and precious foreign ingredients from places like Brazil and France, they did not bake too much stock in advance.

Gram replied, "That Brazilian sugar is a real problem. That's what's giving us the flavor, I've told you." Gram panicked while he heard her mixer running in the background. He could imagine her weathered, eighty-four-year-old arms hoisting up that big bowl of cake batter.

"I know, Gram. I'm on it. Dr. Page says he's introducing me to his daughter this weekend. And hopefully, she can help us with this customs situation. Just hold tight."

"We've only got eleven bags of the pure Brazilian cane left. But at the rate we're going with this sales uptick, we'll have to use beet sugar. The weaker flavor will hurt business, J," she warned. He hated hearing her worry.

He lowered his voice, so the ladies didn't overhear. "I know. I'm doing all I can."

The moment he put the phone down, the Sag Harbor Dears all flashed grins sweet enough to season Jerrell's pastries.

"So are you taking care of us or what, Sonny Boy?" one of them inquired.

"Yeah, we'd hate to call up Bake Factory. We're trying to support you. A young Black man doing a lovely thing. You did tell me that's why you came to Sag Harbor, right? Why Douglass Page invited ya?" Emma asked.

"Of course, it is." He laughed off his nervousness. "I got you. Don't worry." Jerrell beat his brain while wondering exactly how he had it.

"Excellent. Here's what we need," Emma said, handing him a list of *sixteen* items they'd jotted.

He held his breath to keep from hyperventilating as he took it. "No problem."

Heart thumping, feet tripping, he backed toward the door.

On his way to go unravel this predicament, his gaze hit the firehouse wall. It was lined with portraits of Black girls dressed in billowing white gowns, smiling and posing inside a circle of Black elders.

One particular face struck him.

Framed in long waves rippling past her shoulders, her eyes innocent but determined, with her lips curved in a taunting smile. A crown sat fitfully atop her head. It was the girl he'd just sent crashing to the pavement. Her friends had called her "Maddy". He looked at the names under the picture to locate her full name.

Madison Page.

So, this demanding debutante on the sidewalk was a darling in Sag Harbor. Known and respected in this tight-knit community, who'd been coming here for years, and was probably loved and adored among all the people Jerrell needed as customers.

And she was likely uppity as hell, he concluded.

Thankfully, he'd never have to see this chick again.

The last thing he had time for, during the most critical gamble of his life, was another Christian Louboutin-wearing, high society snob who thought her shit didn't stink.

"You got this, Rouse," he muttered to himself under his breath, giving the dear ladies a wave and pushing out of the building.

He spent the next few hours on the phone while waiting for Kami to arrive with the orders, calling top sugar refineries and chocolate factories around the world. This entire Pauletta's concept was based on exotic foreign ingredients he'd brought back from his international travels. Without the richness of pure cane or the creamiest fudge from England, he would sink. It separated rich desserts that melted on one's tongue from cheap, grocery-store paste.

He secured a shipment from France. That would hopefully take Gram through the next couple of weeks—Christmas and New Year's—and then they could start figuring out Valentine's Day.

Then, he called the six customers whose orders Rashad still hadn't delivered.

Among the calls he made was Douglass Page, the kind gentleman who'd helped Jerrell start his business. He would get his order first.

At eight o'clock that evening, Jerrell did a dance as Kami pulled the delivery van into the driveway of his rented house.

"Girl, you're the angel bringing me to Heaven. I'm so glad to see you."

"More like pulling you from this grave you've dug for

yourself," she said, jumping from the van. She was dressed in all white—white fur-trimmed trench coat, white turtleneck, and tight white jeans.

"Damn, you wore that to work?" He noticed a second vehicle pull up to the curb, a gold E350 Mercedes, with one of Kami's friends behind the wheel. Astonished, he turned to his older sister. "Wait a minute, you're not going to help me with these deliveries?" he half-whined.

"Nope. Got plans."

"Like what? Reading Maya Angelou on a Saturday night?"

"I already told you. I'm not getting in the middle of this. It's all on you, baby brother," she said, skipping to her friend's car. "You told us you could do it. You have your van now. So get it done! Call me and let me know how it's going!"

"But she's your grandmama too!" Jerrell pouted.

"Yeah, and I was perfectly happy with her selling pies to her church friends down in the Boot. You decided—not me, not Daddy, none of us, but *you*—to move her to New York and take it to another level." Kami threw up the deuces. "Have fun with that."

Minutes later, Jerrell maneuvered the van down the street to 32 Eastville Avenue. The different-sized clapboard houses all seemed familiar. He got out and searched for his first delivery. Douglass Page.

Cool, he thought.

This was Dr. Page's residence. Jerrell and his benefactor could chat at last.

Entering the biting night winds, he took a pecan pie and liquored red velvet cupcakes to the door. Had he been to this house earlier?

Jerrell was so tired his memory might have been tripping.

A graceful, older woman threw open the door. Nat King

Cole's melodious vocals blasted at him, and the aroma of toasty cinnamon and spices hugged his nostrils. The woman looked old enough to be his mother and seemed like a mirror image of someone else.

"Oh, you must be Pauletta's!" the lady said. "Come on in and warm up a little. We've been waiting for these! Can't wait to dig in."

Loud yelping and laughter floated from another room.

Jerrell offered his most formidable smile. "I hope you enjoy them, ma'am. My grandma puts her foot in these goodies."

His eyes danced around the airy, two-story picture of simple elegance. Vintage fisherman's trappings surrounded Jerrell. The worn wooden foyer cabinet, rickety coat rack, and chipping paint on the stairs seemed to hold secrets. The rustic floorboards and doorframes were humble. He stopped himself from kicking off his shoes and joining them for hot chocolate. Instead, Jerrell diverted his attention to the lovely lady in front of him.

"This is Dr. Page's residence, right? I was hoping I could speak with him."

The lady's lips pulled back in a breezy grin. "Yes, it is, but he's not here. He's out somewhere with the fellas. Who knows? Probably the firehouse, or the barbecue smokehouse. If you have time, I'm sure they'd love to have another betting man in the building."

Jerrell massaged his disappointment. He'd really wanted to see Dr. Page. "Oh no, ma'am, I have more deliveries to make. Maybe next time. Thank you."

One of the main reasons he'd come to Sag Harbor was the possibility of meeting Dr. Page's daughter, who worked on the Senate Foreign Relations Committee.

Jerrell was hoping she could make some calls. He needed to get that Brazilian sugar off the docks in South America and onto a boat. He backed toward the door.

"Would you tell him Jerrell's sorry we missed each other?"

"Certainly. And if the kids like these, I'm sure we'll see a lot more of each other." Mrs. Page's eyes crinkled with her relaxed smile.

Had she been drinking?

Apparently, Dr. Page hadn't told his wife everything about Pauletta's budding business. Jerrell wouldn't be the one to spill it.

Suddenly, the woman reached for his jacket. "Oh, zip this up, son. Can't go out in that winter with nothing over your chest."

Jerrell chuckled, reminded of his mother and grandmother. With gleeful shouts in the next room, he thought of his own family he was missing tonight. He prepared to leave the warmth and reenter the cold, burying a moment of loneliness.

"Of course, ma'am. Y'all have a good night."

"Mama, will you please get in here and tell Reet her bows suck? This girl can't tie a bow to save her—"

Jerrell looked up.

Smooth, honey-colored skin, long fluffy locks flipped into a messy, kinky bun, descended the stairs. Her amused amber eyes danced under a million lights refracting through the chandelier.

That face. From earlier.

Maddy.

Jerrell rubbed at his pounding chest, where Santa's reindeer seemed to be taking flight.

Her happy, socked feet halted. A wintry freeze set over her slackened jaw.

"What is this?" The young lovely's gaze fell to the baked goods Mrs. Page carried.

Hold on, Jerrell thought. *No.*

The pieces came together in his mind.

She was Madison Page? Dr. Page's daughter who worked in the *Senate?*

Jerrell prayed the man had another daughter.

"The dog-walker is also cooking our *pies?*" This younger version of Mrs. Page asked. Her face melted in disgust.

"I'm not a dog-walker," Jerrell replied.

"Oh! That's why you seemed familiar." Mrs. Page slurred. "I kept asking myself why. You were just outside our house earlier today!" The mother looked from her daughter to Jerrell, and in her increasingly tipsy state, began suppressing a laugh.

"You walk dogs *and* work at a bakery?" the young woman asked pointedly. "Where are all your pets? Do you have them in the kitchen while you're cooking our food?"

Jerrell's face began turning hot.

"Maddy Marie!" Mrs. Page snapped. "That wasn't necessary." But the woman's eyes dropped to the pastry boxes she still held. Her neck cocked back at Jerrell. "Well, you don't, do you?"

Reminding himself that he was standing on her turf, he answered, "Ma'am, I already apologized for what happened earlier. Those were not my dogs. And these goods are airsealed and packaged in a professionally maintained kitchen."

"Actually, no." Maddy corrected him. Her eyes became darts shooting at his chest. "You didn't apologize. I'm still waiting."

She reached the bottom of the stairs. Strutting to stand two feet from him, she brought with her a sweet vanilla scent that curled up his nose. Yet her heart-shaped face was unsmiling. Her frosty eyes iced him without saying a word.

Slender curves, perfect and shapely in her leggings, velvety skin, all sent Jerrell's mind into an unexpected Christmas fog.

He turned to her mother, Mrs. Page. "Could you tell Dr. Page I'll catch up with him soon?"

"Sure," Maddy replied for her mother. "And hopefully, by the time you see him, you'll be a better deliveryman than you are a dog-walker."

Irritated, Jerrell sucked his teeth, and peered down at his lovely pest. "I wasn't talking to you."

"She won't remember," Maddy returned. Her head tilted to the side, and she flashed him a vindictive grin. "So maybe I'll tell him. Maybe I won't."

Mrs. Page eyed the two of them, chortling before she left them to their pissing match.

Jerrell rolled his eyes. "Maybe tomorrow you'll wake up on the right side of bed."

"Good thing you don't have to worry about my bed," Maddy shot back.

"I feel bad for the poor dude who does."

They traded attitudes one last time, and she reached for the doorknob.

He snuck in a nice eyeful of her back landscape.

But the reindeer in Jerrell's chest crashed when Maddy shot them down with her final smirk.

"Bye."

OUT OF EACH OTHER'S HAIR

MADDY

"Seriously? That chocolatey slice of cake from earlier today, with the dogs?" Lana asked.

Maddy and her friends enjoyed hot toddies near the fire-pit in the Page family's backyard. She retreated into the plush cushions of their built-in patio chairs. Outside their wooden fence, the ocean waves crashed ashore.

Maddy hugged her blanket tighter and rubbed at her bruised knee that responded with tender pain through her sweatpants. "Yeah, he was standing right at the front door. And got an attitude when I asked him!"

Lana almost spit out her liquor. "Girl, no, you didn't have to go there. You could have just accepted the pies politely and sent him on his way."

"Nope. Those damn pies cost Mama a fortune—$20 each! For a pie! And $6 for a cupcake. Now you tell me who's crazy," Maddy insisted. "I bet those aren't even the real prices. He's probably overcharging and putting the extra in his pocket. I mean, how much money could he be making walking dogs and driving a delivery van?"

Her sister Marguerite's hand hugged her protruding seven-month pregnant belly while she laughed. "Now see, that mouth of yours… why you still ain't got no husband."

"Don't. Have. Any. Man. Speak correct English, as if Mama sent you to a forty-thousand-dollar a year prep school, because girl, I'm shocked *you* found a man," Maddy snapped back at her little sister.

Chrissy shook her head, chiming in. "She's right. He should've apologized. And then he showed up here with dessert. Uh uh. That's a big nope."

"That sexy mofo can pop up at my crib with food anytime, *and* his dogs!" Lana said, rubbing her thighs. "He was sexxxyyyyy. I will walk the hell out of his dog, do you hear me?"

Laughter broke out around the fire.

Inside the house, Chrissy's kids watched a movie and played with Maddy's niece and nephew for a sleepover. Her friend reached over to grasp her arm, cutting into Maddy's thoughts.

"You have not changed one bit. Little skinny, bossy ass telling everybody else what to do. My girl!" Chrissy held her mug out and the two of them toasted. "Go for what you know. Make those fools move out of your way. That man needed to respect how you were already in the space and moved around."

"Exactly!" Maddy declared, tipsy and sitting up straight in her chair to emphasize her point. "Even if it was a mistake, it was his fault, and he should've accepted it. That's being civilized. But so many men don't know the word now."

Marguerite's face wrinkled in disagreement. "Girl, please. Your clumsy ass wasn't paying attention and you fell. You wouldn't be so bothered if you were getting some D on the regular."

"I do get some, excuse you."

"Yeah, but it's just standard, so-so dick. It's not that good," Maddy's sister said slyly, making sure the kids were still indoors.

"There's more to life than chasing men, girl," Chrissy added.

"Like what?" Lana asked, to which she and Reet burst into laughter.

"I have better things to do with my time, and that's why I make more money and I'm more accomplished," Maddy bragged to her little sister, reverting back to one of her tried-and-true lines for when Reet started throwing her ring in Maddy's face.

"It's also why your first two engagements walked out on you. You and your know-it-all big head. Maybe if you learned to shut up sometimes, they'd stick around, and you wouldn't have to sit there and pretend like you don't want nobody."

Mouths dropped across the fire, leaving Boyz to Men and ocean waves to fill the gaping silence.

"Forget you, Reet," Maddy fumed, feeling the heat rise up her face.

"Love you too, babe," Reet replied, smacking and digging in her heels. "But you need to hear it from somebody. May as well be the girl who had to wear your funky hand-me-downs for eighteen years. Stop flapping them lips and start putting 'em on some wood. And guys won't be cringing from you at the front door."

Maddy's younger sister made sure no kids were within sight, before she tongued the rim of her cup, flicking it back and forth to represent another sexual motion.

"Ew!" Maddy cried.

"See, that's your problem," Reet stated matter-of-factly.

Lana guffawed as her hand flew into the air for a high-five, and they gripped each other's hands.

Maddy simmered that her co-worker was a little too comfortable in agreeing with her younger sister.

Chrissy shook her head, unable to control her own laughter. "This is too much. I wasn't ready for this. We were supposed to be roasting marshmallows with our folks and shit."

"Oh, damn!" Lana said from inside the kitchen.

Maddy jumped up. "Lana, what is it? You alright?"

They found Lana, crumbs falling from her mouth, white cream cheese icing on her fingers. She held a red velvet cup cake. "This is the shit!"

The others broke into more laughter, doubling over.

Maddy chuckled. "Where's the dog hair?"

Lana's tongue licked up the icing around her mouth. "Oh, hell nah. You should taste this. Ecstasy! I need another one, but I won't hog them all. I'll order my own. What's this dude's number?"

Maddy smirked at her co-worker. "Girl, you just want to walk his dog."

Lana stuck out her tongue and laughed. "Well, since you rejected the job, I guess somebody should help him out!"

Maddy sucked her teeth. She wouldn't touch that guy with a ten-foot pole. "You enjoy. I'll pass."

"Maddy, really?" her father chastised after Reet gleefully relayed the delivery story to him. "You know better. That's not how you treat guests."

His daughter scoffed. "But he wasn't a guest! It was unprofessional to show up at our house delivering our food in the same clothes he was wearing for his dog-walking job, Dad. You would never let me do any mess like that!"

Dr. Page chuckled, stringing up more Christmas lights at the firehouse. "Give that poor man a break. He's just trying to keep his head on straight, and you're busting the man's balls."

"Wait, what's the saying you used to raise us?" Maddy switched her tone to mock his voice. *"I can't think of a time when incompetence was ever in season.* Wasn't that it? Or is it that saying we all learned when we pledged? The one about excuses? Excuses are tools of incompetence…"

"… that build bridges to nowhere, and monuments of nothingness…" her father continued, a wide smile spreading over his face.

They finished the last line of Juan Pablo's poem together. "And those who often use them, seldom amount to anything."

Maddy handed him some cord. "Now tell the truth. If that had been me making people fall, and then taking hairy food to somebody's house, would you be so nice to me?"

He laughed again. "No. But the dessert was immaculate, Maddy Marie. In fact, I heard everybody enjoyed it a lot."

"Well, if that's not sexist, I'm not sure what is." Maddy huffed. "If I do it, unacceptable. But since he's a guy, 'give that man a break.' Hypocrite!"

"Get over it. I taught you to be gracious, no matter how other people act. I see you're still working on that part." He reached for more lights.

"Well, somebody clearly didn't teach Dog-walker. I'm not

knocking his hustle. But I never knew of a time when incompetence was in season. He needs to show some respect for his customers and change clothes when switching between his five thousand jobs. It's not hard."

"Between jobs, Maddy? What makes you think that's his job?"

"Because he was doing it, maybe?" She fumed, pursing her lips.

Lana's laughter rang out from the other side of the fire station. Surrounded by two guys in her trademark hip-hugging jeans, she intentionally leaned over so her butt crack would show, and her cashmere sweater would fall open to display a full bosom of her Christmas presents. Maddy chuckled to herself, glad her co-worker wasn't bored.

"Oh, hello, Mr. Dog-walker, welcome back. Did you bring us anymore treats?" Lana's voice suddenly said behind them, in that sultry tone she used at the club.

Maddy unwound another strand of lights.

"Lana, stop playing. You keep talking, but one of you will cough up dog hair eating all that crap, and when you do, I won't say I told you."

But Lana's eyes dropped and rose again, peering behind Maddy at an object that was apparently catching Lana's attention.

Lana continued, "I couldn't stop feening for those cupcakes last night. What did you do? Sweeten them with your finger?" She clearly was not talking to Maddy.

Dread filled Maddy's chest.

She edged around.

There he stood.

A long black wool coat draped over his broad shoulders, leather newsboy cap shoved over his smooth, shaven face, he ignited a woodfire in a black turtleneck and dark gray dress slacks. As if he'd just stepped off the runway in Paris. In his arms were more boxes of pastries.

Maddy ratcheted her jaw back up, tongue in.

"Dr. Page, finally, I never thought I'd run into you," Dog-Walker called, looking past Maddy to her father.

"Jerrell! How are you doing, son? Thank you for bringing those over on such short notice. I wanted the fellas to try some of these. We'll get you a little business buzz, some word of mouth while everybody's in town for the holidays."

Maddy stared from one to the other, aghast that Dog-walker had indeed returned. And apparently, had made friends who'd kept her in the dark. She glared at her dad.

"You two… know each other?"

Her father's tense smile tightened over his lips. "Yes, sweetheart, believe it or not, I do have a life outside of you kids. This is Jerrell Rouse. His father is Charles Rouse, our investment manager over at Masters Bank Manhattan."

Maddy couldn't help the scoff that escaped. "Really?" she asked. *A dog-walker with a banker for a father?* "You mean, nice Mr. Rouse who brings his wife down to Virginia Beach for vacation?"

"Yes, really. *That* Mr. Rouse," her father replied, throwing her a warning look, before he turned to Jerrell. "I heard you met my daughter yesterday. Jerrell, this here is Madison Page. Please forgive her… unlady-like mannerisms. We found her wandering in a field as a toddler and have been trying to tame her ever since."

Lana snorted as Maddy's oxygen became ensnared in her chest.

"Maddy, I hope everything is alright, and I didn't cause you too much inconvenience," Jerrell said, removing his kidskin black leather glove and offering her his hand. Smooth, unblemished, and moisturized with clean-cut, manicured nails.

She took it and made sure to keep her eyes trained on his, no sneaking glances at his chest. "No. No inconvenience at all." Fake smile.

"No dogs today, as you can see," Jerrell quipped, a tiny flash of venom in his eye.

"Yes, my vision works just fine." She removed her palm from his warm touch.

"Let me introduce you to the fellas. Come on, son. Maddy, you and Lana finish up over here," her father said, handing her the lights. "Say, everybody, here's our guy! From Poppin' Pauletta's!"

No sooner than they turned did Lana's hips hump the air right behind Jerrell. "Oh, damn, those lips! The long hands. Big feet! Oooh weee."

Maddy cut her eyes away from her father's friends, gathering around and embracing Jerrell. She yanked apart the lights, irritated now.

Lana shot her a cutting stare. "What is your problem?"

"*No dogs today, as you can see,*" Maddy repeated his words mockingly. "Ugh, how cocky is that?"

Her co-worker gave a cackling snicker. "Girl, you busted that dude so hard. Put him down and showed him your *whole* ass, just because of your ruined jeans and nails. But today, he clapped back and let you know what time it is. He is the son of a banker. Not some mutt from the other side of the tracks, and not some rich airhead that you can kick around like all those other ones. He's got mmmoneyyy." Lana's hips swayed as her neck kept rolling. "Just go on and take your medicine. And while you do that, I'm going to bed him."

"Well, you have all the fun with that. And make sure you get a shot after." Maddy rolled her eyes, wrestling the lights.

While she grappled with her irritation, a thought crossed her mind. *No.* "Daddy wouldn't."

"Wouldn't what?" Lana still eyed the guys on the other side of the room.

Maddy ignored her. She noticed her father's friends offering this Jerrell stranger a Cognac, to which he put up his hand and refused with a gracious smile. They were too chummy. A sinking feeling burrowed into her stomach. The men leaned their heads back and laughed. Why hadn't Daddy mentioned this guy?

"Girl, why are you mad-dogging that man so tough?" Lana asked.

Maddy sucked her teeth. "Because I don't have a good sense about this."

Her father couldn't. He would never try to set her up against her wishes. Just, no.

They weren't going to push somebody else on her, to leave her holding the emotional ropes when it became an embarrassment.

Lana's eyes swung from the men back to Maddy. "Girl, you tripping."

If only Lana knew. She didn't have to worry about her family dipping into her love life.

"Maddy!" her father called as they returned. "Jerrell here has a few more deliveries to make and is having trouble finding a couple of the houses. Why don't you be a dear and show him the Turner house and the Merediths?"

Maddy's bottom lip dropped. So now she had to be his chaperone? Who was she? The mansitter?

She tilted back on her heels. "So, he's not very good at

walking dogs, or delivering food?" She turned her attention to this Jerrell guy. "How do you manage to keep either of your jobs? Are your bosses aware what kind of employee they have working for them?"

Jerrell's eyes narrowed and he looked about to yank her and throw her out the window.

Just as annoyed, Maddy dismissed his hurt feelings, because she was right.

Her father started, "Now, Madison Marie, you don't have to—"

"My *boss*?" Jerrell retorted with an edge. "An employee? Either of my *jobs*? I *am* the boss. I do the hiring and firing, and I'm quite satisfied with my performance. Since you're asking."

Maddy was at a loss for words. So, he wasn't a dog-walker. Or a deliveryman.

Lana smirked, sucking her teeth, clearly enjoying the exchange.

"Well, good for you then. Congratulations. Daddy, I have plans for brunch with the girls. All he has to do is pull up GPS on his phone and it gives walking instructions."

Again, Jerrell's eyes flickered. "Actually, it's cool. I already tried GPS and that's steering me wrong, but I'll just ask around. Dr. Page, everybody, nice meeting you. You all have a pleasant day."

Ugh, Maddy thought at his apparent play for sympathy.

Lana jumped on the opportunity, audibly scoffing loud enough to let Jerrell know she was in his corner.

"I'm new here too. My first time visiting," she said, stepping up to Jerrell and shaking his hand. "I'd love to see some of these cute little houses. I can come with you, and we'll explore this place together." Lana then shoved her hands in her back pockets, so her breasts pushed against her cashmere sweater.

"Yeah, exactly!" Maddy piped up. "They can tour while I wrap up here, and when Lana is done, she can meet me." She and Jerrell avoided one another's gaze.

"Or," Maddy's father intervened. "You can show our new friends around, on your way to your brunch. Because that's what we do here." Dr. Page's eyes squinted in that *don't you dare embarrass me, young lady* look. "Isn't it?"

Maddy tried to keep her face together as she grabbed her coat. She and her father both exchanged *we'll discuss this later* glares, before she stomped outside to get Jerrell.

This was only a few minutes, Maddy told herself. In a few short minutes, it would be all over, and she would hopefully never see this guy again.

"The Turners and the Merediths. That's pretty easy. Should take us no time."

Jerrell didn't bother looking at her. "Don't trouble yourself, lady. The hired help wouldn't want to inconvenience you."

She rolled her eyes at him. "Stop pouting and be strong as I was yesterday when you literally ran me down with your canines. Come on. We'll be out of each other's hair in a minute."

BOTHERED

JERRELL

She wasn't wearing makeup or the glamorous coat and boots from yesterday.

Still, he was all too familiar with her kind, the snooty types who'd made fun of his Cajun Louisiana accent when he first arrived in New York during middle school. Now Jerrell stared at a bare-faced girl who had just wandered out of a Disney picture.

"Um," he said as he lost his words. "What?" Jerrell had been too busy fuming at her condescending remarks.

"Does this order go to the Merediths or the Turners? I'm not clear on house numbers, only locations," she replied.

Without warning, Maddy leaned over Jerrell's arm to view his cell phone digital GPS. An earthy aroma of coconut oil and vanilla tickled Jerrell's nose. Her cottony head brushed against Jerrell's chest. Gone was the perfectly blown out hair from the day before. It had now frizzed, tightening into little coils around her edges and inside her bun.

"Oh!" Jerrell snapped out of his stupor at her being so close. "Yes, this order is… let's see," he said, swiping through the app. He'd overheard the girl trashing his competence, and then she'd written him off. So, why was he breathing hard like a nervous schoolboy? "Wow, Deidre—uh, the sales associate—must've been really busy. She forgot to put the names with the orders. Only the addresses."

"We'll just walk over and figure it out when we get there," Maddy said, her simple all-weather boots taking off. "So how long have you been, um, delivering pies and walking dogs?"

He didn't bother correcting her as they crossed the street. Like she said, only a few more minutes, and he wouldn't have to see her anymore.

He'd figure out another way to address his Brazilian sugar issue.

Residents yelled out greetings to Maddy, and she eagerly waved at people she'd apparently known for years. Her mouth opened wide to scream for her longtime friends driving into town. She even broke into a little line dance that someone else did with her on the sidewalk. Their arms entangled, apparent glee decorated their faces. It seemed like, at will, Maddy could shed her stiff alter ego he'd just encountered.

Jerrell cleared his throat in a mock cough to regain her attention.

"Oh, yeah, sorry," Maddy said, saying goodbye to her neighbors and their children. "I'll for sure catch you guys later."

"Wait, those boxes!" one of Maddy's friends called. "What are you holding? I've seen those before! Is that Pauletta's?"

"Cupcakes!" her little girl screamed, eyes lighting up, feet leaving the ground so fast they might have floated. She clapped before pulling on her mother. "Mommy, pretty please, can we get some?"

Jerrell flashed Maddy a proud glance. Incompetence, huh? Meanwhile, Maddy gave his boxes a passing look.

"Sir, you wouldn't happen to have extra with you, would you?" Maddy's friend asked him, gazing past Maddy to catch Jerrell's eye.

"Ma'am, I'm sorry, but our orders for the weekend are already in."

Dr. Page had been right, and he was grateful he'd come to Sag Harbor.

"Oh, mannn," the girl pouted.

The mother inspected Jerrell, before turning to Maddy. "Is he a friend of yours? You should bring him to the ball next weekend. He's cute."

The one thing Jerrell and Maddy could do, without disagreement or awkward tension, was agree that they were definitely not interested.

Bumbling explanations tripped over one another, as they made clear that no dates, no interest, no nothing was happening between them.

The woman's suspicious eyes slid from Maddy to Jerrell and back. "Tehe. Okay. Well, see you two later. Jerrell, we'll… call to your store."

"Perfect," he replied.

The woman snuck Maddy a not-so-subtle side grin before her little girl led her off.

Maddy charged ahead.

Jerrell felt his arm arrested as Maddy's friend Lana clung to him.

She batted her long, bushy eyelashes at him. "So, you were going to tell us about yourself and these sweets."

Jerrell gaped, still at a loss for words. "Ha. I was?"

"Yeah, all this love you get from the neighborhood… must

be damn exciting, huh? Soon as you step up, people treat you like some kind of hero, all happy to see you," Lana gushed.

"Oh, well, I'm not the one putting in the hard work. Actually, it's—"

"Exactly. Of course, you're not," Maddy cut in, her boots still stomping ahead. "I mean, you only do the smiling and hand-shaking. But the real labor is likely on some poor, overworked, underpaid woman back in your kitchen. Who puts in all those hours, sweating away, one day after the other, in a godforsaken uniform, and gets no credit at all. While you show up and be the hero," Maddy spouted in an uninterrupted stream of consciousness that caused both Jerrell and Lana to roll their eyes.

"Wow," Jerrell replied, breathlessly. This girl had no off switch.

One moment she seemed so pure and angelic, and the next, a demon on the loose. But Jerrell didn't have time. A few more minutes with this chick. "Um, yeah, whatever you say."

Her friend Lana squeezed against him. "How often do you let your own kids eat your dessert? I'm sure your wife can't keep her hands off of it, right?" Lana asked, still making her arm quite comfortable in his.

"I'm pretty sure you probably already guessed that I don't have kids. Or a wife. You were only asking to be polite, right?"

Lana sucked her red bottom lip and thrust her chest out again. As if she hadn't made her intentions clearer back at the firehouse. "Of course. And I have plenty of time to be polite while I'm here keeping Maddy company. Polite conversation. Polite drinks. Polite...." Lana shrugged. "Whatever. We don't even have to be polite," she added with a chuckle.

He laughed again as his cell buzzed away in his pocket, reminding him more deliveries remained.

Meanwhile, Maddy's wellies kept marching toward one of the beachfront spreads. His eyes automatically drifted to her shapely thighs moving underneath tight, thick leggings, barely covered by her all-weather tan parka. Eager to be rid of him quick, she practically galloped.

"I think this is it," Maddy said, walking up the steps. "Right? House number 32? The Merediths."

He checked his app. "Yes, this is it."

The owners threw open the door, their exuberant faces greeting Maddy.

Once again, Jerrell watched her face light up, running into their arms.

The woman beamed, "Girl, I'm so proud of you! I see you on TV all the time! Sitting behind powerful senators, whispering in their ear, covering their microphones while you all discuss important, top-secret stuff."

"Come down and see me anytime. I'd love to give you a tour of the Capitol and take you around. And Myles would enjoy it too. How are you doing, smart man?" Maddy gushed. "Jesus, you're almost taller than me."

Damn. So, this *was* the daughter Dr. Page had been talking about.

Well-connected, entrenched in her community, influential behind the scenes for businesses. Jerrell had been praying all day that maybe his ears had fooled him.

People's faces brightened when they saw her. So she wasn't a demon all the time. Once again, he found himself disrupting the gathering, feeling bad as he cleared his throat.

"Oh, yeah," Maddy said, flicking her eyes over her shoulder at the apparent inconvenience of his presence. "Did you guys order cupcakes?"

Finally, half an hour later, he was delivering pies to the Turners. By then, his friend Deidre had practically killed his cell phone battery with her constant calls about the influx of holiday orders.

"You need to hire somebody else. This is becoming a lot, J. I only flew up here temporarily to help because you're my boy, but you should really do something," Deidre rambled on while Maddy spoke to neighbors.

In a whisper, he rushed his best-friend off the phone. "Call you back in an hour. I'll work it out. Bye."

He couldn't miss a chance to meet more potential customers, who would spread the word to others.

"Well, alright, looks like we tackled them and you're home free now," Maddy said, wrapping up her social calls. She happily lifted up onto the balls of her feet, and did a perfect spin in her boots, even on the sandy sidewalk. Clearly, she was thrilled to walk him back to his van.

Jerrell's older sister had taken dance, and her pirouettes were still on point, legs still maintaining their tone. "Ballet?" he asked Maddy.

"How did you guess? My dad told you?" she replied.

He was sure her luminous smile wasn't for him, but the from people she actually respected.

"Just a hunch. I'm home free?" he clarified. "Or did you mean *you're* home free?" And rid of him now.

"Yes, you can go back to," her eyes fluttered several times, "I'm sorry, but I forgot where you're from."

Of course, you did, Jerrell thought, buttoning his lip.

"Do you even have to go?" Lana almost whined, batting her thick, super-glued eyelashes at him. "So much to do around here. When do you get off?"

Maddy lowered her head and snickered. "Well, I'll leave

you two to it. Good luck with the rest of your deliveries, Jerrell."

Did she just blow him off?

And drop him with her friend?

As Maddy broke into a light jog through the yards, Jerrell's gaze followed. His imagination toyed with what else those legs might do.

A throat cleared next to him.

Oh, yeah.

"I hear they serve excellent lobster right up the road. If you're off from running your company soon, we can check it out. Or even if you stop working late," Lana said, practically gluing her extra-long lashes to him.

Jerrell unhooked Lana's arm from his. "I'm sorry, but I still have a ton of work to do. I'll have to take a rain check."

He should have been happy to watch Maddy skip away from him. So why was he bothered?

CLEARLY STILL SALTY

MADDY

"And another one!" Maddy cried, throwing a reindeer horseshoe over a stake.

She threw her arms in the air at the neighborhood crab boil, where they played games under a heated tent. In mockery of the guys, Maddy, her mother and Chrissy all leaped up and banged their chests together.

"Oh, my goodness, are you kidding me?" Dr. Page complained to Reet's husband, Xavier.

"No, clearly, they are not playing. It's supposed to be a fun little game, and these women came to play for real," Xavier replied.

They danced, yelled, and bragged, hugging it out when the men lost by four points.

Minutes later, Maddy struggled to pick up the crab from the pot boiling over the fire pit.

"Oh, here, let me help you with that," Mrs. Emma said, grabbing another pair, and together they maneuvered the sea delicacies from the soup of thyme, parsley, white wine and more spices. "There you go."

Maddy released a relieved laugh. "Thanks, Mrs. Emma. Teamwork goes a long way, right?"

"With the right team, yes. That's what we are, girl," Mrs. Emma rubbed her shoulder against Maddy's, giving her a wink. "You going to The Madames breakfast meeting tomorrow morning, before the debutante rehearsal?" she asked. "We are really looking forward to having you there. I think a couple of members have issues they wanted to discuss with you. About yachting licenses and the private spa down in Virginia."

The Madames gathering!

Maddy had almost forgotten that her mother mentioned it. "Oh, Mrs. Emma, I had to bring some work with me." She scrunched up her face, expressing uncertainty. "I may have to skip it."

She hated letting people down, but the Senator's memo was imperative. Nothing else came before that. Especially when Maddy's co-workers were gunning for her job, buttering up the Staff Director and Chief of Staff in her absence.

"I'm sure you're a busy girl and all, but do try to join us if you can. No pressure," Mrs. Emma murmured. A semi-retired judge and the vice-president of the prominent Madames, Inc., secret sorority, Mrs. Emma practically lived in Sag Harbor full-time now, just as Maddy's grandmother had in her later years.

"I'll do my best, Mrs. Emma," she replied, cringing at the prospect of waking up at 6 a.m., to do work, and then make a sorority breakfast at 10 a.m. Not to mention that debutante rehearsal started at 11 a.m. "Sag Harbor means the world to me, so I'll try."

"Is that why it took so long to come back? Hm? We've missed you," the elderly woman's eyes picked away at Maddy.

Maddy sucked in a big gulp of unforgiving ocean air. Right up the beach was her grandmother's favorite rock where she liked to sit early in the morning. "And you all were in my thoughts. But I needed the time. Everything around here reminds me of her."

Mrs. Emma gripped Maddy's arm. "Of course. But Estaire was such a force in this community, and we could use somebody to resume her duties, to bring people together."

The elderly woman's face could have squeezed lemons as she linked her arm through Maddy's, and her wrinkled eyes peered at the younger woman. "People up and down the East Coast are starting to say that Black Hamptons is *dead*."

That news felt like gritty sand in Maddy's eyes.

Worked up and balling her fists, the elder continued, "We need fresh blood here. To organize the meetings, lead the clubs, bring in more investment dollars and new energy. We old folks are winding down, and it's hard getting these busy young folk to put in work."

Maddy loved the Hamptons that her family helped build. But how would she do what her grandmother's friend asked?

"Thanks, Mrs. Emma, I'll think about it. But Capitol Hill takes a lot out of me."

"I don't mean to scare you, dear," the older woman continued. "I'm just putting something on your mind to consider, because you look a little more… tense than you did the last time we saw you. At Estaire's homegoing."

Estaire's granddaughter blinked fast to beat back emotion. So much had changed since GeeGee's passing—another failed marriage engagement, rough competition on the job, plus a string of embarrassing set-ups and bad dates.

Across the fire just then, through her tears, Maddy saw a strapping figure. Smooth chocolate cloaked in black wool, stood a few yards from her. The moisture in her eyes dried up, evaporating in front of the flames.

"What is he doing here?" she murmured.

"Who?" Mrs. Emma asked, her gaze following Maddy's. "Oh, it's the guy from Pauletta's."

Maddy recognized who it was. "But I thought he finished making his deliveries already. I helped him."

"Oh, I hear he's staying for the next few days," Mrs. Emma replied, nudging Maddy. "He's such a nice gentleman, don't you think?"

The next few days? Maddy's food stuck to her throat.

Dog-walker was, once again, throwing his head back and enjoying conversation with her brother and father, who turned around and tossed her a quick glance. Across the tent, she traded suspicious eyes with her mother and sister. What was going on?

Should she go speak? No. It would seem like she cared he was here. But if she didn't, she would seem like the spoiled brat sitting in a corner pouting.

"Mrs. Emma. I'll see you later," she said, kissing the woman's cheek and rising to go find one of her friends.

"Hopefully, later means in the morning," Mrs. Emma called with a sly wink.

"Tehe," Chrissy chuckled as Maddy approached her. "So, I guess you're coming over here because you heard."

"Heard what?"

"No, young lady, get away from that table. Don't go near the food when I'm not there," Chrissy chastised her children before returning to Maddy. "He's doing a pop-up shop through Christmas." Her friend sipped on her drink. "Sure is strange how comfortable he is with your dad."

The two exchanged suspicious looks. Chrissy knew Maddy and her family well enough to share concern that Maddy's father might be up to something.

"Daddy has always stayed out of my love life. It's not his style to hook me up. Now that would surprise me."

Chrissy shook her head, and her eyes started glistening with emotion in front of the orange flames. "Consider yourself lucky. Why do people think that a man is something special just because he dresses up really nice and says the right things?"

Immediately, Maddy suspected her old friend was referring to her recent separation from her husband. Maddy had served as Chrissy's bridesmaid at Spelman almost ten years before. Chrissy's quick marriage happened between exams at a campus chapel during finals week. After Chrissy had learned she was pregnant in their junior year.

Maddy attempted to gas her friend up, changing her voice to a fake British accent. "Because they wouldn't know special if it bit them in the arses, Madam Chriselle."

It worked. Chrissy's face lit up, as it did when they used fake accents as kids and pretended they were from different countries.

"Do you know if Kevin is coming this Christmas?" Chrissy finally asked the question Maddy had hoped to escape.

Maddy sipped champagne to wash her old crush from her throat.

It had been twenty years since he'd tortured her in front of his friends, on the beach, in the daylight. Kevin Middleton.

The entire ocean could have been filled with champagne, and it still wouldn't have been enough to drink away Kevin's ruthless torture of her. "Please, Lord, I hope not. I can actually look at myself in the mirror now and not barf for liking him."

Chrissy sprayed out her liquor as her amusement erupted. "Girl, no! You used to *love* that dude."

"I was an idiot."

Chrissy's gut kept shaking.

"I thought I heard crazy women somewhere!" another voice cried.

Maddy and Chrissy turned. "Oh, my God!"

Adella, another childhood friend from their younger heyday, came racing through the yard before bear hugs and screams proceeded. "It's been too long! Since your engagement to Kelly, right?" Her head swung from side to side. "Well, where is he? I never got an invitation to the wedding. What's it been? Two years?"

The others' faces froze, eyes darting around, as they squirmed at the memo that Adella clearly hadn't gotten.

Maddy swallowed. "It didn't happen. But that's alright though, because I see something else did pop off!"

Adella held up her left hand, blinking numerous times, as if she was emotional. "Oh, this happened over Thanksgiving. Our date is this March."

Squeals and more screams ensued, and a stunned Maddy threw her arms around her old friend.

"March?" Maddy said, her eyes fluttering in shock. "That's in three months. Oh, my God! Were you going to invite us?"

Maddy gazed at the sparkling rock that must've been three carats.

"It's Harry Winston," Del said, tearing up.

And still, Maddy got a weird vibe from her old friend. Something didn't feel right. But Maddy wouldn't rain on her parade. "This ring is… is beautiful! Let's celebrate! So where is he? When do we meet him?"

A tall, stocky guy greeted her, and his lips parted into a slick smile. "I'm Desmond. And you are Maddy. Adella talked about you the whole way here, hoping you would be in Sag Harbor. A pleasure to finally shake your hand. So, you work on Capitol Hill, huh? The political shark with two masters' degrees who wrote to the president as a kid and got them to preserve a history museum?"

Maddy grinned at Del. "Girl, that wasn't me. It was these hard-working Sag Harbor families. Folks like my g-grandma." She fought off the clogging of her throat.

Del squeezed her arm. "Miss Estaire was such a force around here."

"That she was," Maddy replied.

A lifetime ago, her grandparents would've been coming in from a night stroll with the dogs around this time. Pain flashed through her heart that GeeGee would never walk through their family's gate again.

"You alright, girl?" Chrissy asked, throwing her arm around her friend's shoulders.

Maddy wiped away a threatening tear. "Yeah, I'm managing." She held up her mug as Lana walked to each one of them, pouring refills. "To a damn good time this Christmas."

Del and Reet gushed about wedding arrangements and party planners for the baby shower.

But as Maddy stared at them all, something about Del's new fiancé seemed off. Like there was an awkward distance between them.

Maddy turned to chat up Desmond so he wouldn't feel left out.

And she could've sworn her eyes fooled her. It must've

been the alcohol, so she blinked several times, but Maddy's vision was not tripping.

As Lana's full curves strutted around the group pouring liquor in their cups, Desmond's eyes ogled her butt.

"I don't have a good feeling about Del's new fiancé," Maddy noted to Chrissy, and tossed back more champagne. Desmond eyeballed Lana's butt so hard she thought his eyes might detach. "And she doesn't look all that happy."

But Maddy would keep quiet, and not rain on Del's parade.

"Don't look now, but your dog-walker is coming over here," Chrissy noted, motioning ahead of them.

A slight ripple rolled through Maddy's chest.

"Good evening, Ms. Maddy, how are your hands and knees holding up? Just wanted to come and check, make sure you were alright," the rich male voice returned.

Maddy stared into his mocha eyes, dancing before the large fireplace. Any other time, he wouldn't have been a bad-looking guy. Any other time than when she hated him.

"They're fine. Did you get all your deliveries out okay?" she asked, forcing herself to be cordial.

"I did, thanks." He folded his arms across his broad chest. "I came over, hoping we could bury the hatchet. I appreciated you helping me find those last couple of houses today, despite what happened. My offer for coffee still stands. Tomorrow morning. My treat."

Did he really think he could get off that easily?

"Would this coffee be your tacit admission you were wrong and that you need to make up for it?" Maddy asked.

Chrissy snorted and started choking on her champagne.

The dog-walker sighed. "No. It would be a simple act of good will toward somebody who's clearly still salty about it."

"Oop," Chrissy said, even as she coughed.

Maddy's stare tightened, as she avoided his perfect-fitting wool jacket buttoned over a taut chest, with an elegant silk scarf donning his neck.

"Much as I'd love for you and your dogs to jump all over me again with no apologies, I have a busy schedule in the morning. Sorry."

A DIAMOND

JERRELL

ould that be your tacit admission? Jerrell seethed the next morning at his store in New York City.

This girl's words ran on a constant loop through his mind.

Who was *she* supposed to be? To sit on her high horse and pass judgment, as if she was Judge Mablean? And even if she *was* Judge Mablean—

"J! Damn, dude, you're smashing them," his best-friend Diedre admonished, rushing over and rearranging the pecan pies in the box. "What is up with you? You've been slinging these poor boxes all morning. What did the pies do to you?"

He rubbed his eyes. "My bad. I'm in my own head. This is a lot."

Deidre snickered. "Yeah, we warned you it would be. Like, literally, everybody told you, but you had to go out and be Mr. Badass. You already knew what you were signing up for, and it's actually going way better than you hoped. So, tell me why you're abusing the product today."

He shook his head. No stranger would take up space in his thoughts. "Nah, nothing. It's just stress."

"No, that's a lie. Somebody got under your skin. Who was it this time? Your mom? Your dad? Roland?" she asked, referencing his oldest brother, the sibling with whom he fought most.

"Nobody. Let's pack these boxes in the van so I can roll out. After that, I probably won't see you for the next week. You'll be running the shop here, while I look for somebody else to take over," he replied.

The thought of entrusting a stranger to track sales, handle the in-store money, receive shipments, and do it responsibly was too daunting. Who would care about his grandmother's product, and growing this fledgling operation, the way he did? But he simply could not be in two places at one time.

Deidre threw him a long, suspicious stare. "Oh, wow, this is serious. Must be somebody I don't know, because if it was your family, you would've spit it all out by now. Some girl's got your nose open, Boo Boo?" Deidre asked, walking out with him to place boxes in the van. "Wait a minute. This man, Dr. Page, his daughter. Has he introduced you yet?"

Jerrell remained quiet as he reentered the backdoor to the kitchen.

"You met her, and she said no. She won't help you," Deidre guessed.

"No," he muttered. "I haven't asked."

"Oh, my, I wonder why that is. Did you show her your sparkling personality, and she's already told you to get lost? So now you've shot yourself in the foot before you even started. How close am I?"

"I invited her for coffee, and she said she was busy."

Deidre's mouth fell. "Daaayum, I must meet this chick.

This goddess who has stopped Jam 'Em Jerrell in his tracks. Who didn't fall for those pillow lips, Al B. Sure jawline, and Atlantic Ocean waves. For her to even reject your coffee, you must've really stepped in it. And she has clearly checked you so hard you're wearing your mad all over you this morning."

"I'm not mad," Jerrell lied. "And I am *not* trying to jump her." He hoisted up his final box. "I just need to figure out how to attack it is all."

"Boy, when a woman likes you, there is no such thing as 'too busy.' Don't challenge everything that comes out of her mouth."

"But I don't—"

"This is me you're talking to," Deidre chastised as her eyes narrowed. "Be the good guy working hard for his grandmother, not the crusader who sets the world on fire."

She knew him so well. He wrapped her in his arms and kissed her forehead. "I could never repay you enough for being here. Thanks, sweetheart."

"But you will damn sure try," she retorted as he burst out of the door.

At ten o'clock, he arrived at the *Oasis Cove Hotel* for the debutante rehearsal that started at eleven.

He'd hired the Turners' grandson, Myles, to help him ring up sales while Jerrell schmoozed. Today was Myles's first day, and Jerrell began showing him the ropes.

"Hello, Mrs. Emma, what are you doing up so early on this fine morning?" he called as he set up in the foyer.

"Why, good morning, Jerrell. Oh, our secretary ordered you for our breakfast. I can't wait," she said. "I'm the vice-president of the Sag Harbor Madames chapter. We will be presenting the debutantes, as we've done for over fifty years."

He enjoyed watching her eyes rove over the boxes and

light up with anticipation. "Oh, The Madames? I've never heard of the group."

Her eyes twinkled as if she knew a secret he didn't. "You're not supposed to, dear. It's a private, secret club. No open acceptance. No applications. Invitation only. Just for us ladies who wish to stay to ourselves."

Jerrell marveled at yet another secret Black club. Just what did these organizations achieve for the greater good if no one knew they existed? But he kept his activist lip buttoned and released a laugh.

"Tuh, that's kind of mysterious. Like something out of a conspiracy book—the *Da Vinci Code*. Or the *Illuminati*, or *Skull and Bones* at Yale."

"Or maybe just a few women who don't plan to destroy the world, but make it better," Mrs. Emma replied with a little wink, before taking a blueberry and cream cheese muffin and cup of coffee.

A figure entered the walkway.

With perfect posture and confidence, her every move seemed regal, even as she stomped the sand off her wellies on the floor mat. Graceful fingers coolly unbuttoned her jacket, revealing the shimmering burgundy Christmas sweater falling over her breasts and hugging her slender waist.

Damn, boy, stop it, Jerrell said to himself as his chest tightened. *She's a headache,* he reminded himself, jerking his vision from the fluffy curls enveloping her face.

Maddy looked up. Clear disdain hit her upon seeing Jerrell.

Her eyes slanted into sharp daggers. The satisfaction Jerrell got from watching her disappointment was priceless. She eyed the pastries set on the table between them.

"Good morning, Ms. Page," Jerrell said, delighting in her

discomfort at his presence. "So, this is why you were too busy for coffee with me. Why am I not surprised you're a member of a super-secret sorority that takes no applications?"

"Everywhere I am now, you seem to be there also," she noted, removing her coat.

As she did, Jerrell's eye wandered to the bump on her back. Tight and sculpted, a fair size four…*grip*-worthy….

He averted his gaze before she turned around.

Laughter from elderly women drifted through the doors, enlivening the empty foyer.

Jerrell lost his scowl and returned his lips to a smile, extending warmth in his eyes. "Come one, come all. We whipped up some goodies for your special event today."

"And hopefully, you won't choke them with it," Maddy murmured under her breath. Just loud enough for Jerrell to hear. She then did that perfect spin again and headed toward her exclusive, ultra-rich girls' club.

Jerrell planted his hands on the table, leaning over it. She needed a piece of his mind. "Woman, look, you seriously need to…"

He jumped. Did somebody pat his butt?

As the ladies greeted him, the occasional fingers found their way to his chest. As the younger members' eyes roamed over him, Jerrell could've been a slab of meat in the frozen food section.

Past all the fur and feathers, inside the ball room, Jerrell observed as so many women wanted to talk with Maddy, get her thoughts on a situation, or receive advice. She reached out her arms to embrace one woman after another. They hobnobbed, clutching one another's hands, tapping each other's faces with broad smiles. It was the family reunion in heaven.

"Man, sorry if it's none of my business, but," Myles started, eying Jerrell, "maybe you two wouldn't be so mad at each other if you just asked her out."

Jerrell snickered. "Hmph. It's not like that. We're not… we don't…"

Not in a million years. Her type, wrapped up in all these pointless clubs and groups, simply wasn't for him.

It was all very cute and swank, but he wanted a woman he could hoop with, and looking through the lace, boots, and silk, that was not Maddy.

Though her figure wasn't half bad.

Teenage debutantes started entering. Hesitant, bashful expressions on their faces, they clutched their jackets and purses, gazing around the foyer, staring at the pictures on the wall. The nervous girls fidgeted, not knowing what to expect, as they chatted, primped in compact mirrors, and paced the floor.

Jerrell used the time to call Deidre and Gram and check on things back in Brooklyn.

"How is it there?" Deidre asked. "Did you throw yourself on the ground yet and beg forgiveness for whatever idiot words flew out of your mouth?"

"Girl, bye," he replied. "You know there is no way in hell I would ever—"

The double doors swung open, right in Jerrell's face, giving him an unobstructed view of heaven.

"Hello? J?" Deidre spoke from the other end.

"Yeah," he responded mindlessly, his thoughts levitating at this new distraction.

"No way you would ever what?" Deidre repeated.

"Mr. Rouse," Mrs. Emma said, shining her eagle-like eyes on him. "We have a small emergency. The gentleman scheduled to practice with us couldn't make it. Could you do me a favor and assist please?"

"I'll call you back," he said to Deidre, shoving his phone in his pocket. "Sure, Mrs. Emma."

Jerrell entered the ballroom, and at the center stood a diamond.

Surrounded in billowing cream, her bare shoulders out, pearls embroidering satin that cupped her breasts, layers of tulle sweeping around her, she was indeed a goddess.

A transformed Maddy almost looked like… a good person.

Her eyes finally bounced up, finding Jerrell.

Shock smeared Maddy's happy expression when she realized he stood beside Mrs. Emma. Her mouth dropped in a silent protest.

Behind them, teenage girls gasped. Murmurs suddenly filled the ballroom. Jerrell overheard one of them. "Oh, they're going to be so gorgeous together. Like a Princess and her shining Knight."

Gold drapes and voile fabric cascaded from the outer ceiling, sweeping to the multi-tiered crystal chandelier. Its ethereal golden light cast a halo over Maddy's head. Jerrell's consciousness warned him to avert his eyes, to think of something else, and not give her the satisfaction of his attention.

But had he looked away, his insides might have sunken.

Shining knight?

What did these women want him to do? His breaths sped up in his chest. He had gargled, right?

The girls' eyes glittered under the golden luminescence shrouding the room, their eyes all falling on Maddy.

Jerrell wondered how someone appearing this angelic could be so…

"Good morning, ladies, I'm Madison Page, and I'll be a

judge of this competition, to be concluded at the ball on Saturday evening. I am also The Madames Miss Debutante Queen 2008. Unfortunately, last year's queen could not join us this week, as her grandmother is in the hospital. Since I happened to be on hand, I'm standing in."

As Maddy spoke underneath the chandelier's glow, her eyes danced from one girl to another.

"I received this honor from the women I admired as a child, and it was among the greatest privileges of my life. When we break away from our parents to start college, we leave for a vast, and at times, overwhelming world."

Maddy's gaze deepened, hands clasped together, as if gathering her thoughts.

"And in that vast world—filled with all its trials and challenges—we often question ourselves, and doubt who we are. But my time as a debutante is one of the moments that affirmed me most. Right in this room. Here in Sag Harbor, it's okay to thrive, to discuss wealth, expand your holdings, build your startup, enjoy luxury and leisure, nourish your souls. Among the Madames, my right to soar was never up for discussion or debate. Here, prestige is not simply possible. It *is*. So, ladies, welcome. To a place where your greatness is not a question. But a certainty. You will never have to apologize or explain yourself, because you are with friends. Celebrate yourselves, as we celebrate you."

A hush gripped the college women. Some of their eyes misted. Finally, they applauded, beginning to wrap their arms around one another. Their eyelids snapped shut, as they seemed to internalize Maddy's speech.

Jerrell had to admit, the words had kind of spoken to him too. Only a little.

While waiting for them to call him for whatever they

needed, he watched Maddy demonstrate the presentation at court, instructing the girls on parading, curtsying, table etiquette, and dress attire.

Maddy presented a proper curtsy with the grace and regality of a swan. Her foot sweeping behind her, she extended the bend of her arm in a ballerina's second position. Her back was ironing-board straight, her body dipping low, almost to the ground, bowing her head as would a member of nobility before a royal court. Finally, she returned to standing in first position. Her admirers clapped once again, the girls' illuminated eyes aglow.

The warmth of these young souls transported Jerrell's memories to his own freshman year, when he showed up to Alpha Beta Kappa's interest meeting. He'd floated on the same cloud of giddy expectation. And once his legacy status to his father and brothers cemented his acceptance, Jerrell's nightmare began. Now, a lone shiver ran down his spine when he remembered being hazed.

To him, all of this grandeur seemed like a nicely wrapped facade.

Yet, in the midst of the girls' heaven, stood a very real and stunning Black Fairy. Her glorious dress swung from one side to the other, and she cast her spell on the entire room.

Jerrell's own pulse galloped, and he felt himself drawn into the allure. His misgivings clashed with visions of this resplendent being who practically floated before him.

"And now for you, Jerrell," Mrs. Emma whispered, as her manicured hand guided him forward.

WHO HURT YOU?

MADDY

"Oh, that's all right, he doesn't have to..." Maddy's voice trailed off. She turned to her mother and sister, her eyes pleading with them not to abandon her. "Mama, you can demonstrate the dance with me."

"Honey, you know how my foot gets when I stand on it too long. It'll go fast." Mrs. Page backed away. "It's only a few minutes."

A desperate Maddy swung to Reet.

"Girl, how will I do the waltz with you in this big ole belly?" Reet lowered her voice. "Just keep your fat lip buttoned, and everything should be fine."

She scanned the ballroom, seeking her dad, in hopes he had stopped by, as he'd said he might. She could use him as her instructional partner. But the father-daughter rehearsal wasn't until tomorrow.

Maddy's eyes landed on the man strutting toward her, who seemed to wear all the discomfort on his face that she felt.

She swallowed uncertainty, rejecting the urge to ask if he'd bathed after walking the dogs. She held out her hands. *Keep your fat lip buttoned*, Reet's voice snickered in her mind.

"You know the waltz, don't you?" Maddy asked.

A chastising glare was Jerrell's response, as the dog-walker or dessert delivery man, or whatever he was, slid his right arm around her shoulder blade. She lay her left hand atop his shoulder, while their opposite hands clasped. In the curve of his arms, her forehead hovered precious inches from his smooth, pillow-like lips and shaven chin. Maddy resisted an urge to rest her head against it. A lavish aroma of sweet baked goods mingled with his cologne that smelled like Italian cypress trees, all teasing her nostrils. The sweetness and forests stopped her breath in her throat, compelling her eyes to his.

The waltz music started, and in unison, he stepped forward and she moved back. In the background, Mrs. Emma began explaining the dance in the shape of a box. Against the backdrop of her voice and the melody, Maddy inhaled his invigorating aroma of Italy and sensuality.

His scent reminded her of wanting to go camping with someone who loved nature as much as she. And how she'd never made love in a cabin in the woods.

Stop it, she chastised herself, diverting her eyes from his skin and switching her thoughts to another subject.

The Senator's press conference, the China technology delays, South America… her mind raced.

Okay, so he could dance a good waltz.

Back, sideways, forward.

Don't screw it up.

She remembered to hold her head high, spine straight, shoulders relaxed. While the polished Capitol Hill staffer radiated on the outside, on the inside, Maddy stiffened as if she were thrown into ice water. Why did he have to smell so delectable?

"Are my dancing skills up to snuff, Princess?" he asked, shaking up her thoughts.

"They suffice," she answered, turning from his mouth. Away from errant fantasies of what it must feel like.

"Glad you think so," he whispered with mint-flavored breath that caressed her forehead. His feet floated alongside hers, his arms holding her to the right side of his solid chest, so their knees did not bump. "You women sure know how to put on a show for these girls who don't know any better."

"Don't know any better? A show?" she asked under her breath while fixing her face, as her mother liked to say. After all, she needed to appear pleasant. "What are you talking about?"

"Getting these young, naive girls to believe in some fairy-tale that doesn't exist. It's setting them up to get hurt."

"What fairytale? Did you not hear what I said a moment ago? The Hamptons are a refuge from a world that's already hurtful. We endure enough hell everywhere as it is. But then, how would you know?" she asked, as her tulle dress swayed, brushing both their feet. "You're probably used to other folks doing hard work, while you show up with your good looks and fine threads for people to fawn all over you."

Jerrell smirked, his nimble legs moving against hers, a muscular arm sweeping her to the side. "So, you think I look good?"

His amused eyes needled hers.

She scoffed. "Of everything I said, that's what you took away?"

"It's the only thing you said that was worth taking."

A tiny laugh escaped her chest before she could capture it. *Dammit.*

She couldn't allow him to think she enjoyed his company. "You just proved my point. Girls like us come to Sag Harbor, to escape from you small-minded people."

"Small-minded," he repeated with a scowl.

"Yes."

"Have coffee with me."

"You still haven't apologized."

It was his turn to laugh before his lips spread over his pristine teeth. "I have nothing to be sorry for."

"Then why are you offering to appease me when you're innocent?" Maddy examined him now.

Unflinching, he returned her stare. "The incident was still unfortunate."

"No. You're used to saying or doing what you want to people, not apologizing, and expecting them to accept some pathetic consolation prize."

Jerrell smirked. "Aha, so you're a psychologist, huh? Tell me something. *Who hurt you?* Who played around with that little heart in there, and you never got over it?"

His questions were icepicks chiseling at her while they danced.

Thoughts of her old crush, Kevin Middleton, immediately flooded her head. Maddy quickly kicked them aside and held her composure.

"Nice way to deflect. I appreciate the offer, but there are plenty of other women you can knock around. They'll like it, and you won't have to apologize or even buy them coffee."

Before she knew it, his hand tightened at her waist, and he drew her closer to him, so his skin brushed hers.

Jerrell murmured against Maddy's hair, and the cream of his voice somehow slithered down her abdomen. "You're right. They do enjoy it. *All* night. I won't hold it against you that you haven't let me knock *you*."

He pulled back and his eyes shoveled hot coals into hers.

She laughed out loud. Her smartass dictionary of comebacks left her. And at that moment, a bright flash went off in their faces as a local newspaper photographer snapped them.

He continued. "It's just coffee. For now."

"I'll be busy," she insisted, even while her panties started getting sticky in her pretty dress. And it wasn't from sweat.

"But I haven't given you a day or time yet," that voice coaxed again. His scent taunted her again. His defined chest muscles kept sweeping her breasts through his sweater, chipping off another piece of her resolve, *again*.

"Unnecessary. Since you can't apologize, I'll be busy until the end of time."

Even as she rejected him, he was funny. The conversation tickled Maddy, taking her mind off her Staff Director's questions she was up researching at 5 a.m.

Still, she was no weakling. She'd promised herself she would leave Sag Harbor with a clear head. No more dudes pulling up in their pricey cars, iced out wrists, and name brand threads, caking strong and pretending to be the real deal when all they wanted was a trophy wife from a family with a reputation.

She was so caught in the tit-for-tat exchange that a pang of disappointment shot through her when the music ended.

Applause and eager murmurs filled the ballroom. Maddy performed another formal curtsy. She swept out her hand, and to her surprise, Jerrell's arm slid under hers to help her balance. His forearm lithe and firm, it steadied her as she lowered and rose again.

"Thank you," she whispered.

"Tomorrow morning. You can thank me then."

She rolled her eyes. "Busy."

Young women rushed to approach them. "Oh, you two are so beautiful. A King and Queen," one of them said.

"Like the President and First Lady," another debutante chimed in.

"Sir, what is your name?" a debutante asked Jerrell. "Can you talk to my boyfriend? He thinks stuff like this is stupid."

Maddy gazed at her pigheaded counterpart, gloating that she'd been right. She enjoyed watching Jerrell's stunned silence, and how those lips seemed to stall in the face of these young women wanting a better class of man for themselves. She removed her long gloves, wearing a slick grin, and left him standing in the crowd.

Once she entered the dressing room to change, Maddy's heart knocked in her ribs.

With cypress trees and bakery sweets still lingering on her skin, she wondered if this thump in her chest was from over-exhilaration on the dance floor, or from him.

When she glimpsed at herself in the mirror, her mouth was open, breasts heaving, and the skin above her collarbone pulsating from her excitement.

Her mother entered the dressing room, wearing the grin of a Cheshire cat, and reached to unzip Maddy's dress.

Maddy stared at her mother's reflection. "Quiet."

The older woman sucked her teeth, her eyes twinkling. "I've never seen your face glow."

"Mama."

"All right, fine." Her mother threw up her hands. "That's it."

The room fell silent. But in Maddy's head, Jerrell's voice kept waltzing on her nerves.

Who hurt you? Who played around with that little heart in there, and you never got over it?

MADDY CAKES

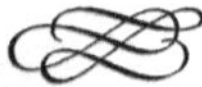

MADDY

A couple of hours later, Maddy joined her childhood friends for afternoon lunch on Adella's family yacht.

From Adella's private dock, they set sail as soon as Maddy arrived from debutante rehearsal and boarded her friend's 60-foot Sunseeker Renegade heated yacht.

With the weather in the reasonable forties, clouds floating under the sun, and the waters smooth and inviting, the group of childhood friends feasted on sturgeon roe, Ecuadorian shrimp, and Chesapeake blue crab. They washed it down with Dom Perignon Oenotheque Rose. Goose-down coats, cashmere scarves and a heated canopy, shielded them from winter's bite.

"We haven't gotten updates on you in a while. How did you come out with that property in Miami-Dade you wanted?" Maddy asked Adella, who was a surgeon by trade but whose father started her out with commercial real estate at an early age.

In ten years, Adella had expanded from New York to more

urban areas booming with growth and immigrants starting businesses.

"Oh, girl, I bought that property a long time ago. It's giving some of my biggest returns. Hair shops, nail salons, and beauty supply stores will never go out of business. Do you hear me? I mean never," Adella laughed, holding out her champagne flute, to which Maddy clinked her own glass.

"Wait," Lana said, shaking her head. "You rent property to those foreign people who sell weaves in the hood and who show no respect for us at all."

Chrissy, Maddy, Adella and the six other Sag Harbor friends who'd joined the cruise, all exchanged uncomfortable looks. Maddy's insides twinged, and she prayed that Lana didn't carry this conversation any further.

"Oh, sure. They're paying their money to a Black woman," Del said. "What's wrong with that?"

"And you use it to buy up more properties and make more profit," Lana asked.

"What else would I do with it?" Del replied.

"Well, do you give back to the communities that spend at your locations? How much of that profit returns to your 'urban' customers that pay for this lifestyle? For boats like this?" Lana pressed.

"That Indian wet and wavy on your head is what you get out of it," Del snapped. "I don't owe you or anybody else any explanations about my business or how I operate. And I damn sure won't justify myself to you. Now, I didn't force you to come on this boat. But since you're on it, you can show some respect."

Chrissy and Maddy exchanged another awkward stare, in which Chrissy questioned why Maddy brought an outsider to Sag Harbor.

Indeed, Maddy had not expected this. Lana was the life of the party on the D.C. night scene when they got out for Congressional Black Caucus week, or when they'd partied for homecoming at Howard or Hampton. But then again, Maddy had never brought her around the exclusive bourgeoisie, who discussed land, venture capital, and investment funds.

Lana's hard work on community projects and equal justice issues had drawn Maddy to her five years prior, when Maddy first arrived on Capitol Hill. Back then, Lana had been on the Hill for a year, and they connected because of their passion for helping people. But since Maddy kept her country club life private, this was the only time an issue had ever arisen as to their different backgrounds.

"Oh, wow, the Love Boat's gotten all quiet and everything. My bad, I didn't mean to stir anything up. It was just a question," Lana snickered, sipping her champagne.

When she reached for the Dom to pour herself more, Del jumped from her cushion. Grabbing the bottle first, she pulled it from Lana's reach.

"Oh, damn, it's like that, huh?" she asked.

Maddy tried to subtly warn her co-worker to chill.

At that moment, Chrissy's eyes dropped to her cell phone buzzing in her hand, and her jaw fell again.

"What?" Maddy asked.

"Well, my, my, I thought you were getting rid of the man, not falling into his arms," Chrissy said with a smirk.

"Girl, don't do that," Maddy protested, trying not to get worked up. "What are you looking at?"

Chrissy passed her phone, and Maddy chafed at seeing the screen. A screenshot of the Madames' social media page was filled with photos of Maddy in her strapless pearl and tulle Vera Wang. And next to her, a strapping male figure with broad shoulders and muscular thighs. An adoring cluster of women surrounded them, clapping and gawking. Maddy's eyes rolled into her head.

"Who sent you this?" Maddy asked.

"My little cousin is a debutante. Said you gave a phenom speech this morning. Had everybody tearing up." Chrissy sat back with her champagne and tossed her childhood friend a knowing look. "So, I guess he's your date now, huh?"

Lana looked at the photo over Maddy's shoulder. "Yeah, y'all cute. You may as well let him hit."

"No, believe it or not, that is not every woman's goal in life," Maddy said with a laugh, hoping to lighten up the vibe.

"Why not?" Lana asked.

Maddy thanked the heavens her sister Reet hadn't joined them because of her pregnancy. She would have been all over this conversation, and Maddy was in no mood. "I'll have a much better time with my parents. No surprises, and no goofy hook-ups. And I'll leave here with peace of mind."

After steering the yacht back toward the shore, Del joined them to see the photos. "Damn, Maddy, you and him are feeling that dance. I haven't seen you look like that since..." Her eyes shot up to Maddy's.

Maddy swung her focus to the ocean reflecting the midday sun, grateful Del hadn't spoken *his* name.

The late afternoon weather was growing chillier. Del's other friends spurred polite conversation to fill the tension between Lana and Del.

Once again, while Del steered back toward land, Maddy turned to her new fiancé Desmond to interact with him. But before she could open her mouth, she caught a covert exchange between him and Lana. The zipper on Lana's jacket had dropped a couple of inches, revealing the ample rack on her chest. And she had freshened her lip gloss, apparently while Maddy and her friends chatted. Once they realized Maddy was glaring at them both, they refocused their attention elsewhere.

"Were you able to get your senator the answers he needed this morning?" Lana asked Maddy, an apparent move to deflect from what Maddy just saw.

Maddy was too livid to form an answer.

No. No, no, no. Not to Del. Of all the people for this to happen to, not Del.

Maddy's head could have fallen into her lap with gloom. If this guy was cheating under Del's nose, what was he doing when she wasn't around? How often?

After they returned to the dock and disembarked, everyone helped Del with tying up dock lines and cleating.

While they looped the line into a cleat hitch, under her breath, Del whispered, "I'm not feeling her. She can't have dinner here tonight."

"I understand. She'll leave Sag Harbor in a few hours," Maddy muttered back. "My bad for bringing her. She's always so cool, so I wonder what's up."

As she scanned the group, laughing and chatting while exiting, Maddy noticed Desmond was not helping his fiancé with the cleating. Rather, he palmed his phone. His eyes roamed toward Lana, who met his gaze, before they both returned to their phones.

Maddy's chest wrapped into a giant knot. How would she handle this? When would they hook up? Lana was leaving tonight. And her departure would be perfect timing.

She approached Lana as the group entered Del's yard and headed to the kitchen.

"So hey, are you ready to head out?" Maddy asked.

"I thought we were eating?" Lana asked, before recognition flickered in her eyes. She laughed. "Oh, I see. I'm not welcome at her dinner now."

"But you're scheduled for your train back to D.C. I'll take you to the station," Maddy offered, throwing a goodbye wave to Chrissy, Del and their other friends.

"Girl, please tell me you high-class folks aren't all sensitive over a simple question? Much money as that chick's got, she must hear questions all the time. She doesn't have some kind of script or something? Like what we give the senators?" Lana asked, getting into Maddy's rental car.

"Lana," Maddy replied in disbelief. They had traveled together a few times over the years, for Capitol Hill staff cruises, skiing and golf resorts. So this sudden irritating change in her confused Maddy. "Whether or not she can answer… that's not the point."

"Well, excuse the hell out of me," Lana retorted.

"So, I'll take you by the house and we'll just pick up your bags."

"Oh, didn't your mother tell you? We talked this morning while you were in the shower, and she invited me to stay through Christmas so I wouldn't be without family. It was real nice of her."

The narrow street of Eastville Avenue seemed to close in on Maddy. Her mother had done *what* and not spoken to her first? "But what about you not having anymore time left for vacation?"

"I called in sick," she said, scrolling through her messages.

Maddy glared at the phone resting in Lana's hand. She fought the urge to snatch it and view who Lana now messaged. But a vulgar picture of a man appeared on the screen, for which Maddy wasn't ready. Disgusted, she turned her head, retraining her eyes on the street.

"Why were you looking over here? Mind your business," Lana said.

Maddy fumed, wanting to tell Lana to leave anyway. To do so would cause awkwardness when they got back to D.C., where they ran in the same circles, attended the same social gatherings, and sometimes traded info or collaborated on assignments. She couldn't ruin this connection. But hadn't Lana already tested it? Aside from that, the atmosphere needed to stay calm and festive for the next two days.

"Girl, be careful. Because Del is a good friend, I've known her for years, and she *is* my business. Don't put me in a bind."

Something had to be said. Maddy and Del went too far back, and though they didn't talk often, it wasn't necessary. Maddy knew Del would drop anything and be by her side, because that's how awesome she was.

To that, Lana clicked her tongue.

On the drive back to her home, Maddy ruminated on how she would broach the subject of Del's fiancé with her, or even if she should.

They passed the firehouse and a surprising line of people poured out of the building, spilling onto the sidewalk. Maddy hadn't heard of any events happening there tonight. Closer to the entrance, disgruntled neighbors huffed. Strangers she didn't recognize also intermingled with those she did. A few residents walked out the door carrying the characteristic plum and white boxes that Maddy now associated with Jerrell. Some looked satisfied. Others, not so much. Maddy pulled the car over.

"Girl, can you drop me at the house first?" Lana asked.

"This will only take a minute while I see what's going on. If you don't want to wait, I'm four houses away. It's within walking distance. You'll be fine," Maddy replied and got out.

"But I placed my order three days ago, over the phone," one neighbor in line complained.

"I put in mine last week!" another customer added.

"This is ridiculous. I'm only standing here so I can get my money back," yet an another resident bellowed.

"Whoa! Where do you think you're going? The end of the line is down there," someone fussed at Maddy as she attempted to squeeze inside.

"I'm not a customer. Just trying to help," she explained.

In the firehouse, Jerrell's customers shifted from one foot to the other, waiting as Jerrell, Myles and another worker hustled to get the pastries wrapped, boxed and rung up on the register.

"Hey," she said to all three workers. "Should I ask how it's going?"

Jerrell looked up at Maddy, did a double-take, and threw himself back into work. "Don't come here gloating. I don't have time."

"So I see," Maddy replied, staring at the infuriated faces. As she realized what must've occurred, she took off her jacket. "What do you need?"

He was moving so fast, interacting with customers and checking orders on his tablet, that he could barely answer. "The line. Ask whose orders we can fill tonight, and what we can deliver first thing in the morning."

Maddy drew back, a little stunned. It sounded like torture. "First thing in the—"

"Yes," Jerrell answered, panicked and tense while he hustled, eyes focused on his task. He didn't explain how she should do it. "The very first thing. No further delay." She got the sense he was talking more to himself than her.

A spare sheet of paper in her hand, she rushed to the line. "Good evening, how are you? We apologize for the inconvenience and appreciate you waiting. There's been a little confusion and we are doing our best to straighten it out as soon as possible. We hope within the next twenty-four hours. Would you tell me what you ordered, so we can try filling it tonight, or first thing tomorrow?"

"I'm having a brunch at my home. Those brandy brownies should have been waiting on me already!" one person called out.

As she wrote names and receipt orders, two or three at a time, she moved back inside to search if they'd been prepackaged, and if not, what pastries were still available. While Myles wrapped food, made 'thank you' notes, and boxed it all, a third worker rang up sales and took phone calls for new orders. For the next two hours, they developed a system in which she tried to do damage control and calm the fury of customers who had paid for pastries they couldn't take home.

At the end of the evening, they all breathed sighs of relief when Myles rung up the last customer. Then, there was another hour and a half of hustle and packing leftover pastries back into Jerrell's van.

No one had to tell Myles it was quitting time. The poor boy had been at work when Maddy attended the Madames breakfast that morning at 9 a.m. He waved goodnight and was out the door before anyone could say it back.

About eight thirty at night now, they finished the last of the clean-up.

"Hey, girl, I'm Deidre, Jerrell's close friend," the other worker said, sticking out her hand.

Maddy hoisted her tired bones to shake it. "I'm Madison, but everyone calls me Maddy. Pleasure to meet you. You must be some buddy to put yourself through all this."

Deidre's hearty laugh rose from deep in her gut as she rolled her eyes at Jerrell. "Yes, in fact, I am. Aren't I?"

This sharp-witted sister seemed to be his reality check. She added another dimension to Jerrell, which rehabilitated him. That, and his hustle Maddy had observed these last few hours.

"Yak yak," Jerrell said, mocking them. "You two have jokes, that's great. Let me treat the two of you to some good seafood," Jerrell offered on the way out.

Maddy's guard rose again. She couldn't sit across from him over drinks, staring at his lips, laughing and joking, making herself vulnerable the next time she saw him. Besides, tomorrow morning, she had to wake up early and work.

"Today's been a long one, and I might not make it through the meal."

"It's only an hour. My probation officer is right here—and her big foot that she'll use to kick me. So, what could I say wrong?"

At the foot comment, Deidre gave him a playful shove. "Actually, these feet hurt, so you're on your own. Pleasure meeting you, Maddy," she said, leaving.

Jerrell's friend tossed him a discreet expression before walking out, as if she were leaving to give him and Maddy privacy. A half-grin appeared at his lips. They'd been discussing her.

"I have an early day tomorrow and I should head out too," she announced, reaching for her shoes. She would check work emails before going to sleep, in case a few landed in her inbox while she was out.

"It's only 8:30," he protested. "Y'all have a nice little community—restaurants, sports bars, game rooms, jazz clubs. Why don't you show me around?"

"As you made clear earlier today, there are lots of women who'd love to," she replied, and stretched to grab her boot. But exhaustion dragged her limbs until she felt too lazy to get up and retrieve it.

Jerrell's knee settled on the floor next to her, his face inches from hers. His long fingers picked up her foot, massaging it. The feel of his firm pressure against her tired flesh sent tremors through Maddy's other body parts.

The aroma of Tuscany and vines entered her head again, flirting with her imagination, parting her mouth. His scent drew Maddy's attention to his curved jaw, and eyes that were already absorbing her.

His voice low, no longer playful, he replied, "But I'm not asking any other woman. I'm asking the one who rushed in today to see if we were okay. Who volunteered to help a brother who ran her down with dogs. Nobody else. Just you."

She swallowed. Maddy hadn't expected this.

Gliding around her calf were his long fingers that held it steady, igniting her nerves that shook past her knees and into her thighs. He slid on her boot.

Maddy wrestled to keep her cool. "Are you admitting guilt?"

He reached for her other foot, massaging it. Slow torture. Sensuous and intentional. He cupped her other calf, holding her flesh like ripe fruit, and slid on her other boot. Maddy's leg remained in his hand that stroked her skin over her leggings.

"Yes."

Her breathing stopped.

"I'm sorry, Ms. Madison Page, that I wasn't more careful on the sidewalk, and knocked you over."

Her brain waves were still too stunned to remind her lungs to breathe. Still on his knee, Jerrell stared into her, unwrapping her.

He had removed her only defense.

She inspected every part of him for whether he was running game. But instead of cockiness, Maddy found his eyes penetrating hers.

He raised from the floor and offered his hand. Warm fingers closed around hers, and Jerrell pulled her up. They were close enough for his scent to waft into her nostrils, for his breath to graze her skin. Maddy's gaze danced with his.

"Thank you." Her heart beat so loud she might not have heard herself say it.

His chest rising and falling, he lifted her hand to his lips, kissing it as his eyes stayed on hers. "You're welcome."

As they walked out and he led her to her rental car, he reached past Maddy, opening the driver door. Again, his scent splashed into the sea of her thoughts, and dropped anchor between her breasts.

Maddy forced herself to get in the car.

He sucked his bottom lip, gazing down at her. "Goodnight, Maddy Cakes."

INFURIATING & BEAUTIFUL

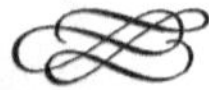

JERRELL

"**P**lease, oh please, come have dinner with me, baby, I'll carry you home on my back. You need me to rub your feet? Want me to cook for you?" Deidre mocked Jerrell while they worked in the shop with his older brother, grandmother, and great-aunt. "I was standing there with my jaw on the floor, like, wow, this dude has left the building!"

"No! That's not what I was doing," Jerrell shot back.

The entire kitchen broke into gut-shaking laughter at his defensiveness. Three days before Christmas, at four o'clock in the morning, all that kept them awake was humor and stories.

"Don't tell me this dude threw his jacket on a puddle so she could walk over it!" Jerrell's older brother Sheldon joked, joining in the shenanigans.

More guffaws bounced across the kitchen, as their hands mixed batters, whipped eggs, and brought their grandmother's pastries to life with an early-morning grind.

"The girl came in and helped when she didn't have to. I was showing appreciation," Jerrell said.

"You wanted to show her more than that," Deidre retorted.

"Who is she?" Sheldon asked. "And what does she look like?"

"Her looks don't matter! How is her heart?" Gram replied.

"She's the daughter of Douglass Page, Dad's dentist," Kami answered. "Our folks holiday with them and play golf when they go down to Virginia. And she's a staffer on Capitol Hill. On the Senate Foreign Relations Committee. That's why J is being such a good boy with her. He needs that sugar to leave the dock in Brazil."

Jerrell shook his head, going over a list of names he would interview for store managers and delivery van drivers. "Y'all are doing too much right now. It's not like that."

He checked price lists and ran budgets, rubbing his eyes after being up all night. In the kitchen's corner sat only four large, knee-high bags. They could not do without that Brazilian brown sugar.

"I gotta get out of here and shower up for work," Sheldon said, offering Jerrell a bear hug. "Real proud of what you're doing here, little brother."

His older brother's arms wrapped around him gave the youngest sibling in the Rouse family a small dose of reassurance.

"Thanks. Appreciate you helping, man. I'll see you in a couple days at Mom and Dad's."

"No prob. And when you come, please keep your bottom lip in. Bring some of your stuff. Don't push. They'll see things on their own now that you're moving up a little. Be cool," Sheldon advised, referencing the big blow-up over Thanksgiving between Jerrell and his folks. Right after his father heard from colleagues that Jerrell had turned in his two weeks' notice at Earl Lynch Bank.

Boy, do you know how hard I had to work to get your ungrateful ass into Brown? His father's larger-than-life voice boomed between Jerrell's ears, ricocheting down his rib cage to his heart.

He squeezed Sheldon's shoulders a final time. Then, Jerrell lifted Kami from the ground and swung her, the way she did to him when they were kids in Louisiana.

She grabbed his face. "You're going to be fine. This is coming together faster than you hoped. Imagine when Gram's desserts are flying off grocery store shelves. We won't know what to do with your colossal head."

"Thanks, Kam Kam," he said.

"Find some time to call Mom. She's worried," Kam suggested.

Jerrell hadn't spoken to either of his parents in almost a month, ignoring his mother's phone calls after she'd sat in appall through Dad's tirade. Her soft murmurs of his name, in hopes he would stop, didn't count. Everybody had been there —all four of Jerrell's siblings, niece and nephew, and a couple of aunts visiting from Louisiana to deliver Gram to Jerrell for their joint venture. In fact, Gram's was the only voice that had been powerful enough to shut Dad's down.

"He's not your boy anymore! You get out of his way and start letting him live his own life. Maybe that's what's been wrong with him all along. Always hurting himself to fit in your shadow."

The argument kept screaming through Jerrell's consciousness.

Kami and Sheldon walked out. To freedom and security, at a well-known, established employer that would deposit a guaranteed check into their bank accounts for Christmas, with a bonus. For what must've been the five-hundredth time since he left the bank and started his own company, Jerrell nursed a moment of doubt. He wondered if he was as stupid as his father said.

The freedom of making his own moves and decisions exhilarated him. It blew him away to see customers' faces light up and kids jump in the air. How their eyes rolled and mouths chomped when they tasted chicken-stuffed crescents or brandy brownies, was sometimes sweeter than money.

But Jerrell had gotten only four hours of sleep a night since starting, sometimes less.

There was no one else to pass the buck to, no secretary to help multi-task, and no reliable structure already in place that he only needed to repeat.

He was the assistant, janitor and system.

At 5:55 a.m., the bang of cabs driving over the pothole on the street, reminded him he was no longer on the sixteenth floor. Boots and hard sole shoes clapped on the sidewalk, and squeaky brakes pulled to a stop at the corner. Far from posh offices with sleek glass desks, catered lunches, and expense accounts. The New York streets were his office now.

Gram squeezed his arm.

"How are you holding up around here?" he asked her. "Is the work too much?"

"Pfft! We are up to our eyeballs in this here kitchen. All this flour and sugar, going home with it all in my hair, on my clothes, under my nails. And I wouldn't have it any other way. Most fun I've ever had in my entire life. Especially seeing my food flying out that front door."

Her upbeat energy differed from the depression he'd heard in their phone calls over the summer. Joy danced on her face, lighting up her eyes.

The sight of Gram lifted some weight from Jerrell's chest. "I'm glad you came."

"So am I. I'm happy you're financing my fun time before I leave this earth," she chuckled. "But listen, what's going on with this Brazilian sugar you like so much? When will you talk with your new lady about it?"

Jerrell thought of that issue himself. He couldn't just spring up on Maddy, who already had barbed wire wrapped around herself, and request a favor. "Not my new girlfriend. I will ask as soon as I can."

"Well, stop taking forever. This sugar won't ship itself," Gram admonished.

By 8 a.m., Jerrell was making the rounds to drop off delayed orders from the day before, arriving at homes as he apologized and thanked customers.

A figure in all-black workout gear crossed the street, a sight for Jerrell's tired eyes. She jogged at a healthy pace, condensation curling around her head in the morning cold. Tight, well-sculpted calves, inward-curving waist, back straight, arms close, fists balled, she was ready to take down any attacker.

Jerrell creeped ahead in the van, intrigued.

Maddy's firm butt cheeks had his full attention. His heart speeding up, he swallowed and wondered, for a moment, if he should blow his horn. It would scare her, and she was in a deep zone of concentration.

Perfect.

He took in the view for a few more seconds, waiting until his wheels lurched just behind her. And he blew long enough to stun her, but not so long that it upset neighbors. As Jerrell had hoped, the pay-off came in her practically having a seizure and leaping a foot into the air.

Jerrell doubled over the steering wheel and cracked up at her expense. This moment was worth his chaotic early morning.

Maddy panted from the workout. Her initial scowl and confusion soon turned to relieved laughter as she realized it was him. Fresh-faced vigor glistened on her sweating cheeks and forehead. Her mouth forming an "o" as she still exhaled, the pristine princess was a sight Jerrell could stare at all day. He slid his window down.

"So not cool. I will get you back for that," she called out. "Trust."

"Hop in here, and help me do some real work," he offered.

Hands plugged against her tight hips, she replied, "I don't accept rides from strangers." Her smile still lingering, she started walking.

"You know we're not strangers anymore," he said, as his eyes appreciated her firm rear end once more. "Or at least we don't have to be."

She surprised him when she stopped again. "And why do you want to be friends with someone who you think is too privileged and uppity?"

He delivered a sly smile. "Maybe I want to dance with the devil."

Even as she turned her face away, he could see her chuckling.

"Good day, Mr. Rouse." With that, Maddy took off with her morning jog.

How was somebody so infuriating and beautiful all at once? Any other woman, he would have written off already. But not her.

Jerrell waved to the residents he now recognized. Their open-mouthed smiles and relaxing demeanor were melting his notions about the exclusive Black upper class. They put up decorations in their yards, walked in from helping one another decorate homes and yards, hauling the larger decorations on their trucks, all while shouting out greetings or a cheer for their favorite sports teams. Circumscribed, the clapboard houses projected no airs.

From what he'd noticed so far, locals were most comfortable keeping daily life low-key. Even people who came from out of town to stay in vacation homes took off the furs and jewelry when they arrived. Jerrell marveled. They went out of their way to remain unseen. To keep this little piece of heaven to themselves.

Inside, Mrs. Emma Vincent and the ladies played bridge. He prayed she didn't ask him to walk her dogs again.

Not only was Jerrell dog tired, but Myles sat in a chair, eyes glued to a game on his phone, and he hadn't greeted a couple of customers. The entire mix-up the day prior was because of Myles somehow failing to enter an accurate order. The ripple effect of his accident on all the other orders and products had turned into a pastry nightmare.

Jerrell was still trying to figure out how to broach the subject with the young man. He'd been that age too once.

"Well, hello there, Prince Charming," Mrs. Emma called, peering up from the bridge table.

Seeing Jerrell, Myles shot up, pocketed his phone, and began taking orders.

"Good morning, Mrs. Emma," he replied, hoping his voice didn't sound tired as he felt. Unsure what to expect after the big mix-up the day before, he approached the Sag Harbor Dears. Multiple sets of eyes peeked at him over their cards. "What did I do to deserve that title?"

"Oh, you haven't seen it yet?" Emma asked.

Another lady lowered her hand to eyeball Jerrell. "He can dance the waltz with me anytime."

Jerrell's jaw fell slack as Emma passed him her phone. Plastered on the Sag Harbor social media page was a snap of smiling, giddy debutantes. In the middle of them all, he and Maddy danced across the floor, she in her wide-skirted tulle gown and he in some standard slacks and a black wool turtleneck. Like a fairytale couple out of a made-for-Hollywood movie.

In a dreamy photo, Maddy flashed a beaming grin for cameras. Jerrell almost chuckled out loud. That woman had shot daggers at Jerrell the entire dance, but the image projected two people on cloud nine. He saw no hints of the knife fight that had almost gone down between them.

"You know," Mrs. Emma started with a raised eyebrow, "Later today, after she's finished with the debutantes, she'll be having story time with the neighborhood children down at Santa's Shop. They're setting it up at *The Ivory* restaurant tonight for dinner."

"I was up all night working on this food. Once we're finished here, I'm heading to my rental to crash," he replied.

Mrs. Emma's eagle eye narrowed. "Young man, please. I know lovers in denial when I see them. She'll be playing Mrs. Claus tonight. My husband, Virgil will dress as Santa Claus. However," she said with a wink, "we can make other arrangements."

Maddy's surprise and giggling just a few minutes ago still pawed at his insides.

"Thanks a lot for that, Mrs. Emma, I appreciate the tip. But Maddy's so busy with all she has going on, I don't want to bother," Jerrell replied.

On the outside, he wore his saddest face for the Sag

Harbor Dears to sympathize with him. But the wheels of his mind turned. Since Little Miss Goody-Two-Shoes was too busy to get off her high horse, he would accept Mrs. Emma's help.

CHRISTMAS TOWN

MADDY

"Come on, Mrs. Claus, Mama Claus, it's time to go!" Maddy's brother William urged them from the car as their family arrived at *The Ivory*.

Smells of salty ocean mingled with seafood that sizzled in local restaurants and bars. The Black-owned *Ivory* was in a predominantly white enclave of Southampton. For tonight, the restaurant closed to all but the Black establishment and social circles from the Black communities of Nineva, Sag Harbor Hills and Hillcrest Terrace.

Maddy's niece and nephew took her hand, pulling and jumping, swinging her in every direction. As they did, she recalled a long time before, when she and her friends had also anticipated this magical event.

"Wait a minute. How are you Santa Claus's wife, and you have not married anybody? You're our auntie," five-year-old Elijah stated, trying to figure it out. "Why aren't you at the North Pole getting my presents ready?"

Maddy's brother William smiled a sheepish grin, while she

shoved him in his ribs. "Did you put them up to asking me that?"

"Of course not! Dude's smart as his daddy," William shot back.

"No, you mean smart like his granddaddy, because that gene skipped a generation," Dr. Page cracked, sliding his hand around his son's shoulders.

"Well, little boy, the real Mrs. Claus is at the North Pole, getting your toys ready, and helping Santa recheck his list to make sure you have been nice." Maddy jumped at him, tickling him as they entered the doors. "Because if you aren't kind to your poor auntie, guess what!"

Elijah burst into laughter. "Okay! Okay! I'll be good."

Scents of hot cookies and cake hit her nose soon as she walked inside the five-star Ivory's heavy gold and glass doors.

"Oh, my sweet Lord," Mrs. Page whispered, her eyes illuminating at the North Pole-themed Christmas town atmosphere, with hanging meteor lights, white trees, fake snow on the ground, life-sized gingerbread men and candy canes, and mechanical reindeer. "The Turners have outdone themselves this year."

"Yes, ma'am, they sure did. What an awesome treat," Dr. Page joined in, marveling.

The maître d' took their coats and greeted them, escorting them to their tables.

He turned to Maddy. "And you must be Mrs. Claus! You're every bit as beautiful as in the photo. Just follow me."

Taken aback, Maddy asked, "The photo?"

"Oh, yes, the princess shot everybody's talking about. You and that Vera Wang gown that made you look like a Black angel, dancing with that handsome prince." He was speaking so fast while hastening to the backroom, that Maddy struggled to catch his words.

Stunned, she pushed her legs harder, cranking her neck to hear. "I'm sorry, but how did you know about this picture?"

"Oh, that gorgeous photo is everywhere. And in the *New York Tattle Society* page."

Maddy felt the heat rise in her Mrs. Claus suit, and now it seemed too tight and irritating. She told herself the image was no big deal, that it was only a dance.

At the threshold of Candy Cane Forest, she stopped in her tracks.

His back to her, tonight's Santa Claus patted children's heads, asking them what they wanted for Christmas, and posing for photos. Mrs. Emma Vincent's husband, Virgil, always played the role of Santa Claus, for many years. But this new man's strapping figure was too tall for Mr. Vincent.

She swept aside worries of the dog walker and the photo and approached her partner for the evening. "Well, hello there, I hope I'm not late. You seem to be great with the children."

The man stood and turned around.

Decked in a red suit, black boots, Santa hat, and a long white beard hanging from his chin, Jerrell smiled.

Maddy's face fell slack as his gorgeous, wide-toothed grin unfolded like a sparkly Christmas card.

"Thank you," he said, "I spent a summer in college teaching English to kids in Senegal, so I have a little experience. Plus, when I find time, I still mentor guys at my old high school in Brooklyn. You know... when I'm not walking dogs."

Was this a joke? Who around here was trying to set her up?

Her chest dived into little somersaults that she couldn't

control. Tiny fireworks exploded through her, and she wondered what was going on. Had she put on enough makeup? Was there lipstick on her teeth? Did she blend her powder into her skin properly?

"Oh, damn," Jerrell continued, relishing that he'd stunned her, "for the first time since we've met, you don't have something smart-ass to say. Color me shocked."

ALL THE WAYS

JERRELL

Jerrell's blood flowed so fast it could have been the Niagara Falls ripping through his veins.

Mrs. Emma reached for Jerrell and lowered her voice. "Now you make this count, young fella, you hear me?"

He laughed. "Make what count?"

The elderly woman winked. "You know what. I'm old, not blind. Don't pretend you're not interested. Every time she shows up, you turn into fudge in the middle of that cake, melting everywhere. You won't stop looking at her. You think we can't see?"

On the other side of Mrs. Emma, Maddy stood. Skirt swirling around her thighs, boots enclosing her tight calves, leggings hugging her skin, her lithe waist encircled by a black leather and rhinestone belt.

But no, Jerrell had no feelings. He had not been waiting all day for the scent of coconut, shea butter and sweet vanilla to transport him to paradise. She was just another woman. And a spoiled one at that. Sharp, feisty, and so unbothered by him it kind of irritated him.

The moment Maddy saw him, she became a deer frozen in the woods, uncertain whether to stay or flee.

Jerrell offered his arm. "Don't worry. You only have to be married to me for an hour."

Maddy peered at the older women who'd helped Jerrell arrange this. As she faced her mentors and godmothers, Maddy wore an accusing expression as if to complain, *you all stabbed me in the back.* Then she placed a stiff hand inside Jerrell's arm.

His hand slid over hers.

Her mouth fell open, as if ready to protest.

"I just wanted to see if they were as soft as they felt yesterday," he whispered before sliding on his white gloves. "My bad. It slipped."

Before she could register a complaint, he led her out, and little children screamed, jumping and clapping as soon as Santa and Mrs. Claus entered the main dining hall. Maddy and Jerrell wore gigantic smiles. The children's excitement bounced off the walls as cameras flashed and the speakers blasted Christmas music.

First was story time, and surrounded by their elves, Mr. & Mrs. Claus took turns reading from Christmas-themed books.

Jerrell observed Maddy throw herself into the stories, lurching forward in her big seat. With her eyes enlarged, she acted out the scary, intense parts while the mesmerized children at her feet jumped. Her drama skills tickled Jerrell, with her voice changes and exaggerated arm movements. Laughter spread over the group as Jerrell took over, giving Maddy's entertainment abilities a run for their money. He added a flare of his own to every word, pausing for a moment to ask a little girl to read a couple of sentences for him.

"What do you think the elves did next?" he asked, raising his shoulders and hands in the air.

Adults chuckled, snapping their cameras and shooting video. When the stories finished, Maddy rounded up the large bag filled with gifts.

A natural smile dawned across her face. Their excitement infected her, and her every movement added a slight hop, or an extra bang. Jerrell couldn't tell who was more thrilled—the kids or Maddy.

"Auntie Maddy, since you're Mrs. Claus now, I hope you hooked me up," one rambunctious little boy declared, taking his gift from Jerrell. He stared from Maddy to Jerrell and back to Maddy. "So, are y'all boyfriend and girlfriend? This means I can get Christmas anytime I want?"

"Elijah Page!" Maddy admonished, trying to hide her own amusement.

Jerrell burst out laughing at the embarrassed roll of Maddy's eyes. The entire room joined him, guffaws erupting all around them.

The little boy dodged as his mother tried to pull him away from Santa, and he ran back to his table.

"Good to know at least the men in your household have some personality," Jerrell muttered to her.

"The women in my family have all the sense," she said, grabbing another gift and calling a new name.

Jerrell made sure his hand brushed Maddy's. Manicured nails, cut just over the fingertips, painted a deep crimson, they flashed around the presents and whipped over the children's shoulders. So immersed in what she was doing, she remained oblivious to Jerrell's occasional glances and touches.

Across the room, Jerrell's gaze met that of an attentive Dr. Page, who stared at him now. He seemed to catch Jerrell checking out his daughter, and the older man hid a cryptic expression under his thick mustache and crinkling eyes. Very self-aware now, Jerrell smiled and returned to his Santa duties.

"Daddy!" one boy in the group screamed, jumping up and running over the other children. "That's my daddy right there!" The little man's elation caused him to trip over another kid's hand.

"Son! Haha! Come here. I told you I'd see you," a man said, stepping from among throngs of parents.

In ignorance, Jerrell awaited the next kid. But to his surprise, Maddy froze. Jerrell followed her eyes to the beautiful father-son reunion unfolding in front of them.

"Psst. Maddy Cakes. Gift?" Jerrell murmured.

The warm and cozy gathering seemed to ice over. Like a wind chill had just blown in from nowhere.

"It's not your time yet. Thursday at noon and not a minute before," a woman snapped whom Jerrell recognized. She snatched the child from his father.

"But I want my daddy!" the boy screamed, squirming to leave his mother's arms.

"Chriselle, not here," an older woman warned, turning to the father. "How dare you show up here where you have no business?"

The man whipped out a piece of paper. "Wrong. A judge told me I can be with my kids and visit a couple hours, so I'm not going anywhere."

"You got a lot of nerve bringing her here," Chriselle hissed.

Jerrell recognized the woman now, and the dread on Maddy's face confirmed it was her friend Chrissy.

"Hold on," Maddy said, dropping the next gift and rushing toward the melee.

"I should be here to watch him with Santa like you!" the man growled.

Maddy's arms waved them outside, as she joined the elders who worked to calm the tension.

Jerrell turned to the curious children who'd been so eager just moments before. Time to improvise.

"So, who wants to pin the reindeer on Santa Claus, huh? Who's got first?" Jerrell called, clapping his hands together. Fortunately, Jerrell remembered the boy's name from a cupcake order a few days prior. "How about Blake! Little Blake. Wasn't it your turn to open your gift?" Jerrell asked in a booming voice. "Ho ho ho, bring your parents on over here, and let's see if you have skills. Come pin this reindeer on Santa."

Maddy walked a sniffling, teary-eyed Little Blake back to the center of the circle.

"My daddy's not going to leave me, right?" Blake whimpered to Maddy.

"He'll be outside waiting for you to tell him what Santa got you. You don't want to let your dad down, do you?" Maddy asked in a soothing tone that Jerrell would have loved to hear her use with him.

Little Blake shook his head, fresh tears brimming to his eyes, and another sob rolled from his throat. "No. Please let him stay."

"He's not going to go. Pin the reindeer on Santa, while I go get Dad," Maddy murmured.

"You promise, Aunt Maddy?" Blake sniffed.

"I am Mrs. Claus tonight, sir," she said, pressing Blake's

nose, "and that over there is Santa, and if you're nice, Santa will make sure your daddy can watch."

Maddy's eyes darted to Jerrell, with a desperate plea for him to help her out.

"Ho ho ho, Santa loves the daddies. But has Little Blake been a good boy this year?" Jerrell asked.

"No!" a small girl answered for him. "He fights all the time at school, and Mommy has to go get him."

"Shut up!" Blake said to the kid who was obviously his younger sister.

The boy's words strummed the strings over Jerrell's heart. Jerrell had gotten into scuffles as a kid when he moved from Louisiana to New York, after his father's promotion. "Well, Blake, everybody gets a second chance with Santa." He lowered to one knee, next to Maddy, and both their hands encircled the boy as they consoled him. "Try it, man. Pin this reindeer on Santa. And let Mrs. Claus go make your wish come true tonight. So your daddy can see."

Maddy looked to Jerrell with gratitude before she rushed from the dining room.

The other adults joined in, music blared again, and one of the other children blindfolded Blake.

"Hot!" they cried, laughing and taking pictures as Blake searched with the reindeer.

"Cold!" the kids laughed when Blake veered in the wrong direction.

Unsteady in his footing, groping at the air in front of him, Blake's mouth shook with apparent fear. His eyes covered, dried tears on his face, he seemed lost.

Jerrell remembered every bit of what that felt like. As the child shook his head, he seemed about to give up and take off his blindfold.

"Keep going, son," a male voice called from among the cheering. "You can do it! Get that reindeer on Santa Claus. Don't quit."

Maddy had reentered the room with both of Blake's parents and the father's significant other that he'd brought.

Blake's lips spread into an eager, open-mouthed smile, and he kept groping through his blindfolded darkness.

"Hot!" the kids screamed. Within seconds, Blake found Jerrell, and Jerrell couldn't resist giving him a bear hug.

"I told you Santa Claus would help you out," Jerrell said, turning to Blake's parents. "Mom and Dad, get over here and let's celebrate your magnificent little boy that came from both of you. Look at how talented he is."

Chriselle and her estranged husband Blake appeared to swallow rocks as they trudged to opposite sides of Blake and Santa.

Maddy went to stand at her friend's side, locking her hand into Chriselle's and squeezing, as they all posed for the photo.

At the end of the night, Mrs. Claus leaned in her chair, massaging her feet as families filed out.

"Heaven, it's been too long since I wore these boots."

"You surprised me out there. Those kids were feeling you. If I didn't know any better, I would've guessed you were trying for an Oscar."

Earlier tonight, Maddy had transformed into someone else, as if she lived at the North Pole, and Jerrell had loved every moment.

"You weren't so bad yourself."

"If only you were that nice all the time," he pondered aloud, plunking into the other seat.

"I am. To those who deserve it," she half-moaned in her

tired state. She removed her Santa hat, revealing the slender curve of her neck.

His exhausted shoulders slumped, and Jerrell took a breather before loading his van. "Maybe people are more worthy than you think."

"Or maybe more of them should do better and earn respect. Excuses, excuses," she sighed.

"… are tools of incompetence…" Jerrell replied as if the line lived on his tongue.

He watched her eyes blink upon her seeing that he knew the poem.

She continued it, often recited in Black fraternities and sororities. "… and those who often use them…"

"… Are seldom good at anything," Jerrell finished. His hand moved across the arm of the chair where hers rested.

"What did you pledge?" she asked.

"ABK. And let me guess… Delta Theta Tau." She matched the profile—snooty, prissy, and elitist.

She drew back, faking offense. "Excuse you. Alpha Phi Gamma."

Now it was his turn to show surprise, laughing with genuine shock that she'd joined a more down-to-Earth sorority, the one that was known for community activism. "Wow. Sorry, I just can't see it."

They both scanned the room, realizing that, other than the cleaning crew, they were the only people left in the dining hall. Even the owners, the Turners, had cleared out.

"You don't have anybody to help you load up your desserts?" she asked. "Where's Myles?"

"Oh, he headed to a friend's house. You know how that goes. Kids are so eager to work nowadays," he said with a chuckle. "But it's cool. I'm used to doing it myself."

"Without staff to assist? I thought you hired and fired?" she asked.

"Good workers are hard to find. My friend Deidre is here from Louisiana, helping me get things off the ground while I interview for someone permanent. She runs the shop in Brooklyn, and I hustle here." He thrust himself from the chair to clear out the cake dishes.

Fatigue wore him down now. After thirty-six hours of no sleep, Jerrell was dying to hit the hay.

"You look like the wind outside is going to blow you down. I'll help you with some of those," Maddy offered, coming toward him and taking a few platters. "Wow, there's not a single slice of dessert left."

"Hmph," he scoffed. "You're surprised?" Jerrell paused a moment. "Have you had any of this?"

Maddy's bashful expression was his answer.

He continued, "Oh, damn, you are going hard on ignoring my product, huh? Everybody all over town has tried my dessert but you."

She helped him push the cart through the kitchen where employees still washed dishes and put away food.

He turned to the restaurant crew. "Hey, folks, who in here hasn't tasted my desserts yet?"

Workers nodded their heads with approval. "I've got some cupcakes to take home to my kids."

"Does anybody have extra? So this woman can see what she's missing," Jerrell inquired.

"No!" Maddy retorted. "You all are tired and ready to clock out. Don't let this man talk you into giving up your food." She glared at Jerrell. "That is just like you, asking these hard-working folks to give up their stuff."

She turned to open the backdoor, so they could wheel the

cart through.

Behind her back, a worker passed Jerrell a piece of the Fatally Fudgy Fudge Cake, and he moved fast. When Maddy swung around again, he stood right beside her.

But he hadn't intended to stand so close that her face rammed into the fork he held. Part of the cake smeared her cheek, and a few morsels with icing swiped her lip. Her annoyed eyes could shoot bullets into Jerrell.

The mess on her cheek broke him into guffawing. "I didn't mean to do that! It was an accident!" He explained through his chuckles. "But here. Since you're standing there…." He felt bold enough to push the fork of remaining cake into her shocked mouth that already hung open.

She was beautiful. And helpless, cornered between the door and the cart of dishes, unable to move.

"Why are you feeding me? I'm not a puppy."

"You do act like one, though. Jumpy, snappy, whiny." His voice lowered as he slid frosting on her nose. Jerrell watched her fluffy lips chew. He scooped another piece of cake off the saucer and closed in once more.

Maddy's hand swiped his fork aside, and he came right back at her again, smearing icing over her jawline, and against her cheek.

"Now what? See," he teased. "You're too slow."

Horror escaped her open mouth, and he shoved in another forkful. "Good girl. That's it."

She huffed through curled lips. Pinned against the wall, her eyes wild and annoyed, looking like they wanted to scorch him, she sent Jerrell's self-control out the window.

"You are going to get it, I promise," she muttered.

Jerrell wiped off some of the icing and stroked her cheek. His face was only inches from hers, as he wore a sly smile and kept his voice low. "And I look forward to all the ways you'll give it to me."

He pulled a clean fork through his lips and winked.

Maddy's face froze like a trapped buck.

No smart aleck comeback catapulted from her mouth.

"We should let these workers go home," Maddy murmured instead.

As if recognizing that she needed to put her mental armor back on, she inched away. Her playful, vivacious mood clouded over, and the chinks in her gear tightened around her again.

They entered the cold, and Jerrell's breath froze in his throat. Inches of snow had piled up on the parking lot, still flying from the sky and swirling at their faces. It rose above their ankles and surrounded the tires on his van. He had not yet purchased all weather tires!

"Snow!" he shrieked.

"Hey, why is your vehicle light on?" Maddy asked.

He rushed to the van where he'd left the door ajar. "No!" he huffed.

He jammed the key inside the keyhole and tried starting the ignition several times. It wouldn't start. This couldn't be happening. His head fell against the steering wheel, and he wanted to kick himself. He remembered how he'd gotten distracted when he saw Maddy in her Mrs. Claus outfit. Right as he was bringing in the last set of pastries. He became so engaged in the event—well, who was he kidding, wrapped in her—he forgot to return and lock up the van.

Maddy's eyes fluttered at realizing no one was in the parking lot mingling anymore. Everybody had gone. "My family just left me." Her face sank further. "And I forgot my purse with my cell, wallet, and everything."

Jerrell let her borrow his phone to call her folks to come and help them out, but they were too afraid to return on the icy night streets.

"I thought Chrissy was bringing you home," her mother explained. "You were busy with her and her kids, so we figured she was your ride. Your father and Will can try to get you tonight, but the streets have already started freezing fast. There are plenty of hotels there. Stay in one and call me so I know you're safe. We'll pick you up tomorrow when they clear the roads."

Jerrell couldn't believe this. How was he so stupid? On the other side of the van, the door flung open again and Maddy got out, allowing a blast of wind and snow into the already chilly van.

"What are you doing? Where are you going in all this?" he asked, staring at the face of a chocolate angel that could have been standing atop a cake.

"To get a room."

"With what money?" he challenged.

Her head swung toward him. "So, you're not coming? You know I'm good for the money. I'll pay you back tomorrow."

Jerrell thought about it, debating whether to call the 24-hour roadside assistance to come and give his battery a jump. How would he drive to the shop in the morning to pick up tomorrow's deliveries? These next few days of sales would make or break him.

But his eyes were closing from exhaustion.

And standing in his sight was a demanding, rebellious lioness whom he wanted to tame.

Maddy shut the door between them, starting off in the harsh weather without an answer from him, as to whether he would pay for her hotel room.

Through his rearview mirror, Jerrell watched as she wasted no time, legs high-stepping through the snow. Jerrell had a mind to teach her a lesson and leave her by herself for assuming he would follow her. He should've called roadside assistance and gotten ready to operate his business first thing in the morning. It was what his father and older brothers would have warned him to do.

But Maddy's sashaying hips were a siren's call, clearing his head of all better judgment.

YOU'RE LYING

MADDY

"Thank you so much, Mr. Davies," Maddy said, almost with a plea to the *Oasis Cove* hotel manager who'd known her and her family going back decades. He was checking to find her a room in his booked hotel three nights before Christmas.

She couldn't believe her folks had left her at the *Ivory* alone, without saying a word. She'd thought they were still outside mingling. On her tired feet, eyes darting around the grand entrance, she concluded her parents and the neighbors had arranged this. The dance with the debutantes, her mother's and sister's big smiles all smug. The Madames circulating the photo of her and Jerrell up and down the Eastern seaboard. Her father's cozy embrace of this guy. The coincidence of Jerrell popping up to take Mr. Vincent's place as Santa, while everyone kept Maddy in the dark. All a setup. Her mother had promised no ploys or scheming behind her back.

"Ah!" Mr. Davies exclaimed, looking up from the computer. "We have something."

"Oh, my God," she sighed with relief.

"We found a very nice room that is very worthy of you, and," he leaned forward, "I'll set you up with a deal since you're only here riding out the snow."

Smugness settled over her as she turned to the high-minded Jerrell, who she suspected had come only to watch her beg him for money. The scowl on his face confirmed she was right.

"Must be nice having Daddy's connections," Jerrell muttered under his breath.

"I'm afraid there's a snag though, Maddy," Mr. Davies said, staring at Jerrell. "We can only make one room available. Not two."

Her satisfaction tanked. As she opened her mouth to press for another suite, she stopped herself. How could she implore the man to try harder after he'd just helped her at the last minute, during Christmas? With a warm smile, she accepted her fate—stuck in a snowstorm for the next few hours with a man-child.

Minutes later, when they stepped into a signature suite at one of the Hamptons' top hotels, Jerrell let out a low whistle.

"Ah, we're fancy, huh?" he asked. "Daddy's girl got all the—"

"Enough with the Daddy's girl noise," Maddy snapped, maybe harder than she intended. "I have my own money; I do my own work. People know me and respect me for my accomplishments, separate from my family. So stop treating me like I'm some *dimwit*."

She had dealt with the "poor little rich girl" label her entire life.

"Alright, my bad," he said, moving to start the fireplace. As the flames danced against his face, he held out a drink toward her. "Truce? At least to get through tonight?"

Kicking off her boots, she rejected the liquor. "Truce. But I'll get up early tomorrow, so I shouldn't. I'll take a bottled water."

"Of course, you will. Do you ever relax?"

"Only around people I trust," she shot back, standing inside the restroom as she removed her itchy stockings. Air on her skin felt so good. Her stomach growled, and other than Jerrell's cake, she'd eaten nothing all day, not even at the event.

With no pajamas, she had only the Mrs. Claus dress and hotel slippers. She tried not to notice Jerrell's eyes sweep across her figure. Now self-conscious, she hadn't shaved since the week before, in case she and Sherman got together while she was still in D.C. Her legs weren't a bushy forest, but neither did they shine like a glistening beach, the way she liked them. But why did she care?

"You can borrow my T-shirt," Jerrell offered.

"No, I'm fine in this," she replied.

He laughed. "Woman, we are two grown people. I've seen plenty of women. What you have underneath is no different."

Maddy answered him with silence, while she ignored the low pulsating between her thighs.

She called room service and ordered a crab sandwich, performing her good deed for the day by also placing Jerrell's order. In front of the crackling fire, she warmed her still-iced feet and legs. The next few hours would fly by, she told herself.

He took off the Santa suit, hanging it in the closet, rather than throwing it around, so he wasn't messy.

Maddy averted her eyes and refocused them on the fire.

But her attention slipped to his body in the mirror, where the hotter flames burned across his chest and back. A white shirt covered taut, sculpted muscles. Slender and toned, it was the physique of somebody who cared about himself.

Oh, no, she thought, *I am not scoping him.*

She shifted her gaze again, refusing to turn weak or vulnerable tonight.

A few awkward moments passed once she eyed the bed between them.

His easy laugh was unnerving. "You *have* been in the room with a man before, right?"

"That's not for you to worry about. Where will you sleep?" she asked, making clear it wouldn't be with her.

As if reading her mind, he stepped forward, stopping inches from her. The fire now danced in his eyes. "Wherever you want me."

She fished through her brain in search of her voice. "Good. I want you over there on the couch."

Jerrell reached over her, his bare arm brushing her shoulder, warm breath heating her skin, and took his drink from the mantle. "I think you're lying. The way you were just staring, I could've sworn the couch is the last place you want me."

Maddy's insides quivered. So, he had good comebacks. As she searched for a righteous comeback to fend him off, none came. Her blood was too busy pounding her ears, while the throb between her thighs screamed.

His serious eyes cast all her doubts into the flames. A soft, golden glow highlighted his mouth that confronted her, his jaw line curving toward her, and his muscles that begged to be gripped.

She hadn't ever felt this weak. Nor so wet. A sigh escaped her throat, and she tried to be strong. "Stop gam—"

In one quick motion, Jerrell set his glass down, slid his hand around her neck, and easily pulled her to him.

Before she could open her mouth again, Jerrell covered it with his. His tongue wasted no time finding hers, and he pushed the flavors of whiskey and sweet cake frosting onto her tastebuds. Dipping and swirling around her tongue with confidence, his motions ignited a storm in her nipples and thighs. Jerrell's soft insistence was every fantasy she'd wished for and never known.

His hands cupped her neck, making her yearn for him to cup more of her. Tension in the Capitol Hill staffer's neck muscles dissipated under the relaxed touch of his fingers kneading her flesh. All her objections and pretenses fell into the flames as his lips sucked, tasted, taunted hers. His kiss awakened parts of Maddy she didn't know existed, and not one of her muscles moved to stop him.

It was Jerrell who pulled away. His wet lips brushed her forehead. "You're gorgeous. And I won't lie, Madison, I want you."

Every pulse point on her body clamored, while her brain tried to process this new reaction to a man she couldn't brush off or yawn at. His fingertips still held her neck. Why did his touch feel like warm marshmallows on her flesh? Her head still spun from his tongue, but she dug deep for her brain. She was the one who was usually in control. But he'd pulled the rug from under her.

"You want me, or want to get to know me?"

"Stop acting like you're not catching feelings for me," he replied, while the irises of his eyes clutched Maddy.

"I'm not," she whispered against his chest. But her raging body parts screamed she was a liar. She needed to balance herself. She made the mistake of laying her palms on his pecs. Solid, lithe, and sturdy.

God.

Jerrell's thumb caressed the delicate skin along her throat, right where her carotid artery pulsated.

"Then why does someone so disgusted with me breathe so hard?" He kissed the temple of her head. "Whatever man hurt you, I'm not him."

A knock at the door broke his hold on her.

Jerrell tipped the server and brought the tray of food to the bed. He gave Maddy her portion and then surprised her by taking his plate to the sofa, as she'd requested.

They ate in silence, as she tried to pretend what just happened didn't really happen.

She bit into her crab sandwich, on tough baguette bread that crumbled all over the sheets. "Crap! This looked so much better in the photos."

Jerrell ignored her, smacking up succulent, buttery lobster meat from his dish and then digging into a hot baked potato swimming in chives and garlic butter sauce. His plate appeared far more amazing. But if Maddy ordered again, she would have to wait another thirty to forty minutes, and she was ready to pass out. She took more bites of tough bread and cold crab, as more crumbs sprayed everywhere. Resentful, she chewed through the near-styrofoam food.

He pushed lobster meat through his lips, pulled his fingers out, and sucked the butter off each one of them, loud enough that she rolled her eyes. He slurped a swig of whiskey. As she battled to keep her own food from falling apart, she watched him go through his entire plate, until only a few bites of corn on the cob, potato and lobster remained.

He then rose from the sofa and brought his plate to the bed, sitting next to her.

Thrown off, she flinched and started to scoot away. "What are you—"

"Here. If you don't want it, I won't waste my time. I need to sleep. You're not the only one who rises early," he said, holding the lobster to her lips.

"I can feed myself," she insisted, as her uncertain vocal cords undermined her.

"So can I." He swiped the lobster meat across her mouth. She tried to grab his arm. He jerked away, and she missed. He brushed the delicacy over her chin and neck.

Maddy shuddered. Her jaw fell as he moved toward her, leaning so close his breath mingled with hers.

"Madison Marie Page." He slid lobster across her lips. "Rhodes Scholar. National Merit Scholar."

She gasped, and as she did, he pushed the crustacean inside.

"Summa cum laude graduate of Spelman College. Bachelor's in Political Science, Master of Public Administration and Business Administration from Oxford University." Each time he spoke, he swiped the meat over a different inch of her skin, his touch searing her flesh. "Former President of Alpha Phi Gamma Sorority." Another swipe of buttery lobster across her chest, just over the rim of her V-neck bodice. "Former Student Body President at Grassfield High School." He dipped the lobster in butter sauce, and Maddy didn't object. "Former Madames Debutante Queen." He swept the lobster along her jawbone, following it with his eyes. "Former White House Intern. Senior Legislative Assistant for Senator Randall Easton on the Foreign Relations Committee." He brought the food back to her mouth. "And of course, daughter of Douglass and Maryann Page."

When Maddy's flesh pulsated in her panties, Jerrell's mouth lingered in front of hers.

Maddy waited, studying his eyes that taunted her, anticipating where he might touch her next. She could only imagine his tongue playing inside her bra, her stomach, her clit.

Jerrell pulled away. "You irritate the hell out of me. You're stubborn and uppity." He shoved the rest of the lobster in her mouth, stuffing it so full she had to jerk from him. "And too hell-bent on your pursuit of justice. It may cost you friends. You're too pure. And can't have fun. Not even when you're supposed to." Maddy chomped like a horse to keep all her food in. "And yet still—don't ask me why—I want to get to know you."

Angry at herself for acting so desperate, she tried to calm her begging body parts. She hadn't expected this. No one had ever been so... so... what was he? How had he learned all her information? Where had he found her curriculum vitae? Who had he talked to?

"Where did you learn all that?"

"Don't worry about it. You're not the only person with connections. And whether or not you like it, you and I have one. That you're still here tells me you want to get to know me too."

Maddy's pumping heart sent her blood raging through her. "*No.* Just because you've got a little game doesn't mean—"

"Woman, I've got more than that. And you want to find out what. Now, are you going to get off your high horse and eat this or not?"

Fighting every shred of her common sense, Maddy opened her mouth and allowed him to feed her the rest of his food.

Still nervous, feeling very self-aware, she laughed aloud when he pushed the corn cob too high into her nose.

"Yeh, girl, shuck that corn," he chuckled.

Each time Jerrell's steady fingers smeared more butter along her lips, he tenderized her. No awkward silences lingered, no reaching for words between them. To the contrary, Jerrell's hands and relaxed tone reinforced that he did not fear her.

But all of Maddy's fear came creeping back. Did he plan to use her? Was she some kind of conquest? A check off his bucket list? Kevin Middleton all over again? One thought after another sped through her mind, as Jerrell slid the last morsels of crab and potato in her mouth.

"Stop thinking so hard," he murmured. "You don't want to hurt yourself."

She glared at him. "It wasn't myself I was thinking of hurting."

Jerrell's stare intensified, his eyes flashing at Maddy. "Well, be careful before you think to hurt me, because I just might like it."

She sucked her teeth. "I wouldn't be so sure."

"I am. Just admit you've been wrong about me."

He leaned toward her. She jerked back, terrified he would kiss her again, and she'd lose the ounce of fight she had left.

"I'm not. I know it."

"Let's see. You assumed I was a broke dog-walker who you could talk down to and push around. Then, you figured I was some delivery driver working two jobs. You thought I didn't have any connections, or money, or a career, and I wasn't worth your time. And then you concluded, because I wouldn't apologize for what happened, I'm some conceited boss who abuses my employees. And every time, you've been wrong. Aren't you the one who owes me an apology?"

Maddy shifted in the bed, getting under the covers to warm her feet. "No. Goodnight, Mr. Rouse."

As if collapsing, he rolled onto her bed. She shrieked, pushing him.

"What are you—"

He kept rolling, smashing her underneath him. Was he going to attack her? Take her by force? She shoved his heavy shoulders and tried to kick him off, but his legs pressed against hers.

He now lay on top of Maddy, his lips hovering over hers, so close the seafood and potatoes on their breaths mingled. The nearness of him, his body heat trapping hers, sent electrical jolts through her joints. The covers separating them weren't thick enough to blunt his heart beating on top of hers. Maddy's eyes tumbled into the dark forests of his, so deep she searched to navigate inside them. Along her hairline, his fingers teased her skin. His eyes open, as if daring her to fight back, he sucked her bottom lip, slow.

Between them, between her legs, he pressed his long, tough-as-brick erection. Her mouth dropped wider. His stare still unlocked her tough exterior. Maddy couldn't find a working vocal cord in her throat to save her life.

Jerrell rolled off. He landed on the other side of her in bed. A devilish grin on his lips, he nestled his head on her pillow, just inside the crook of her arm.

As she started to admonish him for treating her like furniture, his eyes snapped shut. A small snore told her goodnight. He was already out.

"Ugh," she scoffed, realizing what he'd done.

He'd only fed her so he could sleep in the bed instead of the couch.

Well, she thought while finishing his whiskey, *this was a first.*

MADDY AWAKENED FROM A DREAM, snuggling in warm, goose down covers. Expecting to hear her niece and nephew downstairs, and her sister's loud cackling, instead she heard crackles of a peaceful fire. Sounds of shuffling and a muffled voice pulled her from remaining sleep. Hints of daylight peeped through the blackout curtains.

"Mhmm. Yes, sure," a male spoke on the other side of the room.

Oof, she remembered. *That's right.* Jerrell. He sat at the small desk a few paces away, his back hunched over it, scribbling.

The digital alarm clock on the nightstand displayed it was 6:57 a.m. Not even sunrise.

He couldn't make his phone call elsewhere? Or on another planet? So she could get an extra couple hours of much-needed sleep. As she tried to doze off again, he appeared over her.

"Hey."

She pulled the covers over her face. Lord only knew how she looked. As far as romantic first encounters went, the two of them were batting a thousand.

"Sorry, but I have to go. My pop-up needs to start. I'm already behind for the day," he murmured, tugging at the covers, to which Maddy clung.

"Good thing I'm not stopping you," she grumbled underneath.

"Your mom called. She won't be able to pick you up until this afternoon. And we have to check out of here by eleven. I can't come back and grab you then, so…"

"What about your van?"

"I had roadside assistance give me a jump. I'll meet you downstairs," he said, slapping her butt over the covers. With none of the fanfare from the night before.

He'd been up that early? How had he awakened before her? She watched as he hustled through the room. He wore a different sweater and a pair of crisp jeans, throwing on his heavy leather coat. Where had he gotten those fresh clothes?

Jerrell's gloved hands clapped together, stunning her as he mimicked a drill sergeant.

"You're on borrowed time now, girl! Chop chop!"

After freshening up best as she could with complimentary hotel toiletries, she trudged toward the elevators.

Yearning for a hot bath, maybe even a mani-pedi, she thought out her day. At some point, she needed to round up her girls, Adella and Chrissy. After the fiasco with Chrissy the night before, Maddy wanted to check if she was all right. She would do it after Jerrell dropped her off.

On the elevator from the twelfth floor, she waited as people got on. *Great.* She wondered what these folks were doing up at 7:15 a.m. while on vacation. Yet a third time, the lift slowed again, and the doors opened.

Then a pair of familiar crimson, leather boots with a kitten heel, appeared in front of Maddy. Long, candy apple red nails scrolled through a phone. Thick, rounded legs in tight jeans ascended to a voluptuous, curvy derriere. On top of it rested a possessive claw of wide male fingers.

Maddy's shock threw the air from her lungs.

Lana.

So close to her that his penis may as well have searched her pocket, stood Desmond. Adella's fiancé.

They stepped into the elevator, and Lana remained distracted with her phone. But Desmond's eyes widened with recognition. As soon as he noticed Maddy, his hand fled from Lana's ass. The doors closed them all in, and Maddy suspended into weightlessness.

One of the sweetest and most giving people in the world, Del was the last person who deserved this. Maddy moved not an inch, making no space for them. So, she and Lana stood shoulder to shoulder, with Lana's long weave brushing Maddy's face. Elevator music played as Desmond stiffened under Maddy's glare. She noticed his elbow press against Lana for her attention.

At last, Lana looked up as Desmond's gaze fell down. Turning to find Maddy, Lana snickered, letting out a snort and flicking her hair.

Should Maddy confront them? Was it her place? Or should she walk out?

"Look, mind your own business. Leave your nose out of things you don't know about," Lana hissed as they stepped off.

"I want you gone. Don't return to our home anymore. You'll need to leave," Maddy snapped back.

"No, I don't think so. I already accepted your parents' invitation, and it would be rude to just up and go. I've been making good connections here. So keep out of my business and I'll see you for Christmas dinner." Lana swept her hair around her neck, before strutting toward the hotel's double doors. Behind her trotted Desmond, who avoided eye contact.

In disbelief, Maddy could have swallowed flames.

AND YOU LIKE IT

JERRELL

This morning, Jerrell had awakened to Maddy's thick hair tickling his face. Her dress had bunched around her hips, displaying lace white panties he'd fought not to pull off. Her well-kept feet had impressed him (he checked), and soft, clean-shaven legs, with enough meat on her thighs for grabbing.

He'd laid and watched the quiet grace of Madison Page sleep at his side. The nightmare of his business boarded up had forced him to finally leave her in bed.

It had been a long time since a woman lay next to him whom he hadn't sexed. Only one other woman was so pure and innocent he could wake up and not touch her. Raychelle. Very few women like Raychelle existed. His mother was one.

But for each hypnotic inch on Maddy, there seemed to be fifty irritating character traits to match.

Jerrell was already getting off to a late start, and now he had cargo. With an attitude. Maddy slammed the door of his van and sat stoic next to him.

A pain in his ass was the last thing he needed right now,

while he worried about the lifeblood of his and Gram's new business—the Brazilian brown sugar. He couldn't shirk his plans for the morning to take her home.

Grateful that snowplows had cleared the streets early, he turned from the hotel onto the road. In his own thoughts, he steered toward the city.

"You just made a wrong turn. My neighborhood is down there," his rider blurted.

"I have to head into the city first, pick up my goods." He drove away from Sag Harbor's beach shops and intimate roads that were bustling to life. It would be a two-hour ride each way, and he was late.

"Downtown!" she shrieked. "Why didn't you tell me that before I came with you? I would've called a cab or waited somewhere for my folks."

Yes, that's what he should have done. But a tiny sliver of him—infinitesimal—wasn't ready to take her home.

"What do you have to do today, besides sit on yachts with your uppity friends, eat caviar and order people to bring you more champagne?" he asked.

Out of the corner of his eye, he watched her roll her eyes. "It's none of your business what I have to do. Who do you think you are, hijacking my time?"

"You want me to let you out?" he asked, pulling over. He stopped next to a tiny coffee shop, shoe repair, a store of ornaments and cards, and a small restaurant. "You can spend the morning out there."

Her jaw lowered like a broken gumball machine. He watched her eye her surroundings, and the prospect of sitting on tough, wooden chairs in the cold. She gave in, plunking her arms into one another, across her chest.

Jerrell turned on the heat when he noticed her shivering.

Less than an arm's length apart, irritated silence formed the soundtrack to their ride.

She sat stiff as a corpse for a while, compelling him to check that she still breathed. The longer they rode, he felt a drop of guilt that he didn't tell her they'd be out for most of the morning.

"If you're hungry, we'll get you something in a minute," he said.

She withheld her reply, instead staring out of the window as they rolled through the wintry fields of Southampton, toward the County Route 39 to the city. When she wasn't looking, Jerrell watched her face peer through the frosty glass.

"So, you spent a lot of days around here, growing up?" he asked, attempting to make up for "hijacking her time," as she'd put it.

Another silent moment. As they rolled down the road, Jerrell clenched the steering wheel.

The nerve of this spoiled ass girl.

How could a cool dude like Dr. Page have raised such a brat?

"Yes," she replied, before she surprised him with a big sniff. She turned further from him, so the entire back of her cottony head hid her.

Wow.

So, this was how she would act? Over her schedule being backed up by a few hours?

He had been stupid to imagine what kind of day they'd have if he stole her away for a while. Jerrell fumed for the next half hour as they rode, pressing the gas pedal harder so he could get this toddler back to her daddy and out of his hair. She had twisted so far from him now that her upper body faced the outside.

But her shoulders twitched, as if she tried to conceal wiping her tears.

"Um," he cleared his throat. Was she crazy? He had suspected it but couldn't be too sure. "You good?"

"Yes." Her throat had dried; it sounded hoarse now. Her strong conviction from the night before was gone.

Jerrell fumbled for what to say, as he drove through the quiet, rural roads filled with white Christmas trees.

"You familiar with this area or something? Why do you have an attitude this morning?" he finally prodded.

She sniffed. "The last time I rode through here, my grandma was still alive."

Jerrell's heartstrings tossed in the Christmas winds, and his anger softened. He didn't know what he would do if he lost Gram. His fear of losing her was the reason he'd brought her to New York and financed her lifelong dream.

"Damn. Sorry about that. The two of you visited the city often?" he asked, trying to get her to open up. At hearing her love for her grandmother, he sighed with relief.

"A lot. GeeGee loved theater. Our last visit, I rode up from D.C. It was spring, her favorite season. We stopped and ate at Miss Mayhem's that she liked, went shopping, and saw *A Raisin in the Sun*."

"My grand hasn't ever been to a play. Other than the ones at her church. But not a real one, on Broadway or something. Sounds like you treated her real well."

Her head still turned away from him, Maddy made small motions, again trying to conceal her wiping tears. "She was good to me. To all of us. The best kind of woman there can be."

"What about her makes you say that?"

"Grandmothers hold up the world. They've got all the secrets and understanding," she answered.

The truest words she could have spoken. "One thing we can finally agree on."

"But enough about me," she said. "Talk about yourself. Why are you out here delivering cakes and pies at the butt crack of dawn when you had a good job, and a nice salary and an office on Wall Street? What? You got fired? You came from a financial family. You have means. So, what is this beef you have against people with money? And why haven't I seen your parents at any of your pop-ups? Why didn't they come support you at the *Ivory* last night?"

Jerrell swallowed. He both loathed and appreciated her directness. "Alright, fine. Yeah, my folks are tripping over what I'm doing. My desk job sucked the life from me. I was losing my mind. My dad and brothers love finance, and so do I. Just not…." Now it was his turn to stare out of the glass, stroking the stubble growing on his chin after the last couple of days without a shave. "Not the office part. I looked outside and saw the world passing while I was crunching numbers until ten or eleven o'clock at night. Sure, the money and perks are good. But not when you don't have time to spend it."

"Why didn't you take a job abroad?" she asked.

He shrugged. "I did. Japan. But it was the same thing over there. I did somebody else's work all day, protecting their dream, watching them live. Where was the reward for me? Money wasn't it. I started asking if I would be miserable the rest of my life?" A thought crossed his mind. He eyed her. "You like your job?"

Hey, he calculated, he wasn't a complete user if he segued into the Foreign Relations Committee. While they were here…

"Yes." Her face illuminated at the mention of it. "My work is everything to me. I wake up every day excited to help communities. I've loved that my entire life. There's rarely a dull day."

"So how did you get hooked up with that?"

"No hookups. I jumped on it when I was in college, starting as an intern during my junior year in the president's administration. Put in my application."

"For real? Right in the White House? Or in a Department?"

"The White House. I clerked for his Chief of Staff. I even wrote a brief the president read, and attended a couple of meetings with him where we chopped it up, not just a photo op."

"Get out!" Jerrell exclaimed, impressed. "A memo on what? What could a kid in college have to say to the freaking President?"

She chuckled, relaxing some, the tears on her face drying up. "Working-class Virginians, and technology readiness to reduce poverty. More digital jobs training. Vocation skills should be just as obtainable as getting groceries from the store."

"But how would something like that get paid for? Come on, you're talking to a finance guy. Business owners don't make stuff for free."

"Subsidies and targeted tax cuts, buddy. Making big corporations pay for the profit they earn off consumers. They must reinvest in communities, instead of corporate buybacks and shareholder dividends. You Wall Street guys can't profit off the backs of people and not pay back into society. And I will make sure of it." Her chin jutted out, readying for whatever question came next.

He didn't want to enjoy her fiery passion, but the laughter

he tried to suppress oozed out of him. "Social justice warrior, huh? And a rich one at that. Why don't you take your own money and give it all away?"

"Because I'm not stupid," she shot back.

They broke into chortling as he drove through Long Island on NY 27.

He watched her coat hood fall, and fluffy hair peeped from underneath it. Her slender neck turned toward the glass again, her pillowy bottom lip disappearing inside her mouth, wide eyes drinking in the city skyline.

"How often do you come here to NYC and spend money? Every month? Every week?" he asked.

She shook her head. "Not in four years."

He let out a low whistle. "You missed her that much, huh?"

"There may as well not be New York without GeeGee here." Her voice had gone dry again. "We spent almost every holiday here, and she always made it magical. She took us ice skating. Over there at LeFrak, in Prospect Park." She pointed.

"Ice skating? Black folks do that?" he cracked.

"Maybe not uncultured ones like you, but yeah," she retorted. Her eyes took their own trip to another time. "Each year at Christmas. Us and our cousins. Those were the days."

When they reached the store, Deidre threw open the back-door to scowl at him. Until her eyes caught Maddy in the passenger seat.

"Why don't you come in and grab something to eat?" he asked her.

Deidre's stunned face greeted Maddy as they entered. "Maddy, good to see you again, girl." His best friend approached him with a belt-strap in her stare, ready to whip him. "Mm, you haven't been answering the phone. I see why it's 9:30, and you're just now getting here."

Jerrell turned to Maddy. "Why don't you go up front and grab a pastry? We'll roll out in ten?" He faced Deidre as Maddy took the hint and left them to talk. "Yeah, about that, sorry."

She put up her hand. "Oh, no need for sorries. I handled it already."

Confused, Jerrell's neck cocked. "You handled what?"

A strange young man he'd never seen before squeezed through the door, carrying two boxes of the Sag Harbor orders.

"That," Deidre answered. "I hired a new driver for your Sag Harbor deliveries. I also found a retail clerk to alternate between helping you with pop-ups and working here in the store. So that you can focus on," she peered toward the front where Maddy stood, "more important things. Like running your business." She drilled her index finger into his chest. "Now's not the time for you to get distracted."

"I'm not. There was a lot of snow last night, and the battery drained out."

Deidre's lips smacked in disbelief. "Mhmm."

He kissed her forehead. "Girl, have I told you how badass you are for handling things around here while I grind?"

"I don't need you to tell me that." She sighed. "Are you using this girl, J? She looks all innocent. Comes from good people." His best friend lowered her voice. "And then there's her daddy. Does she even know about you and her dad?"

He turned away, avoiding her chastising glare. "Nnnn... Why is it my job to tell her what her father does?"

Deidre sucked her teeth. "Aww, hell. You like this chick. Your eyes are all dopey, head sagging to the side."

Unable to lie to her, Jerrell's jaw clamped shut. He prepared for the warnings.

"Damn. I haven't seen you this way since... " Her voice trailed off, and Jerrell shot her a warning look. Not to speak of Raychelle.

Sweeping away the sudden pain in his chest, he inhaled. "Where's Gram at? You're tripping."

Deidre continued clenching his jacket. "You are wide open. What does she have that the others didn't?"

Confused, unsure, he shrugged. "All I know is she aggravates me."

"And you like it. She doesn't fall all over you, and you respect it," Deidre theorized, hand on her hip. "Good for you. But what happens if you and her don't work? Where will that leave you with her dad?"

Both of them stared at the lobby area, where Maddy looked out of the window at the snowy New York streets.

To escape from Deidre's cross-examination, he moved to find his grandmother, and introduce her to Maddy. He hoped it would make her feel a little better about missing her own grandmother.

"Where's Gram?"

"She stayed home today."

He whipped around. "Why?"

"She said she needed some time out of the kitchen. I think she met church folks and wanted to visit them for a while."

His heart rate kicked up several miles an hour. How would they prepare food without Gram here cooking it? "Damn. Why wasn't that the first thing you told me? How will we have everything we need? Deliveries and orders ready to go out tomorrow?" he asked, concerned as he checked ovens and countertops. But the boxes already sat ready for transport. "Wait."

"No, we didn't wait. We caught up over the last couple of nights, and I hired an additional cook."

"*Three* new people?" he squealed.

Deidre's face hardened. "Your grandmother needs a break. She's happy doing this. But the woman is eighty-three, J. And you've been beating those streets nonstop. You can't keep killing yourself to prove a point to your dad."

"This isn't about Dad."

"Yes, it is. And now you're caught up with her. How will you do all this by yourself when I leave?" Deidre pressed.

Jerrell rubbed his chin, confronting the question he had been asking himself. The new delivery driver stepped through, toting out boxes marked for Sag Harbor. Now Jerrell worried about the money for these extra salaries. More overhead coming out of his pocket. "You should've talked to me before you brought on three more people," he said.

"I tried. You've had your head in the clouds, running around Sag Harbor with those rich folks, not answering your phone."

"I'm grinding, trying to drum up word of mouth and make this work." His sagging eyes must have gotten him a little mercy, because Deidre's face softened.

She squeezed his arm, the pressure reminding him of how he needed a massage. "Have you asked her about the sugar?"

His gaze fell to the tiles on the floor.

Deidre concluded, "And now that y'all are sweet on each other, you can't."

The realization was a heap of snow covering Jerrell's chest, and he couldn't shovel it off.

The ask would be off-putting, like he'd only hung around Maddy for a benefit. Had he been in Maddy's shoes, he would no doubt think he was being used.

Now his dilemma strutted toward them. Confident and yet questioning, sensual but strong, she brought with her a challenge for his loins and his heart.

"Go," his friend pushed him. "Spend time with her. You're exhausted and you need a break. And then work out how you plan to keep all this above water."

WANTS AND NEEDS

MADDY

A surprised Maddy stepped inside Jerrell's black Range Rover. "What happened to the van?"

"Looks like I have a new delivery driver who'll drive to Sag Harbor now and start handling those deliveries," he replied.

"Your friend is on point and takes wonderful care of you."

"That doesn't begin to describe how awesome Deidre is."

They took off again, through the Brooklyn streets Maddy hadn't visited in a long time, which now opened their arms like old friends. Rows of brownstone houses stretched ahead, reminding her of a childhood throwing snowballs at cousins. Snow-blanketed sidewalks mingled with dirt. Smells of coffee and fresh-baked bread filled her nostrils. Impatient horns blew from lanes of disgruntled drivers. Homeless volunteers rang bells in the cold for donations, only a few yards from Santa Clauses that played a saxophone or a guitar in front of their open hat on the ground.

"When did you come here, to New York?" she asked, attempting to break his sudden stoniness. After all, they'd ride together another two hours. He had kept her talking the whole way into the city, and she figured now it was her turn.

"When I was fourteen. My dad got a promotion. Moved to a house in Fort Greene. Attended Bards. I understand why you took so long to come back here."

"You don't like New York?"

"Nah. I never wanted to leave Louisiana. Begged my folks to let me stay. But I didn't have a choice. Dad meant to give us the life he never had, come hell or high water. Got his promotion he'd worked for. End of discussion. We packed up everything, left my grandma and family behind, and now here we are," he recounted with a hint of a scowl.

"What was so great about Louisiana? Isn't the Deep South poor and…." She let her voice trail off rather than use an inflammatory word like *backward*.

"Poor and what?" he pressed. "Say what's on your mind. I'm sure you're not used to that."

"Not used to what?"

"Honesty. Be straight and speak what you're thinking instead of calculating words in your head all the time."

"I don't calculate anything."

"Yes, you do. Just like a politician."

"Excuse you. Public office and service are honorable. Don't use that word like it's a pejorative."

Jerrell rolled his eyes. "You think Louisiana is poor and what?"

"All right then. Poor and downtrodden. And the national numbers support that. It's the next to poorest state, right above Mississippi. Maybe your daddy was onto something by bringing you some place better."

"I don't know why you and all the other buppy types believe elitist is superior. Love is better. Heritage. Culture."

"You can have all that anywhere, as long as you preserve it and stay true to it. And if you love it so much, why didn't you return for college at Grambling or Xavier?"

"That wasn't my decision either. It was go to Brown or be disowned."

Now Maddy was understanding this low boiling temperature inside him, from the day they'd met. "Come on. A smart guy like you in this town? You must've had the teachers and girls eating out of your hand."

"Not a country boy who'd just landed in the city with a crazy Cajun accent. Not understanding these big city folks, loving my Dirty South rap, socks up to my knees with some shorts, thinking I knew what time it was. I left behind who I was, to become everything I'm not," he recalled as they kept riding.

And Maddy guessed he must have resented it by now. "Nobody's stopping you from going back."

"It's not the same. Can't turn back the clock. Just like New York isn't the same for you. I pledged my fraternity here. My boys at home have moved on. Or they're broke, and here I am pulling up in a Range Rover. With my Brown finance degree, talking about starting a joint venture. Some of my fam can barely put food on the table. Don't get me wrong. A lot of guys from my childhood are doing well. But there are also quite a few who are not. Besides that, most of my frat, college classmates and running buddies, are on the East Coast now. Immediate family is here. Brothers and sisters, parents. And now Gram."

He surprised her, arriving at the LeFrak Ice Skating Rink. "Come on."

"Where?"

"Out here. And show me your moves," Jerrell said, getting out.

He stood in the parking lot, his back facing her as he waited for her to exit the truck. When he turned and raised his arms in the air, he mouthed, *what are you waiting for?*

Unable to suppress her smile, Maddy stared at the white sheet of ice lying behind him, so inviting, packed with fresh snow. Skaters glided in figure eights, wobbling and laughing, the way she, her siblings, cousins and grandmother once did. She threw open the door with a spark of glee.

He rented the skates, and Maddy laced up.

"I thought you had a lot going on today. Deliveries and orders and customers, and all that. Oh yeah, that's right. A bunch of women are at your shop, doing all your work for you."

"Women who know how to do more than get their nails done," Jerrell shot back while lacing up. "Enough talk. Show me how to do this."

"Wait a minute. You've never ice skated before?" Maddy asked, wondering whether to believe him.

"Are you going to show me or keep yapping?" he replied, wobbling. "So, how do I stand on these?"

She grabbed his arm to steady him as they entered the rink, letting others pass them so they entered with enough space. His shakiness sent her into laughing fits, his hands grabbing her waist and shoulders, his knees knocking against one another.

They moved into the rink, and as he waved frantic arms, she laughed out of control.

"Don't let me go," he pled.

Maddy smiled. Before he could realize it, she gave him a fast push across the ice.

"Oh, snap!" he yelled, but he could stand on his own, his athletic legs tightening and sailing across.

She snickered. "I knew you were full of shit."

"How?" he asked, chuckling.

"Because you love to test me."

He skated toward her again, stretching out his arm as if he would grab her, and Maddy evaded.

She spiraled in her skates, demonstrating ease of control on the blades, and floated away from him. "And I remember your folks telling me how, a long time ago, they enjoyed ice skating." She stuck her tongue out at him, enjoying the bit of surprise that flickered on his face.

"Really?" He caught up to her. "They talked to you about me?"

"About their children in general. The way parents do. They discussed the new activities they have learned since they moved to New York. I barely remember the conversation, just polite chatter when we were at the Country Club in Virginia Beach."

"What else did they tell you about their kids?"

He skated closer to her, but Maddy remained out of his grasp, making a subtle point in more ways than one.

"That they were bright. High achievers," she answered, surprising herself as she remembered portions of her conversation with Mr. Rouse. Her father had introduced them on the golf course years prior. "That all of you were different as night and day, bull-headed. But that they couldn't be more proud. Especially your dad, and I could see it on his face. You must have been the debater."

"He mentioned that?"

"Yes, he didn't say which one of his children. But he said the debater loved to go at it about any and everything, to challenge every topic. No matter how simple, he had to complicate it." Maddy swung around, skating backward in time to capture Jerrell's moment of reflection. "And then it hit me, the way you make a problem out of any interaction, the debater must be you."

She started feeling bolder as her legs remembered how to balance, and she took off, gliding faster.

Jerrell skated to catch up. She heard his skates racing behind her. Could hear his breaths as he tried to keep up.

"Somebody hasn't worked out in a while," she noted.

"Ha! Girl, I can outwork you any day of the week."

"I doubt it." She swung her arms, picking up more momentum.

He burst into laughter. "So, you know what you're doing, a little."

"I know what I'm doing a lot!"

The chilly wind licked her face, and she could almost hear GeeGee's voice encouraging her, pushing her to keep her legs strong, strides sure and steady.

They raced several times from one end of the rink to the other.

Best three out of five races. Loser had to pay for dinner. Spectators even formed a cheering section, with women screaming for her to crush him and little boys yelling for Jerrell to make her eat ice.

Maddy forged ahead in the wind, keeping the pressure on and making Jerrell work.

By the fourth lap, he was almost wheezing, but Maddy showed no mercy. Grateful now for her runs through Georgetown, cycling classes and skiing, her body did not let her down.

In the last round, he reached out to snatch her backward.

She skated off, on her way to winning four out of five. But midway, one of her shoelaces fell loose underneath her blade, causing her to trip. And she stumbled to avoid crashing onto the ice, the clumsiest attempt at staying on her feet. Jerrell jumped on the opportunity, thrusting himself forward, nudging her hip and tipping her over, almost knocking her off course again so that she needed to catch her footing once more.

"Cheater!" she cried.

"There are no rules, baby!" His ragged body hauled toward the opposite end of the rink.

Some women booed, yelling, "Disqualified! Not fair. That one doesn't count!"

It didn't take her long to race up to him. "I've still got three out of five, and really four out of five. Doesn't matter. Free dinner!"

He panted, almost wheezing, until he straightened up and focused his eyes on her. "And I'm... getting..."

Maddy chortled, enjoying his breathless torture as she circled him. "Come on, brother. Get it out. You what?"

Even in his pained state, bent over and gagging, he laughed with her. "I'll... have more than... coffee now."

Warm tremors traveled through her skin, unnerving her.

As they returned their skates, Jerrell's chest brushed her back. He reached around her, his long arm enclosing her body. His contact damn near shot electricity through her limbs.

The young, high-school aged desk clerk grinned. "I saw you guys out there racing. You two are cute."

Words eluded Maddy. How did she respond to that? She feared turning around, looking into his face again.

"Thank you," he said behind her, resting his hand on her waist. "Come on. Let's get you home."

Even through her thick puffer jacket, his relaxed fingers on her body were levers on her thermostat, turning up her heat. She sat on a bench to push on her boots, and Jerrell dropped in front of her. He took her boot, placing her foot in his lap, his hands cupped her stockinged feet. "I'm getting good at this."

Icy tingles traveled from the arch of her foot and up her calf. "I think you've been a master at it for a long time. Seducing women. So, they fold as soon as you give them any attention."

His jaw squared, and his eyes stayed glued on her. "You don't want my attention?"

Why did his entire aura have to be so magnetic? Every move, touch, and gaze some gravitational force. Maddy held her tongue, because she didn't want to lie. Instead, she got up.

Once she arrived at his truck, his remote unlocked the door, and she opened it.

A powerful arm slammed it shut, surprising her.

Once more, his chest pressed into her back. Clouds of condensation escaped both their mouths. His heat lingered close to her ear, pushing her heart rate sky high.

"I think you want and need my attention as much as I want and need yours." His reflection picked apart hers through the truck window. "Did you know your mouth opens whenever you want me to kiss you?"

Maddy snapped her jaw shut.

She'd never wanted anything or anybody to the point she was feening. Still, Maddy needed to stay strong. "So, this is the real reason you didn't take me home this morning."

Jerrell spun her to face him, his body towering over hers.

And once again, his eyes nailed her into a trapped position where her limbs would not respond to any of her internal commands.

"Can you blame me for stealing you?" He tilted his head, his lips hovering in front of hers.

Feeling her chin lift, his hand sliding underneath it, Jerrell's eyes stared into her. Maddy was getting lost in him again. Those lips were coming toward her. That skin, she wanted to lick. A magnet was pulling her in. Unapologetic and deft, his mouth overtook hers. Lush, slow, intentional, his tongue sent Maddy into a state of paralysis.

Except for the whimper that floated from her throat.

A tear emerged some place inside her and slid down her cheek. For all the kisses she'd received in her lifetime, none had ever propelled her head to a different planet. Or suspended her in space, where no questions or doubts lingered, only indescribable ecstasy. She felt nothing else, but Jerrell's mouth.

"Ooh, look, Mommy," a child said nearby. "They're kissing."

Her fantasy broken, reminded of the real world, Maddy returned to Earth and pulled away.

The world rotated around her. *No.* She was in a good place. Her focus couldn't suffer right now. She was on her way to the White House, and nothing could get in the way of that. She had no stress. No emotional rollercoasters. Her life was smooth, and her days were even and controlled. Washington, D.C., awaited her, and New York and his fledgling business consumed him.

"You're not my type."

No lies told, she thought.

It didn't matter that he hustled his way through long lines

of disgruntled customers with patience, or how he'd risen to the occasion last night with Blake. Maddy turned her head from him, focusing her eyes on the rink. Her knees buckled, certain parts of her dripped, and her brain worked overtime, sounding every alarm.

Jerrell's lips caressed her forehead. "Baby, you don't know your type."

Right then, his cell phone rang. "All right, I'll be there in an hour. Just sit tight." His intensity returned to her. "Saved by the bell."

An hour later, he stopped in front of her house. "So. What time do I pick you up for dinner tonight?"

Her eyes dropped to her lap as she questioned whether to accept. Sure, he had intellect and drive. And she could even see why Dad had taken a liking to him. He'd walked away from big-time Wall Street to pursue a path beyond making serious money.

His index finger smoothed a couple tendrils of her hair, now sticking from her bun, before it swept her temple. "It's just dinner. Not a prison sentence."

Jerrell was superb at touching her. His piercing eyes made her reconsider her entire life.

"Fine. I'll come and meet you at seven o'clock. At *Sharon's*."

After he came around and opened her door, their eyes iceskated a final time before she walked up her steps.

"Until seven, Maddy Cakes."

She entered her house and collapsed against the door. How would she defend herself from the sexual fire hazard that was Jerrell?

Her sister Reet appeared from the kitchen, a big, mischievous grin on her lips. As if she possessed a weapon of mass destruction she couldn't wait to unload on Maddy.

But Reet's mouth was the last thing Maddy needed. It was imperative that Maddy go to her room and take a few breaths to recover from the firestorm Jerrell had unleashed in her. She had to process why her heart still hadn't landed back on Earth. Maddy started for the stairs.

Reet warned, "Oh, no, baby girl, stay where you are for this."

"Not right now, Reet," Maddy replied, placing her foot on the second step.

Behind her, she heard another set of shoes emerge from the kitchen and enter the living room.

"Maddy. Hey."

That voice.

It opened a door to the most humiliating moments of her childhood—the twelve-year-old foot race, the sham kiss at the beach, and the *Blade and Key* rejection.

She didn't want to turn around but forced herself.

Kevin Middleton.

MIDDLETON

MADDY

"What are you doing here?" Maddy asked.

Not hello, or how are you, or what have you been up to for the last seven years.

"Well, damn, hi to you too," Kevin laughed.

Nothing had changed. Same presumptuous, wide-legged cowboy stance. Same haughty grin. Black, swooping curly hair for days, topping off that vanilla latte-colored light skin that always made him shun women who failed the brown paper bag test.

Maddy remembered all too well.

Stunned that he stood in her foyer, Maddy tried to fake a smile with little success. Her face lacked the energy. "Forgive me if this is a surprise."

"Forgiven. I can understand why," he said, his expression turning humble in a way she'd never seen. "If I were you, a visit like this would surprise me too. I'm vacationing and heard you were also in town. I wanted to come and speak. It's been a minute since Madison Page has blessed Sag Harbor. You've been so busy on Capitol Hill with high-level senators and dignitaries, and now you might head to the White House if Palmer wins next fall. Congratulations."

Maddy swallowed, still wondering why he couldn't tell her all that over the phone. "Thank you."

As she grappled with confused discomfort, a nosey Reet lingered nearby, sipping tea, not troubling herself to leave them.

"Sorry, but I don't think I've heard anything about you," Maddy lied.

Of course, she knew Kevin was an app developer now, making obscene money in Silicon Valley. His name was circulating in a lot of venture capital circles, and a couple of his projects had even crossed her desk for cutting through red tape to sell overseas.

Kevin laughed in his mocking way he had mastered. "Oh, how strange. Reet told me you love my app SocialPath, and you use it all the time to find new friends for golf."

Her cheeks flushed now, Maddy rolled her eyes at Reet. "Everybody uses apps. I have a ton of them."

"Look, Maddy, I'll cut to the chase. I know in the past we've had our differences."

"Differences? Is that what you want to call all your twisted shenanigans you pulled on me?" she challenged.

"Okay, we were kids, and I was immature," he said, turning to see that Reet stood unabashed in observing their conversation from the kitchen door. "Can we go for a walk or something?"

Maddy wondered what she had done for yet another man to pop up, derailing what should have been a drama-free vacation. "No, that's alright. I appreciate you coming by to congratulate me. Have yourself a Merry Christmas."

He shoved his hand in his pocket. Maddy and Reet exchanged silent questions.

Out came a long velvet box.

Unable to believe what she was seeing, Maddy almost choked on her shock.

"Please, Maddy. Just listen for a minute. Walk with me," Kevin asked.

She'd never heard him say "please."

Unsure if she should, her eyes darted to Reet once more, almost needing confirmation. Reet's head nudged Maddy outside.

Maddy followed him out the door, wondering what the catch was. In his hands, he held the precious box she once longed for as a teenager. The box containing the key on a necklace that Kevin and his buddies sported like trophies, representing the society *Blade and Key*. But it had consisted of boys. They started businesses as kids, invested in properties with funds they'd earned and inherited, and loans they borrowed from their parents. They were selective, in a mean way. Only two girls had ever gained acceptance, a math whiz and a computer nerd.

Chrissy and Del had told Maddy not to concern herself with it. They also started a club of their own, which fizzled out within a few months due to them being noncommittal. But *Blade and Key* had endured, with boys often changing the rules for acceptance.

The obnoxious way they'd worn their keys around their necks, even on their bikes, boasting that they knew things the girls did not, ate at Maddy worse than mosquitoes. She should have been over it by now and indeed thought she was.

But the moment she saw the box, the old flood of resentment washed over her.

"I've missed you, Maddy," he started.

"Can't say the same about you, Kevin."

"I deserve that. A long time ago, I was an obnoxious little asshole, and you had to be the smartest, kindest girl I knew."

"I'll stop you there. Save your compliments. What is the point of this?" Maddy had heard enough.

Kevin had taught Maddy the most painful lessons of her life. She would not give him the chance to teach her more.

They strolled toward the Black Whaling Museum. Shoppers waved at them, calling out to them from porches and inviting them inside for plates.

He stared down at his shoes as he walked. "You have toughened up these past few years."

"Do you blame me?" she asked, wondering why she was here, why she had allowed the sight of the velvet box to tear down her wall. Her resolve had endured a lot these last few days since she'd returned.

"No. Not at all," he answered right away.

That did not sound like the old Kevin. Old Kevin would have fired some smart retort, making her want to pour sand in his drawers.

New Kevin continued, "I screwed you over. And I was wrong."

"Tell me something I don't know. That every girl in Sag Harbor doesn't know." They moved toward the dock where Adella's boat floated alongside a few other boats. Snow covered most of the ground still, and the afternoon chill became an evening freeze.

"Okay, how about I love you? How about that?" He turned to her.

Maddy stopped in her tracks. Never in a million years

could she have imagined Kevin Middleton possessing a heart capable of emotion.

"Do you have a fever? See a therapist? Take a behavior-altering medication? Something?" she asked, concerned, cranking her neck.

"No. In fact, I'm clearer now than I have been in a long while," he said, gazing at her.

They stood a few feet from where she had once beaten him at a foot race. But Kevin tripped Maddy before the end, and his friends lied to everyone, saying that Kevin won. At twelve years old, it would be the first time Maddy experienced the gall of men to lie for their manhood. Many more experiences were to come.

"Kevin, what you did to me was not love."

"You're correct. I had a rep to uphold among my boys. And that was no excuse, I know. But you were the most beautiful girl in Sag Harbor. The smartest, most determined, and you always acted like you knew everything, had all the answers. And I had to show you that you didn't."

The Rolodex of her memories was too busy flipping through humiliation after gut-wrenching humiliation. "You were cruel."

"Tell me what boy with a crush isn't? The boys were making fun of me and threatened to snatch my key."

"Yeah, I remember. So you tripped me and caused me to sprain my wrist." Her scraped hand still bled in her mind.

He'd pushed her to the ground, and because she was the only girl in the group that day, no one had been present to take her side. So the boys had declared victory, and that she could not have the key.

Maddy recalled her dad's response when she told him. *So why didn't you trip him first?*

Kevin had introduced her to the calculating power games she'd learn to play at Grassfield High, at Spelman, and then at Oxford and now on Capitol Hill.

"Why do you think my folks invited you to breakfast at the Rockefeller Castle? To make it up to you."

"But when I was sixteen…" The fake-out kiss, where he'd put a frog to her lips while her eyes were closed.

His head dropped to his shoes. "Still stunting for the fellas."

"So, who are you posing for now?" Maddy insisted, cutting through the silliness of their childhood. She shivered from more than icy air, but the queasiness of a humble Kevin standing before her. Kind of like a vulgar comedian deciding he would become a preacher or something.

"You. I want to stunt for you, Maddy. I've dated quite a few women these last few years, and some of them have been very special. But that grit you've got—that fierce independence— it's a sparkler nobody can put out. Beautiful fire. I admired it."

They kept walking, and ahead of them, she saw a small gathering of people along a dock of lights.

Not paying attention, she focused too hard on calculating what he wanted.

She had dreamed of this moment for a long time. As a girl, all the Black princess fantasies in her mind included a beaming and opulent Kevin Middleton standing next to her. But Kevin had had every opportunity.

"This is about money, isn't it? Our families. Sag Harbor legacies. You want somebody whose reputation you can marry. To elevate your clout so the two of you join all the right cliques and circles."

The onerous rules at country clubs could break the biggest egos. Applications asked what job one's grandparents held.

Lineage investigations looked into criminal history. And the exhaustive questions about schooling and accomplishments could make an Ivy League graduate cry. Even the most accomplished women and celebrities could not enter The Madames, and loaded men failed to gain entry to the Master Guardsmen. Heritage was everything, dating back a hundred years and further. Especially among the exclusive Black upper-crust.

"Would that be such a bad thing?" he asked, turning to her.

And there it was. The kicker.

"No," she answered while thinking. "I don't suppose it would."

The icy air hit their faces, and he placed his hand on her arm, closing distance between them.

"Imagine it, Maddy. You and me together, we would be a force. Lie to me and say you haven't thought of it too. The power we'd have. The life we could make. You in politics and me in tech. Taking over everything. One of the most high-profile Black couples from coast to coast."

As he spoke, lights on the dock illuminated his eyes that danced with a giddy anticipation.

Yes, Maddy had thought about it. Too often. And when none of the men in her twenties rose to that level, she'd grown bored. Her relationships had fizzled.

She hated that this hunger in him, like some African warrior-conqueror, attracted her like a gnat to sugar. Or was she a gnat drawn to shit?

"There are plenty of wonderful women out there. You love prestige, Kevin. You don't love me. And you want a prestigious woman on your arm."

"I'd like both," he said, leaning toward her so she saw nothing else but his green eyes. "And I'm being honest. Yes, I crave the world. You've always known that. And it's why you liked me. I picked on you and tortured you because I knew you wanted it all too. Just as bad as I did."

Unable to pry her gaze from his, Maddy processed the truth. Would she be fool enough to let the fantasy take root in her heart again?

You know better than this, Maddy. You've already learned too many times.

As if sensing he hadn't convinced her, he continued. "You thought I didn't admire you? Your favorite color was turquoise, like the water in Jamaica when our families would travel together. You wore this little ring on your finger, of an angel that your grandmother gave you, to keep the devil off. Your favorite dish was smothered lobster she would make. Favorite dessert was German chocolate cake she cooked for you. And by the way, I was real sorry to learn of her passing. I sent you an email, but you never responded."

"Emailed me where?" she asked.

"Your old Hotmail account. Your friends wouldn't give me the new one."

Maddy chuckled at how her crew had protected her. "I haven't opened the Hotmail account in a long time."

"And your favorite place was the horseback riding stables."

At those memories of rolling hills, and stretches of greenery meeting the blue sky, she smiled. "Ha. I didn't realize you cared."

"I didn't know how to care. To us, cockiness was the way to be men. Everything was fun and games. But as I got older, started charting my path in the world, I realized you were a rare one. Not to be played with."

"And what made me so different from the other smart

women I'm sure you've met? Why are you just now showing up after all this time?"

"Your substance. Yes, you have ambition, but life for you is about more than the win. More than a title. Or what's on your resume. You learned that light-years before me. And last I knew, a while ago, you were engaged. I expected to run into you and your husband here. That whole time, I've been kicking myself, wishing I had grown up faster, said something sooner. When Moms told me you were single, I hate to say I was excited but..." He shrugged. "Sorry it didn't work out. But I do get it."

"You get what?"

He grabbed her hand, and once again, could have sent her off the edge of that dock, into frigid waters. Maddy reeled, unsure if his touch would ever feel comfortable.

"I understand dating regular people, with typical thoughts and subpar conversation, who aren't saying anything."

No, No, no, no. Don't relate to me. Not you, Kevin Middleton.

"I'm not sure what you want me to say."

"Nothing. Just give me a chance to show you this is legit."

Lights came toward them, and Maddy looked past him. The gathering of people on the dock approached and encircled her and Kevin.

Boys, whom she hadn't seen since college, now greeted her.

"Hey, Maddy, how are you doing?" Isaiah Grayson, son of a hospital executive and engineer, stepped forward, wrapping his arms around her.

Then came Matthias Graggs, a filmmaker whose parents were both doctors, to hug Maddy. "It's been a long time. Congrats on all you've achieved."

After him was Landon Barstow and Brett Jessup, offering bear-sized hugs.

Then, behind them, were Maddy's girls—Chrissy and Del.

At the sight of Del's face, the thought of Desmond holding Lana's ass sent Maddy to fling her arms around her old playmate.

"I can't believe the two of you came. You two hate Kevin," Maddy said to both Del and Chrissy.

They stared at Kevin. "How could we miss this reunion of all the Sag Harbor kids?"

And then Lenora Bledsoe showed up! She was the math whiz, one of only two girls ever admitted to *Blade and Key*. Maddy squealed at the sight of her. "I thought you were working in Switzerland now."

Lenora's gaze flew to meet Kevin's. "I am, but who can say no to Kevin? Plus, my folks have been hemming and hawing about me coming home. So here I am. Good to see you, love. You got finer with age."

"You too!" Maddy gushed. "Europe has been very kind to you."

Carefully, the men linked arms to avoid dropping hot candle wax from the holders.

Flabbergasted could not describe the suspended state of her heart inside her chest cavity.

"Madison Marie Page, daughter of Douglass and Maryanne Page, for your distinguished achievements and incomparable successes, for your courage and intellect, it would be our great honor and privilege to offer you entry to *Blade and Key*."

Their candlelit faces surrounded her, and they sang the childhood song, *All You Gotta Do Is Jump*. The girls looked on, with Chrissy throwing Maddy a proud wink.

Relishing the moment, she couldn't believe this. And GeeGee was not here to see it.

Kevin stood shoulder to shoulder with his club brothers, cupping his candle against the wind, swaying and popping their heads in rhythm.

Not sleep, not sit, not wait, no time to take breaks. You need to jump. For that money way high. That power touching the sky. That glory don't lay on the ground. Chins up, chest out, head down. Run, not walk. Move, don't talk. All you gotta do is jump.

The words transported Maddy. How did that song still have such an effect on her after twenty years? She should have been over it. But here she stood, all wrapped in the hugs and smiles that formed a blanket around her.

Kevin stepped forward from the circle, holding out the velvet box. Inside lay a small gold chain, glistening at her under the flapping candle flame. At the end of it was a key in the shape of a knife.

She stared in disbelief when he placed it over her neck.

"Still believe this is a game?" Cupping her chin in his hands, his eyes seemed to shine a spotlight on her. "This took way too long, and for that, I'm sorry. We set up dinner for you at *Cal's*. And then a reunion. Private. Members only."

Now she wondered if Kevin had concocted yet another prank, even at age thirty-two. Besides, *Blade and Key* should not have mattered to her anymore. Truth be told, Maddy had made her own way in the world, and proven herself. Maddy didn't need this.

In fact, some of these guys over the years had needed her. She'd received hasty calls for unclassified investigative reports, info on upcoming inquiries and subpoenas, data and complaints against competitors—intel that gave them a leg up in their businesses and deals. This childhood clique had boosted childish egos, and the invitation was de minimis.

So, why couldn't she just spit out the word *no*?

Kevin's expectant eyes awaited an answer, his face never looking more sincere. Candles aglow, the fantasy renewed in her head. A country club wedding, honeymoon in Turks and Caicos, a beachfront house in Malibu, and a home in the mountains—maybe Jackson Hole or Brush Creek. First rate schools for their children, legacy privileges at any college they wanted to attend, private door treatment at banks, and dining among the highest sets. Almost punch drunk on visions of a five-carat rock on her hand, she returned her gaze to Kevin's.

"Uh, I, this is kind of…." Nowhere in her organized, calendared life could she have imagined this.

Maddy knew why she couldn't say no.

"It's okay. Take your time." He lowered his lips to her ear. "But you would be crazy not to think about it." Kevin swooped in now, surprising her again with a kiss. His mouth sucked hers, warm and passionate, whipping her brain cells into a snowstorm of questions.

Was this happening? The guys whose respect she'd craved twenty years ago were finally paying it? Their childhood friends clapped, and Maddy's feet left the ground when Kevin lifted her.

"Congratulations, girl. Happy for you. I remember how we used to talk about this during sleepovers," Del said, her eyes glistening. Next to her stood Desmond, wearing a stiff smile, his hand clasping Del's shoulder. Far different from where he'd placed it that morning on Lana.

Maddy forced her attention back to Del's angelic face. Then, she turned to a tight-lipped Chrissy, who had just warned them both not to marry out of desperation or pursuit of power.

Alarms rang in the recesses of her mind where good sense might have still existed.

"Come on," Kevin said, squeezing her waist, and gazing at her like he'd captured a diamond. "Let's head to *Cal's*. More of our colleagues want to give you your just desserts."

ANOTHER MAN'S ARMS

JERRELL

Jerrell still savored the smell of vanilla and shea butter mingling in the seats of his truck.

The rest of the day, he fought to focus as he instructed Myles, calmed irate customers, and managed sales and orders. But Maddy's lips dominated his head. Her curved, slender legs skating ahead of him, racing hard, had been such a turn-on he'd let those legs stay ahead of him. Of course, he had even let her win, just so he could take her to dinner tonight.

He collected himself as his phone rang again and he answered his sister Kami's call.

"Gram fainted today."

"What? Oh, my G—" He bolted for his shoes.

"It's okay. She's fine," Kami reported.

Jerrell knew what was coming next. "Where is she?"

"Mom and Dad's."

He slapped the steering wheel. "No! She stays with me. That was the agreement. I brought her out here. I'm responsible. Not them. I'll be over there in an hour to get her."

"Whoa, whoa, there fella, slow your roll. The agreement was that she would take all her meds, keep her blood pressure in check, and her diabetes, keep her appointments with the new doctors, and wouldn't miss any meals. And you haven't been holding up your end of the deal."

The truth formed a hurricane of emotions already tearing through him. His voice low, he struggled to maintain calm. "Gram wants to be with me. Not them."

A small whine preceded Kam's next words. "Dad says if you try to come and take her, he will file for a court order and request to become her guardian. Look, J, you know we're proud of what you've tried to—"

"Save it." He may as well have been swallowing vinegar. "She's happy, Kami! Can't you see that? Her spirits are up again. She's back to her old self at the restaurant. If you stick her in some room alone, while people work all day, she will wilt away."

Kam sighed. "You need to figure out a plan. And you don't have one."

"Oh, but Dad's plan of letting her rot alone in Louisiana? That was a brilliant plan, huh?" he asked.

"And this sugar situation. I think you're on your last bag. That may have been the straw that broke the camel's back. It's stressing her out. And I know it's stressing you out. Deidre says you haven't handled that either. She's had to hire new people because you're killing yourself. Can't even take a day off. Little brother…"

He knew Kami loved him too much to tell him he was failing. After all his chest-thumping and braggadocio with his father, now the world seemed to fall on his shoulders. To top it off, tomorrow was Christmas Eve. Two stores to run, more orders to fill for New Year's, and hundreds of deliveries to get out on time. But this was his grandmother's dream, and he'd be damned if he left her at the prison that was his parents' home.

"I'm coming to get Gram in the morning. At five. She doesn't have a guardian right now. Dad can file whatever he wants, and we can settle it in court. Fine."

"J, no," Kami pled. "Just take some time to figure out your situation. You've got a lot on your plate. I'll take a couple days off work, go to the store, and help Aunt Rose with the cooking for the next couple of days. You get some rest. Take a few breaths, spend some time with whoever this girl is that you like. Yeah, Deidre told me. Look, J. You don't want this. Dad is already talking about deducting your college tuition from your inheritance."

"Ugh, that damn man!"

"You're just like him. Both of you, set in your ways. But if something happens to Gram, the family's going to have an issue with *you*."

He turned over his options, feeling the pressure of his father shoving his back against the wall. Since his dad could no longer contain Jerrell physically, he was doing it with his money and Jerrell's grandmother. "Tell Dad to at least let her go to the store three or four days a week, even if it's not every day."

A long pause told him Kami doubted if her skills were that good. "I'll see what I can do." Then the brief pause. There was something else. "So, who's this girl? And don't lie, because I saw the picture. You looked like you stepped out of a fantasy storybook. She's gorgeous. You haven't hit so you can get the sugar?"

Yes, Maddy was gorgeous, in her own defiant, I-don't-need-a-man kind of way. "It's not like that. They needed a warm body, and I was just helping."

"I might come to Long Island, check things out, and see what's going on," Kami teased.

He swiped his hand down his face, assessing how he would get through tomorrow. "I like your first idea better. Would you mind helping Aunt Rose at the store tomorrow?"

"You'll be okay. Just don't steamroll the family while you're trying to put your mark on the world."

Damn, he thought after they hung up.

He wouldn't go back to his father with his tail between his legs or send out job applications so soon after he'd only left Wall Street a few weeks prior. But he wouldn't worry about it right now. He still needed to get ready for his evening out with Maddy.

With extensive arrangements, he would surprise her. Since she felt he was so uncultured, Jerrell would let her know who she was dealing with. He called up *Little Italy*, the most upscale place in Sag Harbor. They would meet at *Sharon's*, before walking to the actual spot. A florist would deliver orange orchids for a table he had reserved against the water. It just so happened he had lucked out, and someone canceled right before he called.

He had only gone to this length once in his life—for his beloved Raychelle.

All his other dates had been straightforward, if he took a woman on a date at all. He'd learned early not to pump women's heads up that way. It only led to torture later, especially when he only wanted to hit. The conversations had put him to sleep, and he often struggled not to check the basketball scores on his phone during the salad course.

But not once had he been in Maddy's presence and grown

tired. She kept him on his toes. It might have even tickled him the way she tried so hard to reject him. Jerrell was not accustomed to that. Rather than trying to woo him, she devoted her every iota of energy to dismantling his ego. And he'd found it entertaining.

At 6:40 p.m., wearing cashmere, covered in a wool coat, and lamb's wool scarf, he arrived to ensure they'd set the table as planned.

Hmph, he thought. *Uncultured guys like you.* She would soon find out.

While standing in front of *Sharon's*, he fired off a few emails to clients, businesses and vendors who'd helped him out the last few weeks. He would try to follow Kami's advice and take a breather, though it was hard. How would he avoid drowning in disaster after Deidre left? His fingers danced across the screen, inquiring about store managers who were trustworthy.

At 7:05, he peered around to make sure Maddy hadn't arrived and was waiting for him in the lobby. He should have gone to pick her up. But she'd insisted on bringing herself. So she was a couple of minutes late? A little more time to knock things off his task list.

But at 7:20, Jerrell worried. Only now did he realize he didn't have her phone number. He would hold off from contacting her father.

At 7:31, he called Dr. Page, who informed Jerrell the dinner may have slipped her mind. Her father would call her to remind her.

This is no big deal. She's just another female, he told himself.

He could have any he chose. But falling back into the chair, he cranked his neck toward the window.

At 7:55, Jerrell sat stunned. So, this was how that felt.

He went to *Little Italy* and grabbed his flowers. On the way out, he questioned who she thought she was. Should he go confront her? At her home, in front of her family? Nah. That wouldn't win him any fans.

He hit Main Street for the twenty-minute walk back to the Black side of town. Grateful he didn't drive, he needed the frigid night air to offset his steam. He was even foolish enough to anticipate they would go for a walk down one of Southampton's most prominent streets.

Among all the questions hammering his brain, the one eating at him most was whether Maddy would have stood him up had he been some big-name political insider. Or a top exec with memberships at high profile country clubs and multiple houses around the world.

Jerrell's leather-gloved hand rubbed his chest. This slight discomfort worming through him was unfamiliar. Was he hurt? This chick was a stranger.

He passed more restaurants on busy Main Street, reaching Eastville Avenue. About a hundred yards away, the ocean waves tossed. More of this New England freeze on his face might snap him back to the task at hand—his business.

He trudged toward the harbor in the cold, simmering over his relationship with his dad, his grandmother's age, how long his savings would last, and….

A feisty woman whose tough facade only intrigued him. Jerrell sighed.

As he walked, a sliver of him might have sworn he saw Maddy's long, thick puff of black cotton atop her head. It blew in the wind over her heart-shaped face and elegant, pointed chin. The dim dock lights must have been deceiving him.

No, as he walked closer, her Mrs. Claus dress from the

night before still peeked from under her unmistakable puffer coat. It was her. Maddy stood alone, shivering.

That was it! She had come. She must have just forgotten which restaurant and misplaced his number. Relieved and laughing to himself, Jerrell started toward her.

But another figure reached her first.

A handsome male slid his arm around Maddy, pulling her against his chest.

Floored, Jerrell watched this dude kiss her like he was familiar, touching her cheek and the back of her head as if this wasn't their first meeting.

No winter air entered Jerrell's lungs. No matter how hard he tried to inhale.

He processed what he saw, debating whether he should call her out and check her ass. But his legs found the strength to turn away.

He'd been right his entire life. No woman matched Raychelle. And he'd been dumb to think otherwise.

Almost dumping the flowers, instead Jerrell saved them for Gram the next morning, one of the few women in his life who would never fail him.

THE SHRILL SOUND of Jerrell's alarm jarred him from sleep at 4:15 a.m. His chest seemed to carry the weight of the ocean when he rose from bed. Instinct made his hands reach to check his phone for messages. His finger scrolled for one in particular.

A couple of screw buddies asked if he was in town.

Why had he set himself up for disappointment? Why

hadn't she been a woman and disclosed she was in a relationship?

For the ride to the City, he turned on his music, punched through news channels, switched podcasts, anything to ignore his burning insides.

An hour and a half later, he waited at the front door of his parents' home for Gram to come out. Of course, his father didn't resist the urge to appear and mad-dog him. Gruff, tall, foreboding, the man thirty-seven years his senior still scared the hell out of Jerrell.

Only now, Jerrell stood eye-to-eye with him, and refused to waver.

Charles Rouse's eyes flared. "You have her here no later than seven tonight. A minute more, and I mean one minute…"

"Son," his mother said, throwing herself between them. The sight of her face for the first time in a month, worried and tense now, massaged Jerrell's exhausted eyes. Her fingers gripped his jacket. "What he means is keep us in the loop, okay? If you get overwhelmed, or if she needs anything, please, call somebody. You hear me?"

He ignored his father, returning his mother's gaze and clenching her arms, wishing he could bury his head inside them now. But he would not dare act like a dejected little boy in front of his dad. "Yeah, I got you. And I will."

Still in her robe, his mother walked them out to his Range Rover, following him as he opened the door for his grandmother and helped her in.

"He wants you to call him, you know," Mom said.

"Why? So he can jump down my throat some more? Tell me how worthless I am?"

"He's worried about you is all. So am I. Boy, you're looking so skinny. Are you eating all right?" she asked, pulling him in close. Her slender, stalwart arms gripped him tight.

Jerrell rolled his eyes, not wanting to state the obvious, but it slipped. "If you and him were so concerned, why didn't you come to the Ivory a couple nights ago? Or one of my pop-ups? It's just on Long Island, not the other side of the world." The youngest Rouse sibling tried not to sound pouty.

His mother's eyes creased as she rubbed him. "Sweetheart, that's not fair. All of this happened real quick."

More like she wouldn't dare undermine his dad by coming to support Jerrell without him. "Yeah, I know." Planting a forehead kiss on her, he would not admit running into the ground so much that he wasn't eating. They absorbed one another's presence in a last hug. "I gotta go. A lot to do today." He pulled away from her embrace. Time to man up. "I will make sure Gram takes all her meds. She'll be back this evening."

No matter how many times he did it, driving out of the yard, watching his mom's hand wave, always turned his stomach to cinder blocks.

"Gram, I'm so sor—"

"Who is this here?" His grandmother held out her cell phone to him.

On the screen, of course, the photo of him and Maddy woke him faster than coffee.

"Gram, where did you get that?" he snapped. "And why didn't you tell me you weren't taking your medication? What are you trying to do? Get both of us thrown in jail?"

"Don't change the subject. This is the girl Deidre was talkin' 'bout? Is she the reason we've been working so hard back in that kitchen, and you've been off with your nose in the clouds, around them biggity negroes, huh?"

"Grandma! There is nothing to tell," he replied. Even at the crack of dawn, she was rowdy, mouthy and pushy as ever. "I've been busting my buns to get this—"

"I'm goin' with you today."

"What? But you need to—"

"You heard me. I said I'll be in Saaag Haaarbor," she insisted, shaking her head and shimmying her shoulders in the passenger seat, demonstrating how she thought it was uppity.

He loved hanging out with his grandmother and wouldn't trade their time for anything. But the following twelve hours of baking and productivity meant the difference between boarding up his shop before New Year's or knocking these holidays out of the park. "Gram, I need you at the store lining up orders for these next few days, getting us ready for New Year's."

"Rose and Kam can line up. Imma be in Sag Harbor meetin' biggity negroes," she replied.

What was he to say? She needed a break. But as they rode out of the city, he got an idea. The sun started coming up. "Alright, fine. But I have to work, and so will you, Mrs. Claus."

"Ha!" she said, clapping her hands together. "Now, you're talkin'!"

Hours later, at the firehouse, his grandmother was stealing hearts. He was thankful the facility had a kitchen, and the firefighters accommodated them, so the pair were rolling. After stopping by his Brooklyn store to snag orders and ingredients, and running by his place to grab the Santa jacket, Gram put on an impromptu show.

Shoppers and passersby marveled to see Poppin' Pauletta on the Sag Harbor sidewalk making dough, whipping up cake batter, talking about her treats and how they'd passed through generations of their family. With her trademark gutsy laugh, she delighted visitors with the disappearing cookie dough and "guess which flavor." They fell in love with her, as Jerrell knew they would.

Jerrell didn't know why he hadn't thought of this sooner. Children decorated their own cookies and cupcakes, posing for photos over bowls of cake batter and mixtures. No one else could have played up the role better. They beamed at hearing Gram's classic Louisiana Cajun drawl.

All the sleepless nights, early mornings and constant stress that had fallen on Jerrell these past few weeks, delivered the reward that afternoon.

His heart twitched that his parents would not come see this for themselves. Even if his father refused to show up and support them, the light on his grandmother's face kept Jerrell going.

In a spontaneous thought, he recalled Maddy's face lighting up the same way, just the night before. On the dock, in another man's arms. Soon as she crossed his mind, a familiar sight appeared in front of him.

"Son, it looks like you're booming right now," Dr. Page said, stretching out his hand, which Jerrell accepted in a tight shake. Maddy's father looked around him at the line of customers ringing up sales with Myles.

"Man, oh my goodness, sir. Yes, Pauletta's is definitely popping." He left Myles to the cash register to walk to a quieter corner outside the fire house. "Dr. Page, I can't thank you enough for all you've done."

Her father's hand gripped Jerrell's shoulder, the way his own father once did. "The moment I tasted your grandma's cooking, and you told me your idea, I knew you had a winner."

Jerrell grimaced. "Yeah, but… Dad doesn't—"

Dr. Page smiled. "Give it time. We can be pretty rough on our own, especially when we see you've got more in you that we need to pull out."

"Well, he's pulling me straight to the crazy house," Jerrell replied as they both laughed. "About your investment—"

"Oh, yes, that's right. My lawyer has drawn up the investment agreement, and I have it ready for you to pick up and review. Pretty straightforward stuff. I give you $35K and you feed me all the desserts I want for life," the lanky Dr. Page joked with a big smile.

They both burst into laughter. "Oh, the documents. I'm sure they're fine, but yes, I would be the fool if I didn't look over them with someone," Jerrell replied, before a realization dawned on him.

How would they exchange the legal papers? Without Jerrell seeing Maddy.

How would it sound if he asked this man to mail them instead? And Jerrell wouldn't ask Dr. Page to go home and get them.

Damn.

Any way out of this would appear to be disrespectful to the hand that helped him. Still, he would rather have eaten the pastries from the ground, after mopping with them, than see Maddy again.

"When should I stop by?"

"Tonight. After you wrap all this up."

Jerrell swallowed. Apparently, Dr. Page did not know what his daughter had done. He forced a smile, replying, "That will work. It'll be my pleasure." His thoughts then switched to the problem that he needed to be honest about. "But remember, I'll be in a bit of a jam without that

Brazilian sugar." He cut straight to the point. "To keep this thing going, we need it off the docks. I've tested other sugars, and that is the one giving Gram's recipes a special kick."

Dr. Page's smile turned serious, and his gaze sympathetic. "You and Maddy haven't talked?"

"About that, sir, she seems to think I'm the devil reincarnate," he replied, wondering if Maddy had said anything else about him that Jerrell hadn't already overheard.

The older man's eyes narrowed, and he grinned. "Things seemed to go well at the Ivory the other night."

Jerrell hunched his shoulders, trying to brush off the sting of the previous day. "Clearly, not well enough."

The wheels of Dr. Page's mind turned. "You should stay a little longer this evening, thaw the ice for you two. Some coffee. Show up with your dessert. And you can teach our family why this food is so special. Nothing obvious, real laid back."

Jerrell was unsure the glacier of ice between him and Maddy could be thawed. Not after last night.

His mind ran in a million circles. How would he act if he saw Maddy again? He thought of how he would approach her. Would he play it off as if he didn't care? Or slide it in somewhere as a casual joke?

No, he would lose his grip, say the wrong thing, and screw his business. At least if he cut the visit short, someone else could later approach Maddy, like Kami or Deidre. Or even his mother.

"Sir, I'll have to take a rain check on the longer visit. I need to get my grandmother back to Dad's and hit a couple of stores for last minute Christmas gifts."

"Sonny, who is this you've been over here talking to for so

long, and you haven't introduced me?" Gram popped up next to them.

"Good heavens, son, is this Pauletta? You've been hiding her," Dr. Page said. Maddy's father bubbled as he met the woman behind the desserts and pastries he loved so much that he'd invested in them.

"Oh, my goodness, I didn't know there was a party going on out here. How come nobody told me?" another female voice spoke and surprised him.

Jerrell whipped around to see Lana, Maddy's co-worker. He looked up for Maddy to be somewhere close by.

"Um, Lana, right? How are you?" he asked, as his eyes scanned the surrounding area.

"I'm good. You searching for Maddy?"

"Well, isn't she your road dog? Didn't you come on vacation with her?"

"Yeah, but we're not joined at the hip," Lana chuckled, swiping her nail across her chin, a glint in her eye that confused him. "I wanted some dessert for myself. But I don't want to stand in that big line. And since we semi-know each other, would you help a sister out?"

Tired, and distracted, he walked her to Myles and instructed him to squeeze in some time for her order.

"Thanks, Babe," she said, running a long nail down Jerrell's chest before walking away.

As he stood trying to figure out his predicament, Jerrell muttered to himself, "Oh, my goodness. Talk about thirsty."

"You think?" Myles replied. "She was practically stalking you, dude. She posted on the other side of that building, eavesdropping on your convo for, like, ever."

Jerrell cleared his throat, unable to believe what he'd just heard. "What conversation?"

Myles threw Jerrell a matter-of-fact expression. "You and Maddy's dad. That woman was listening the whole time. Licking her fingers like you were fried chicken she wanted to wrap in a biscuit."

Now Jerrell reeled. Lana had overheard him and Dr. Page talking?

Maddy still didn't know about the 35K. And now Lana would tell Maddy.

The big boulder already sitting in Jerrell's chest began rolling toward his stomach. But why would Lana care what he and Dr. Page did? After all, what did Lana get out of it? Nothing. And perhaps Myles had just seen it wrong, and she was doing something else, like wiping her nose or putting on Chapstick.

His phone buzzed in his pocket. Deidre.

"Have you gotten your grandmother a Christmas gift?" she asked.

Ugh, he thought, squeezing his head. "You know there's a reason no other woman gets to be my best friend but you, right?"

An unamused scoff was his answer. "I'll take care of it. For her. Not you. But also, I'm having dinner with you and your family tomorrow. Then I have a date. So don't wait up for me on Friday morning at the store."

"A what?" he asked, forcing as much glee into his voice as possible. Thrilled as he was for his friend, Deidre was abandoning him in the middle of the holidays? Traffic would be slow the day after Christmas, when people ate leftovers, and that slowdown was perfect for catching up on orders and work. "I'm happy for you," he said, trying not to choke, as the crowd grew and lots of clapping broke out around his grandmother. "But I gotta go. Let's chew on it tomorrow."

"Whoa, J, one more thing. We switched to white sugar this morning. No more Brazilian brown left."

That sucker punch knocked the wind out of him. He needed to do something if Poppin' Pauletta's was to survive.

He rushed to catch up to Dr. Page, who had walked away.

"Say, Dr. Page! You know what? On second thought, I'll stay longer and do that coffee after all."

AN HONEST MISTAKE

MADDY

Maddy's eyes swam from all the figures on her laptop screen. Dollar amounts. Company names. Products. Events. Dates. She tried to focus on the electronic spreadsheets of American companies.

Trade problems were bubbling in Latin America. Now the Senator wanted answers, asking her to put the wheels in motion for an emergency hearing in the New Year, as soon as the Senate returned to session. While Maddy had been out frolicking with Kevin, the Senator had sent her a barrage of questions about South American countries retaliating against North American business.

They were getting hit with business regulations so onerous the U.S. trade representative had called the Senator the previous night. Now Maddy skimmed reports of major delays and dollar losses.

Too much was on her mind.

At the forefront of her brain was Adella, and whether she should tell her friend what she'd seen. A man staring at other women was one thing, but what did Maddy do now that she had seen them together? She couldn't shake the visual of Desmond squeezing Lana's ass until he recognized Maddy.

Maddy still couldn't believe Lana had been so flagrant and disrespectful. Did Maddy stir up a bunch of mess and tell Lana she needed to go, even in front of her parents? How messy would that be? How would it make Del feel if she learned Maddy abided this?

Lana had shown her a whole other side, almost as if she got pleasure from flaunting her blessed body in front of everyone. They had attended work functions, and on occasion, gone to a social event, or a work trip. Still, Maddy had never seen this scandalous person up close until now.

She needed to find Adella and check in on how she was doing. And give Del a chance to unleash on Maddy for bringing a problematic co-worker to Sag Harbor.

Then there was Kevin. What the hell? Last night had come completely out of left field. No advance email, phone call or any kind of warning.

Only a sudden, "I love you and always have." It sure hadn't felt like love when they were thirteen. She stared at her left palm, still bearing the tiny scar from Kevin tripping her.

He'd called up many of their mutual friends—investors, engineers, tech gurus, and a film director had flown in from Boston, D.C., Atlanta, and even France. She couldn't lie to herself that their bear hugs, songs, and stories hadn't made her heart swell. Two nights before Christmas, surrounded by the old crew, the memories made their childhood come alive again—most of it magical. Or the non-Kevin parts.

But there was no denying it—with hers and Kevin's combined clout, jetsetting would be their round-the-clock life. Everything she had ever dreamed.

She stared out the window, past the backyard, wishing her grandmother was here to help her with this.

Nothing that big ole ocean can't cure, GeeGee always said.

Gran would take her and her collie, Duke, to the water line where they would remove their sneakers and bury their feet in the Atlantic salt water.

However big you think your problem is, remember all that out there, her grandmother would say as they stared at the endless ocean.

Fresh tears in her eyes now, Maddy longed for GeeGee's way of putting every nook and cranny of her life in perspective.

"What are you in here daydreaming about?" Reet's inquiry broke into her thoughts. "You don't need to answer. I already know."

Maddy rolled her eyes. "I thought all of you guys were going Christmas shopping."

In fact, Maddy had been counting on them leaving.

"Not before I come in here and see what happened with Jerrell a couple nights ago. And what went down with Kevin last night? What did you say?" Reet purred, sliding her very pregnant body onto Maddy's bed.

"Don't make yourself comfortable because nothing happened."

"So why was your hair so jacked up when you came home yesterday? Both times. Player, playerrrr," Reet said. "Looks like I underestimated you, you little whore."

"Daddy!" Maddy called. "Will you please come and get your child?"

If GeeGee were still around, she would have told them to butt out.

"Both dudes are fine. You can't go wrong with either. But Kevin is one of us."

"He took twenty years to confess his undying love for me."

"Some guys are late bloomers. So, you going to give him some or not?"

"Not. I said nothing's going down this Christmas, and I meant it."

Reet giggled. "I'm not so sure about that. Drama has a way of finding you at Christmas, girl. That whole Cameron shenanigan last year…"

"Don't remind me," Maddy said, her head falling down onto her laptop.

"What? I think you two could have had something. You and his side chick that confronted you at Terrapin on the third date!"

"Or the year before that, when the Monroes brought their son Ethan, and they asked that night how many kids I'll give my husband," Maddy added.

To that Reet burst into cackling hysteria. "But he took you skiing and whaling in Iceland. And wanted to take you to South Africa!"

"So? Maddy is nobody's birthing machine. She can afford to take herself on trips," Maddy replied.

Reet smacked her lips in protest. "Yeah, that sounds fun. Let me make myself come by the fireplace overlooking the mountains. You just haven't met the right daddy who'll put it on you and make you want to give up them kids. Stop being so scary, girl. You got a lot of tension in you. Let that shit out and enjoy these fine ass men. Especially Jerrell. He looks like he can handle your aggressions." She licked her lips and chuckled. "I think he *wants* to handle your aggression."

"Daddy!" Maddy called. "If you don't get out, I'm taking

my aggressions out on you, and my little niece will be born motherless."

"See, when you talk like that, it makes me not want to tell you the new info I got at the *Ivory* the other night."

"What new info?" Maddy asked, head popping up.

"Oh, no, hunty. You'll just have to wait and see for yourself," Reet teased.

Great, Maddy thought.

That didn't sound promising.

"Anyway, Daddy wants you to come with us. He's waiting for us to meet him down the street."

"Mama promised you all wouldn't bother me while I was working," Maddy grumbled.

"You know she only told you that to get you on the train," she retorted. "And hurry."

Maddy had also wanted to use the downtime for a walk on the beach, and to talk to GeeGee for a little while. But it would have to wait.

She glanced at her laptop screen a final time. Her eyes fell to the research, scanning the impacted industries.

Sugar sat high on the list. That shouldn't have been a big deal, since the United States produced lots of it. Too much foreign sugar entering the country would hurt U.S. sugar farmers. She skimmed farm reports. Despite hurricanes and floods that year, American farmers still produced lots of sugar from beets. She jotted this down in her notes for reasons to refuse a hearing. America didn't need anymore foreign sugar.

But another report caught her eye. U.S. Food and beverage industry relied on sugar imports when farmers couldn't produce enough to meet demand, especially during bad floods. What could it hurt to hold an emergency panel? She included this research in her memo, and recommended the Senator hold the hearing.

"Hey!" her nephew yelled downstairs. "It's snowing! Yay!"

Skimming her report a final time, Maddy emailed it to the Senator.

Half an hour later, Maddy and her family were strolling in the snow, headed toward the shops two blocks away.

Carolers from her grandmother's church serenaded them on the street, and people she hadn't seen in a long time gripped Maddy's hand, their faces beaming. Many of them had attended her baptism, visited her at Spelman, and sent their granddaughters to her for Capitol Hill internships and letters of recommendation.

Her little niece and nephew ran ahead, dipping into the small, Black-owned candy store, jewelry shops, and children's stores in search of Christmas candy and trinkets. Christmas bells and Nat King Cole serenaded shoppers who milled through the streets.

Maddy drifted into one of the candy shops, saying hello to the storeowners who once sold her candy as a child.

Before she left, the storeowner handed Maddy her father's phone. "He was in here a minute ago, buying candy for the kids, and he left it there," the shopkeeper said.

As soon as she took her dad's phone, it buzzed in her hand. He must have rushed out, behind the kids, and forgotten his cell.

She peered at the caller ID. *Tony—Banker.* A banking call the day before Christmas must've been important. She would answer and tell Tony that Dad would call him back.

"Hey, Tony, it's Maddy!"

"Maddy! Your old man told me you were in town. Merry Christmas to ya, girl."

"And Merry Christmas to you. Dad stepped out a moment. But soon as I find him, I'll have him ring you back."

"Oh, I'd appreciate that. He forgot to tell me which account he wants this 35K to come from. Just tell him to call me with that, and I'll get it done by C.O.B. You take care of yourself, all right?"

35K? For what?

"Uh, yeah, you too," she stammered, hanging up.

Was Daddy getting ready to make a major purchase? What kind? He already had the classic Porsche he'd been wanting. And her mother's birthday wasn't for another three months.

Laughter erupted from down the street. A small crowd had gathered a few doors down, where more clapping and cheers filled the sky. Her father, brother and sister were all smiles on the sidewalk, cranking their necks to see a spectacle.

Up ahead, at the firehouse, her niece brimmed with excitement.

"Auntie Maddy, look!"

Among throngs of people stood Jerrell.

Maddy's heart bottomed out.

Soon as she laid eyes on him, their last conversation struck her like a fastball.

Dinner!

Oh, my God!

She forgot!

A FEW FEET AWAY, Jerrell tossed cookie dough in rapid succession at an older woman holding two bowls. She caught them, one after the other, with ease. Adorned in a Poppin' Pauletta's apron, the elder burst with joy. The performer might have teetered over any moment, panting and jerking with quick moves. What on Earth was Jerrell doing to her?

The cold temperatures dropped by the hour. It had to be in the thirties now. But the crowd on the sidewalk kept singing *Jingle Bells*, and someone had pulled out a tambourine, while this poor worker put on a show for Jerrell's business.

"Isn't she good?" her father asked, clapping and looking on. "That lady will be eighty-four years old in a few months."

Even Reet clapped to the beat, wearing a smile brighter than a Christmas tree.

What should Maddy do? Sickened at the thought of standing him up, she fumbled for how to handle herself.

On full display, for all of Sag Harbor to see, was Jerrell's charm and determination, in his exhausted state.

Maybe he didn't care. After all, he'd told her she irritated him, so it might have satisfied him that she forgot. Perhaps he'd forgotten it himself. She feared her face would turn purple with embarrassment, and turned to walk to another store.

"Where are you going now?" her father asked. His expression grew concerned when he saw her. "You look like you're about to pass out. You all right?"

"Yeah, there's one thing I wanted to get for Mama. I'll go buy it and hook up with you guys when this is over."

"Who is that over there needing some Christmas spirit?" the elderly woman's voice called behind Maddy.

Horrified, Maddy tried to scurry off.

"Pretty girl in that big white coat, I won't let you run away from me. Get on over here!" Jerrell's elderly employee beckoned.

Maddy froze, hesitating.

"Yes, you, lovely. Don't make me come over there! Let's turn that frown into a smile. Come to Pauletta," the elderly woman summoned.

Petrified, Maddy's eyes floated around the crowd as her body followed.

Now she faced him.

At the same time Jerrell noticed her, one of his cookie dough balls plummeted. So did his face. The two of them could have been the only people on the sidewalk.

Applause rose, egging her on.

"Go on, Auntie Maddy!" Maddy's three-year-old niece Ella screamed.

Her father's eyes dipped, and amusement curled his lips.

One foot creeping in front of the other, Maddy moved toward the lady with snowy, white hair plastered to her head. Arms outstretched to the sky, not a care in the world seemed to phase this employee.

"Ladies, you come over here and assist," the woman said to Maddy's sister and sister-in-law.

The crowd had grown silent, and Maddy and Jerrell now stood mere yards apart. His eyes avoided her as if she was lice.

The employee instructed Jerrell to toss her two balls of what looked like dough, before she stretched, twisted, threw them in the air, and wrapped them around a little girl until they were long as jump ropes. Then she handed the doughy ropes to Reet and Sandra, Maddy's sister-in-law. At this lady's direction, the crowd began singing *Frosty the Snowman.*

Dough started swinging, one over the other.

"Come on, Maddy," her neighbors and friends cheered.

She hadn't jumped rope in decades, certainly not double

dutch. Her legs bounced as she hesitated, her upper body moved back and forth.

The older woman's face radiated, as would a candle lighting the street. "Nothin' to be afraid of, Baby Girl," she said.

"Oh, I don't th—"

Warm, aged hands slid inside Maddy's. The elder took off, charging into the swinging dough and pulling Maddy with her.

She scrambled to coordinate with the ropes. Surrounded by zealous cheers and applause, Maddy lifted one foot after the other as the two jumped. Astonishment hit Maddy that she hadn't screwed up. She couldn't let an old woman jump better than her, and the lady was still going as if she could do it blind.

This elderly employee seemed to have the time of her life. For a few seconds, cold air mixed with exhilaration, and Maddy escaped into the childlike moment. After twenty years, she couldn't believe she'd lasted this long and still had it!

At the end of the song, the old woman exited the jump ropes without stopping them. When Maddy tried it, she got entangled in them.

"Aww," the crowd moaned in disappointment.

But Jerrell's dear employee threw her arms around Maddy and drew her into a big bear hug, slapping Maddy's back and leading a round of applause.

The younger woman's heart raced as snow fell on their faces. Her adrenaline now swirled in her as if she were a stirred-up snow globe.

"I didn't know how much fun that would be," Maddy said to the woman. "Why are you working the day before Christmas?" She whipped around to Jerrell. "Shouldn't you send this lady home to be with her family? She shouldn't be out here right now. Does she have grandchildren to wrap presents for? This is how you treat your employees?"

Jerrell stood fuming at her, his arms crossing his chest. "Is that really the first thing you want to say to me today? To *me*, about how to treat people?"

Next to him were her father, brother and family. The crowd disassembled, getting in line for dessert orders and begging the old woman for photos.

But the older lady's face flickered, as if she recognized Maddy somehow. "Well, sweet Lord, it's you. You are the one," the elderly employee said, grasping Maddy's hand.

Taken aback, Maddy stared from the worker to Jerrell and her father. "Wh… excuse me?"

"The picture. It's you." The woman's gaze danced toward Jerrell. "Sonny, she's gorgeous."

Maddy rolled her eyes at Jerrell. "You're out here over-working your employees in the cold, for a quick buck? And how does she recognize my photo? Are you using my image for profit?"

Maddy's brother William tossed her a weird glance. Why did it seem they all knew a secret she didn't?

"Sweetheart," her father said, rubbing his eyes. "That's not his employee. It's his grandmother. *She* is Poppin' Pauletta, the name on that there box."

The woman dropped Maddy's hand, stepping back. "And, baby, my grandson doesn't need your picture to make money. He's got *my* picture."

Embarrassment heated Maddy's face.

How many times had she commented on Jerrell's treatment of women and made insulting assumptions about his work ethic?

But what surprised Maddy most was Jerrell had never corrected her.

"Jer—"

He turned away from her until she stared at his back.

Then, he reached out to Miss Pauletta. "Gram, we should wrap this up and get you over the bridge, to Dad's soon. Then I'll go to the store, shut things down there." He delivered the bad news to Sag Harbor residents, that photo ops and purchases would continue for just fifteen more minutes before shutting down.

Jerrell began helping Myles with sales, orders and customers. His face tight and unsmiling, he no longer wore the self-satisfied smugness Maddy was so used to seeing.

She turned to find her family delivering *you-ought-to-be-ashamed* looks.

"Why's everybody looking like that?" Maddy asked.

"Nobody's looking at anything. Dad, you see something?" her brother William inquired.

"No, Son, I see nothing. Sandra, Reet, y'all looking at anything?" her father asked, turning to Maddy's sister and sister-in-law.

"I'm not participating because this is dumb. Stop pooh-poohing her silly behind. What happened last night?" Reet whispered under her breath once they'd stepped away from the others.

When Maddy confessed about the forgotten dinner, her sister's eyes could have become daggers.

"Girl. You're about to mess around and have *nobody*, just like you always do."

"It was an honest mistake."

"I swear for the life of me, that'll be on your gravestone." She reached out and gripped Maddy's neck in a quick hug.

"Don't worry. We'll figure it out. But give him a minute to cool off. I almost thought he would stomp another hole in your face. You're going to have my pregnant ass out in the street throwing blows. I'll see you later."

Dr. Page strolled up and nudged her. "Jerrell called me last night, looking for you. Did you find him?"

In silence, Maddy's eyes fell.

Her father continued, "Is that how you treated somebody who stayed with you in the snow?"

"I took care of myself in the weather, Dad. Got my own hotel room and fed myself. I would have been fine until you all came to pick me up." (Okay, so the feeding part was not technically true, but she did buy the food.)

"But you weren't by yourself. He put his business on hold when he's busting his behind to get it off the ground, so he could bring you back to us, after conditions got bad. What is with you lately?" he asked.

"Ease up, Daddy, okay? We've already talked about this," Maddy shook her head, as her purse vibrated at her side.

"About what?" he insisted to know.

"How hard it is when these guys don't work out," she snapped. "I'm the one who has to deal with people judging me as some kind of failure, not you all."

His face softened.

Texts from Chrissy buzzed on her phone.

Maddy was reminded that she still had her dad's cell. "Oh, here. You left your phone at the candy store. Your banker called you. He said something about $35,000 you're transfer-ring. You forgot to give the account you wanted it to come from," she reported, cocking her neck. "What are you about to buy?"

Dr. Page's expression turned to surprise, as if she'd caught him off guard.

Happy to change the subject from Jerrell, she kept talking. "Are you getting Mom a gift for her big sixty coming up? Why didn't you mention it, so I can help you plan? What is it?"

A mix of reactions ran across his face before he straightened it. "You could say it's for the entire family."

That puzzling answer stomped her. "Oookay."

He looked over her head, at Jerrell. "You sure this is how you want to leave things with him?"

Torn, Maddy took Reet's advice, and started off.

"I need to chat with Chrissy and get Mama one more gift. See you back at the house." Deep in the hidden parts of her, she knew the real reason she wasn't ready to face Jerrell.

A KNIGHT IN SHINING ARMOR

JERRELL

"This doesn't look good," Gram said, staring out Jerrell's Range Rover.

Half of New York City must've been sitting on the NY-27. Headlights twinkled in the distance as the snowfall brewed into a storm. Traffic stood still, brimming with travelers in a rush to see family and run last minute Christmas errands. Three hours into their trip, they hadn't escaped the Hamptons. The snow would turn to ice by ten o'clock. At five hours, Jerrell hated to admit what seemed inevitable.

Fog rolled in, blanketing the city.

"How much further before we're at your father's?" Gram asked.

"Not even halfway," Jerrell muttered.

This portion of the trip should have taken just over an hour.

He flinched. Two cars ahead, a vehicle slammed into another car, forcing him to jerk off the road. To avoid hitting the collision, Jerrell swung his steering wheel, right and then left, to roll past the melee. He and Gram tumbled toward a strip mall parking lot.

"Oh!" Gram cried as they grazed a wooden sign that snapped off his side mirror.

"Gram!" He unbuckled his seatbelt, breathing heavy as he checked that she was okay.

Her hands shook, terror creasing the age lines across her forehead and eyes.

"You all right?" he asked her.

"What are you trying to do? Put me in the grave before I can get rich? So you can spend all my money?" Her biting humor endured even in her distress.

He pulled her in his arms, chuckling while giving her a firm squeeze. "It wouldn't be worth spending if you weren't here with me, lady. Just hang in here. Don't skip out on me now," he said into her kinky hair that was damp from the falling snow earlier.

Underneath him, her frail body still shuddered. Dread crept through him. What would have happened if she'd had a heart attack in this madness? Why hadn't he thought first, before driving her through New York traffic in inclement weather... at *Christmas*? Strong and lively as she might have been, Gram was no longer the sixty-year-old firecracker who had chased Jerrell as a kid.

"Boy, get me out of this mess. Turn this big ole thing around and take me back to where we came from. Let's wait until all this dies down."

"Yes, ma'am," Jerrell replied.

After checking the strip mall sign for damage, making the obligatory insurance call, and speaking with the other drivers, they took off. Grateful for the all-weather tires on his truck, he rode away from the tail-end collision behind them. The driver at fault had apparently been looking at his cell phone in a snowstorm.

On the ride back to Sag Harbor, Jerrell now had to worry about what he and Gram would eat for dinner. He'd been living on pizza, junk, and frozen dinners for the past month. But on Christmas Eve, they had planned to be at his parents' house helping with dressing, macaroni and cheese, jambalaya, and Creole soul-food. Most places had closed early, including the grocery stores. For the cupboards at his temporary Sag Harbor digs, he didn't even keep peanut butter and jelly, or bread.

He wondered where to go for grub. He had already declined Dr. Page's invite to stop by the house. Again.

After seeing Maddy that afternoon, pretending to be so innocent and blameless—jumping rope with his grandmother, for Christ's sake!—he couldn't handle her fake airs. Not even for Brazilian brown sugar.

Another two hours later, at seven p.m., like a lost puppy, he stood on the porch of Mrs. Emma Vincent and rang the doorbell several times. The lights were on, but no noises emanated from inside. No one came to the door. In the snow, he shivered while waiting a few more seconds. But nothing.

Shocked, he returned to his truck. Mrs. Emma had just bragged to him the night before about all the goodies she was planning for Christmas.

Behind the steering wheel, he called a few more restaurants. Those still open required that he order twenty-four hours in advance. His heart sank. Though he'd met many customers in Sag Harbor these past few days, he was best acquainted with Mrs. Emma. Actually, her and one other person. Beside those two, he could always grab convenience store food.

A heavy sigh rushed from his gut. Ten minutes later, he approached the Pages' house.

"Don't mope. This isn't the worst thing in the world," Gram said.

"I'm sorry you're away from the family like this. How often are you in New York? And I'll never hear the end of it from Dad and Roland."

And what would Dad say when he found out about Jerrell's failings as an entrepreneur?

"Grandson, you've been working so hard you don't even know what day it is half the time. In and out, and here and there, and you're worrying your mother sick. You just gave up everything and quit. Take a load off for a couple days. Maybe some space from your daddy isn't a bad thing," Gram ruminated aloud.

"What makes you say that?" he asked with sarcasm. "I love for him and Roland to tell me, over and over, how I put all their hard work to shame, and how there needs to be a black sheet hung over my picture in the Alpha Beta Kappa house," he muttered, shutting off the engine.

Had he even showered that morning? He couldn't remember. And he'd had no time to throw on fresh cologne, at least.

"Jerrell Isaac Rouse. That might be why the Lord has you *here* tonight. And not with your father. Now get in there and be a gentleman, make eyes with that uppity girl, and stop acting like the two of you hate each other's guts," she snapped before exiting the truck.

At the Pages' porch, the door swung open before Jerrell could ring the bell.

Dr. Page stared at him with a knowing smile. "So, you didn't get to Charles's. Snow brought you back to the Sag, huh?"

"Yes, sir," Jerrell admitted, hoping his face didn't appear as ashamed as he felt for not planning better. He stood here in the home of strangers, begging. Something his father and oldest brother had never done. "I've been so swamped… Back at my place… I don't—"

"Say no more, young man. Come on in here. We were just getting ready to eat," Dr. Page said.

Jerrell hesitated, not wanting to impose on Maddy's space.

"You're too kind. We can't tell you how grateful we are, Dr. Page," Gram replied, pushing past Jerrell to get through the door.

Inside the Page home again, his heart thudded a thousand beats per minute. As he swallowed, he became very self-aware, hoping he didn't show it.

Maddy emerged from the kitchen, unaware of his presence as she donned cooking mittens and carrying a steaming dish. Beautiful as ever in a dreamy mohair, candy-apple red sweater, her hair fell around her shoulders in fluffy curls. Her eyes looked up to see him, and shock spread across her face.

Jerrell knew coming here had been a mistake. He should've gone with chicken from the gas station.

His Stacy Adams dress shoes were soggy from walking in snow all day. Water squished from them, forming a puddle on their beautiful wooden floor. In his drenched, socked feet, he looked up, feeling the blood rush to his face, embarrassed.

Dr. Page laughed. "Don't worry. I'll get you a mop." Inside the gorgeous kitchen behind the good doctor, many pots boiled while ovens blazed. "House is kind of old. So it'll be a little hot in here, unless we cut on the air. And that would make the kids cold. You can take that sweater off if you want."

The smell of turkey and gravy filled Jerrell's nose. In a

beautiful home as warm and simple as this, he wondered how Maddy had turned out to be so cold and damaged.

Heavy, weathered wooden furniture accentuated sky-blue paint through the rooms. Bookcases built wall-to-wall, open glass windowpanes formed arches over reading nooks, and beams stretched across the ceilings to give the place an upscale woodsy cabin feel. Little lace doilies on lamp tables, creaking wood in some spots, and knitted quilts thrown over pristine, old-fashioned, rolled-arm white sofas told him this house carried a lot of decades.

"Oh, my goodness, how lovely is all this? I wish I could just pick up this beautiful place and take it back to Louisiana," Gram said in one long exhale.

Jerrell's own eyes also wandered over this quieter kind of Black wealth, to which he still wasn't quite accustomed. Indeed, Gram would be perfect in a homey place like this. Elegant but understated, she could kick off her shoes when she came from fishing or gardening. She could set her pail of worms down, or her fresh catch of catfish and crawfish, remove her rubber boots, and start cooking in a massive stainless-steel kitchen with a sturdy and wide island.

"Yeah, this looks like you. But don't worry. One day, after we take off, I'll get you a house just like this. Even better."

"Really?" another, stiffer voice asked, standing beside him.

Jerrell turned.

His grandmother had disappeared.

In her place, Maddy now lingered. Once again, the brilliant chandelier with crystal faces cast golden flecks in her umber-colored eyes. "Because there aren't too many houses that are prettier than my grandmother's."

God, she was stunning.

Even with an attitude.

Gram had gone off with Mrs. Page, and Maddy's siblings had returned to entertaining the children, leaving the two alone. Her fitted sweater hugged her breasts, swooping into a V-shape, revealing a slight tease of cleavage. Below that was a pair of white jeans that reminded him she took care of herself. Jerrell's chest swelled up with reactions he tried to swat away.

"Do you like what she's wearing? I picked it. She didn't," yet a third voice said from the dining room.

Maddy's eyes widened, and swung toward her sister, who'd been lurking behind them. "Mama! Will you come and get Reet?"

"Maddy's the oldest, but I've got the most sense," her younger sibling Marguerite continued. "You need to know there are some Pages who *do* have sense."

Jerrell cracked up, reminded of his own siblings, and missing them now. He liked the little sister.

Maddy stomped between them, delivering a death stare at Reet that Jerrell knew all too well. How often had he watched his own sisters in these exchanges? Somebody who could knock Maddy off her high horse was a nice reward after his long day.

Maddy turned to him once Reet had left. "Something to drink?" she asked.

"So, you can't dress yourself?" he asked, digging in. She had earned that one. And then some.

"Not funny."

"Neither are you. Bottled water. Room temp," Jerrell said, certain her father had sent her to make nice with him.

The Pages' wall of black and white photos lined the foyer, offering a progressive history of their family's rise. In the picture frames stood iron-faced workers, crowded on a porch step. On a hard dirt yard, dressed in dusty coveralls and ripped work boots, they grimacing at Jerrell.

"Jerrell!" Dr. Page exclaimed, returning. "How about a proper drink? Brandy, whiskey, gin? What are you having to warm up from that cold?"

"Oh, no, sir. Gram's with me, and I wouldn't want to be disrespectful."

"Tehe. It'll be our little secret," Dr. Page laughed.

"Well, if you don't mind some whiskey?" Jerrell whispered, hoping his grandmother was still socializing.

"You got it," Dr. Page said.

Jerrell continued peering at the antiques and photos, wishing he possessed his own family history this way. "Wow, how old is this picture? Who are these folks?"

"Over a century. Taken in 1897," Maddy answered, hands fidgeting at the side of her sweater. "They're my mother's people."

"A hundred years? Have you all lived here that whole time?" he asked, intrigued at the prospect of Black people a hundred years ago, who didn't still live on plantations.

"In this same neighborhood, yes. My great-great grands came North from South Carolina, in the 1890s to escape the Black Codes. They built a tiny house up the road."

She walked toward the hallway, pointing at the pictures along the wall, of Black men standing on docks. Next to them hung large whale corpses, three or four times as big as the workers. The men's faces were serious, chests broad and squared, reflected the pride they must have felt.

"What did they do for money?" he asked, trying to make the most of their being stuck together.

"Whaling."

"Whaling?" he repeated in disbelief. "*Black* people."

"Yes," she replied. "Us. They'd heard about the freedom of the high seas. The danger forced White men to rely on Blacks for their lives. Kind of like men who fought in the Civil War."

She studied each photo of her family's history as if she'd lived it herself. He couldn't resist watching her eyes roll upward, and then down, as she recalled her family stories someone must have taken time to teach her. Maddy seemed to travel elsewhere, forgetting herself. And Jerrell marveled at Black folks who owned photos of their family from as far back as the 1890s.

Her eyelashes fluttered. "The first few years, they stayed in a small house my great-great-grandfather built. In the 1920s and 30s, relatives who weren't interested in fishing, took off to law school and engineering. My grandmother's father was a lawyer who helped local people get their businesses off the ground. When he had enough money, he built this place."

"Wait," Jerrell said. "What about the house down the street? From the 1890s? Still standing, or they tore it down?"

Her eyes lit up. "Torn down. But my great grandfather used the same wood and parts from the first house and put it into this one. The planks from the 1890s house, you can see them here—a little darker next to the newer, light timber." She pointed. "He even had the original wash basins redone and placed in these bathrooms, so we never forget the history and how we started."

Jerrell kept his jaw from falling. Heritage meant everything to him. Especially the last fifteen years, after his father had rushed to leave Louisiana behind.

"Have you ever been down there? South Carolina?" he asked, curious if the swank Maddy could tolerate humidity, mosquitos, and Southern folksiness long enough to survive.

"Of course, several times. Port of Charleston was the

largest slave port in the U.S., and almost half of America's Black population entered there." She paused. "Hold up. You thought I was too uppity to go to South Carolina, didn't you?"

He muttered, "Nah."

"Yes, you did. That's why you asked. You think I'm so trapped in my bubble that I can't handle real folk or concern myself with slavery."

He shrugged. "I don't care what you're trapped in. Though you're definitely caught up in something."

His insides burned at the thought of her kissing some dude on a dock while he waited for her with flowers. He may as well have worn a big "L" for loser plastered on his chest.

At that, she cringed. "Jerrell, about last night, I totally—"

"I'm good. Like I said, I don't care. You have nothing to explain to me." He hoped that sounded as convincing as he'd intended. No more trying to butter her up or put his feelings on his sleeve. He had extended an olive branch, and she'd burned it to a crisp. Jerrell was done.

"I'm sorry. That wasn't cool. It slipped my mind when old friends grabbed me that I haven't seen in a minute," she explained, as her voice shook.

For the first time since they'd met, she appeared humble.

He held up his hand. "Let me stop you. You don't owe me anything. I'm not your man. I was the fool for thinking you might be special."

Her face flinched, shocking Jerrell. Could the witch have feelings?

"We got wrapped in memories from my childhood and…"

While she spoke, a soaring figure appeared inside the Pages' doorway behind Maddy, like a knight in shining armor.

Handsome and strapping, just as tall as Jerrell, the dude

seemed to suck all the air from the room. It was the guy from the night before.

"Childhood memories, huh?" Jerrell scoffed, ready to call her on her lie. "That's what you were doing out on the dock last night? Well, now you can make all the memories you want." He looked behind her.

Maddy spun around to see who Jerrell stared at, and she stiffened, as if indeed caught up in something.

"Kevin," she said in a weak, girlish voice.

Jerrell couldn't just dash off, or he would appear juvenile. He wasn't hurt. Not over some chick he only kissed twice.

No, he'd stay and be a man. Holding out his hand, he introduced himself to this smashing god on Earth. "Jerrell."

"Kevin."

Jerrell motioned at a horrified Maddy. "You must be quite the guy, to have this one's attention."

"Ha! It only took me twenty long years to become that guy. She's a tough one, though. I'm hoping I can keep her." Kevin's smile was broad and luxurious, as if he'd paid a lot for perfect teeth, and could use them as an ATM card to make money fall into his lap.

Twenty years? Jerrell swallowed. So Maddy hadn't lied.

They were thick as thieves, had probably shared a thousand kisses as teenagers in hidden spots, and this man knew all her guarded secrets crammed up in that stony little heart.

But hey, Jerrell thought.

Kevin seemed to be loaded. Another potential customer or even investor. So maybe the night wasn't all wasted.

Right behind Kevin, yet an extra guest strutted through the door, adding to the Christmas roundup.

"Hey, everybody, glad I'm not late," Lana said.

NO

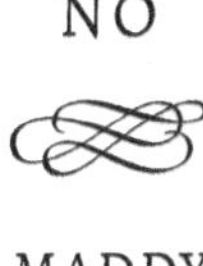

MADDY

ppalled, Maddy's insides slid through the wooden floorboards.

Jerrell had gut-punched her. What did he see? How did he know she'd been on the dock? Well, of course. *Sharon's* restaurant wasn't far from *Cal's*. He must've seen her and Kevin. *Ugh!*

Then Lana strolled in.

What was this? *Nightmare on Elm Street?*

But with Kevin standing there, a gift-wrapped box in his hand, she stared from one to the other. Which heart attack did she address first?

She targeted Lana. "What are you doing here? I thought we talked about this."

Lana's unbothered demeanor could have been a weapon further disassembling Maddy. "Yes, we did. And I *told* you." With that, she marched inside and took off her coat, greeting Maddy's parents.

Maddy wasn't the fighting type. Her family had never entertained drama. But right now, with this level of disre-

193

spect, she doubted she could uphold her class. She rushed to her mother.

"Mama, Lana has to go. Would you please tell her to leave?" But as she posed the question, she anticipated the answer.

Mrs. Page stopped mid-track. "Whatever for? You're the one who invited her here."

"I think she's sleeping with Desmond, Del's fiancé." Maddy shook off the doubts. "No, I don't think. I know. Even after I warned her not to, I saw them both at the hotel I stayed in."

Her mother's face dropped. "Oh, heavens. Poor Del." She picked up the cherry cobbler. "I'm sorry, Maddy, but you'll have to ride this one out. We talked about this. Stay out of other people's business. That's them."

"But what will I say to Del for housing somebody who's sleeping with her man? As if I co-signed on it?"

"Tell her the truth. You didn't help them, and she did it despite you. As long as you and Del have known each other, she'll understand."

With dread sitting like rocks in her stomach, Maddy returned to the living room where Jerrell and his grandmother chatted with her dad, and Kevin lingered.

"Is this a bad time?" Kevin asked.

"Uh," she stammered, accepting his gift box. Her hands shook as she fumbled with the wrapping paper. "No. It's fine."

Actually, was this a rather inconvenient moment for him to show up in her life? Why weren't butterflies and moonbeams dancing through her the way they once did? At sixteen, she would have fallen all over herself. Hell, even at age twenty-six.

Her parents handled all the guests with finesse, and her mother was ever the perfect host, extending her arms and offering food. Without blinking, Mrs. Page could have been a fixture on a housekeeping magazine.

Maddy opened Kevin's box to pull out a gold necklace with a diamond-encrusted crab at the end. Her zodiac sign of Cancer. Her eyes fluttered to his.

"Your birthday isn't until July 2, but consider this a promise of what's coming," he whispered, leaning to kiss her mouth, and Maddy tilted her head down, so they didn't connect.

She could feel Jerrell's glare ripping into her from the other side of the room.

"Thank you. It's beautiful," she mumbled. While he clasped it behind her neck.

As Maddy squirmed, a wide-eyed Reet sat on the sofa and sipped hot cider while enjoying this entertainment.

They all sat to eat, and Lana discussed her work on the Senate Judiciary Committee. Of course, Maddy's mother, a judge, engaged Lana since she was considering a run for political office in Virginia Beach. Maddy had hobnobbed in rooms with people she loathed countless times. She had perfected the art of fake civility. So why did this irritate her?

Maddy and Jerrell sat on opposite ends of the table. Him next to her father, and her alongside Kevin and her mother. Even as volcanic lava flowed from Jerrell's end, scorching her, she tried to focus on what Kevin was saying. A tech deal with a new company out of New York. Licensing with a major studio in L.A. His renovations at his beach house in Malibu, where he wanted to fly her out in a few weeks. Perhaps on Martin Luther King, Jr.'s, birthday holiday. Kevin's fingers stroked hers, and she slid them to her lap.

His moisturized, glistening curls and polished teeth

reminded her why, at one point in her life, she would have ventured to another planet for him.

He whispered, "There's this great place in the Maldives I want to fly you out to. I haven't seen this gorgeous body of yours in fifteen years. We'll put it in a red bikini, slap oil all over it, lay out in the sun, and," he paused for effect, "practice starting a family."

She swallowed, pumping the breaks on asking how many women he'd already flown to the Maldives and practiced with.

The doorbell rang.

God, no, Maddy thought.

When her father answered, a familiar voice cried between breaths at the door.

"Where is she?"

Maddy turned to see Del entering the foyer.

"Del, hey. You all right?"

Del put up an index finger to silence Maddy. "Tell me you didn't know."

Maddy knew the source of torture on her friend's face. "I tried to st—"

Del's mouth careened downward. "How could you?"

"I didn't," Maddy replied. "They ignored me."

"Why don't you ladies take this upstairs?" Maddy's mother urged.

"That won't be necessary, Mrs. Page. I apologize for disturbing your Christmas Eve," Del muttered, seething as she turned toward the dining room, shaking so hard Maddy expected her to combust. Adella's eyes could have torn Lana to shreds. Fingernails digging into her palms and forming fists, arms tense as rubber bands, she seemed to hold in hell and brimstone. "If I see you out on the street," she said through clenched teeth, "you'd better hope I don't catch you."

"Bwahahahaa!" Lana cracked, throwing her head back in an exaggerated taunt, and flipping her hair over her shoulder. "Haaa, how cute is this."

Caught in the middle, Maddy stared down her mother, as if to say, *I warned you.*

Del trekked back into the snowstorm.

"Del," Maddy called. She then turned to Lana, and kicked a chair aside. "Out! Now. Or I will drag you out."

"And I'll help her," Reet added.

"So will I," another female joined from the door that was still open. Chrissy had arrived.

Maddy's mother stood up and faced Lana. "We don't do drama in our home, and I'm afraid you'll have to go, for bringing it here with you."

"I can get her bags," William offered.

Lana scoffed, standing up. She clicked her teeth as she moved from the table.

"You all act like you're better than me, but you're not. You say there's no drama here, but y'all put on more shows than Broadway. Especially those two over there," Lana suggested, motioning at Jerrell. "The only reason he came is to get $35,000 from Maddy's daddy." She turned to Maddy. "And sweetheart, he's only kicking it with you because his product is stuck in Brazil, and he needs you to help him on the Foreign Relations Committee. He's using you. Same as all the others do. Don't think you're special." Lana motioned toward Kevin. "And that one there, he might want you, but he's got somebody else lined up, in case you tell him no. So, Perfect Little Maddy's not so drama-free herself."

No oxygen remained for any of them to breathe. Only Lana's poisonous carbon dioxide filled the room.

"$35,000? Douglass?" Maddy's mother spoke first.

The snowstorm outside blistered through Maddy's chest, freezing over her body until the tears she would have cried were icicles in her tear ducts. Those eyes aimed at her father. "Daddy? I expect this from Mama." She shook her head. "But not you."

"Maryanne, Maddy, this young man needs a little help," her dad explained.

It was happening. Again.

"So, you're paying him to date your desperate daughter?" Maddy trembled.

"No!" Dr. Page replied, his finger shooting up. "I didn't know the two of you would start… whatever it is you've been doing. Well, I kind of expected it. You and him are so much alike."

Maddy's sharpened eyes sliced air until they aimed at Jerrell. Frost dripped from her voice. "Go on. Tell me what you wanted from me on the Foreign Relations Committee. While you were busy laying guilt trips and pretending to be hurt."

He stood up, wiping his mouth before throwing his napkin on the table. He helped his grandmother up. And then delivered a death stare to Maddy that matched hers.

"No."

MADDY AND CHRISSY found Del sitting in her Mercedes, parked in front of the docks where they'd played as kids.

After some cajoling, she allowed them inside.

"Adella, girl," Maddy started, "I would never do something like that to any of you. I swear to God, on my grandmother, I told Lana not to move on him."

"Why did you even bring her?" Del whimpered. "She's not one of us. Not from the old crew. She has nothing to do with Sag Harbor. She's… "She sputtered, sobbing, "… trash."

"I did not know she does this," Maddy replied.

"You said you've worked together for years."

"We hang out, but not as best friends. Del, I'm so sorry," Maddy replied, her heaviness multiplied by all the events of the night.

Del's chest heaved her anguish and labored to exhale. Maddy and Chrissy sat with her, while she let out the despair. Just as they had as teenagers after a bad date, a death in the family, or a huge upset. Like Del's rejection from her dream school of Yale. Or Maddy being humiliated with the frog kiss. Or Chrissy's grandmother making her lose weight as a condition of receiving an allowance.

Del turned to Chrissy. "How did you know I was at Maddy's?"

"My cousin Neera saw your car speed down the street, and we figured the shit was going down. I came to see if you needed backup," Chrissy answered, holding up three brown paper bags. "And liquor."

"Look, y'all, I don't need your sympathy. I want to be left alone," Del said, struggling to get out the words as she started sobbing again.

"Girl, that's not how it looks right now," Chrissy replied. "And don't act proud because I've been there. Hell, I'm still there."

Del fell over, grieving in Maddy's arms, until she hyperventilated.

"Breathe," Maddy whispered.

They all huddled, like the pain was one long wave of electricity flowing through them all.

"It's okay," Del cried.

"No, it's not, but you're strong," Maddy reassured her. "No matter what."

"And once you leave him, you'll be even better. Yes, ma'am, it hurts. But you'll feel so free when you throw him to the curb," Chrissy chided in.

Del rose up again. "I'm not leaving him."

Silence filled the car. Her shaking hands dabbed at her face with a napkin.

Chrissy challenged, "You mean you... are going to stay? And let him make a fool of you? Girl, I—"

"Chriselle, you've been there," Del started, "may I remind you that you stayed with a cheater for ten years? So has my mom. And yours. As well as Maddy's mother. A lot of women have tolerated cheating men. If it doesn't happen with Des, it will with somebody else. Besides, you don't know my situation or have the full story, so who are you to judge?"

Of all Del's words, only three pinned Maddy to the back of the seat. "*My* mother?"

As if realizing what she'd disclosed, Del sniffed. "Forget it. I didn't mean to say that."

"But you did. So, go ahead. Finish. What about her tolerating a cheating man?" Maddy pressed.

Her tears drying up, it was Del's turn to cringe. "No, really, girl. It's none of my business. Your folks are happy now, right?"

The three of them sat stoic against the leather seats, looking up and down the snow-covered Sag Harbor streets that were no longer innocent as they were twenty years before.

As if the universe had reserved the perfect joke, the low radio played Aretha Franklin's heavy *Drown in My Own Tears*, and her gritty voice began raking them over the coals.

"Remember how, when we were little girls, we talked about the castles we would live in when we grew up?" Chrissy asked, drinking from the whiskey bottle, and passing it to Maddy.

Maddy swallowed a big gulp. "Compared to a lot of people, we do have castles. Just not the ones we want."

"And ours are made of glass," Del added, taking a swig.

"I support you, no matter what, Del," Chrissy said. "And you too, Maddy. If you think Kevin is what's best, I'm here for you. My awful marriage doesn't give me the right to piss on others' relationships."

"And I took your concern the wrong way. You were always ready to go to war for me, so I should have known you were coming from a good place," Del replied.

Maddy touched Kevin's diamond pendant at her throat. "Of course, she was. Chrissy is the only one of us who's lived the lie."

"What lie?" Del asked.

"The one where we marry our fantasies—the houses, cars, reputation, vacations, impressive looks. The entire front like we've got it made, when we damn well don't. But we love to front for everybody else. That's what we're really marrying— the front," Chrissy answered, taking a drink.

"Only if you want to lie to yourself," Del replied, another tear sliding down her cheek. "If you accept the truth about your life from the beginning, you'll be fine. My truth is my parents are forcing me to get married."

Her lips trembled, and when she took an extra swig, her shaking hands caused the liquor to splash in the bottle.

The car may as well have sunk to the bottom of the Atlantic, as if the revelation was ocean water closing them in. A ship horn blew in the distance. More snow fell.

The women's arms found one another in the dark.

"We'll help you," Chrissy whispered. "You won't go through this alone."

"Never," Maddy joined.

An hour later, when Maddy walked back in the house, her father awaited her.

She glared at the man who had always been her hero. *Her* fantasy. And now her lie?

"Dad."

"Maddy, you shouldn't have rushed out the way you did. You might have given Jerrell a chance to talk."

"You're my father. Don't take up for him."

The anger on Jerrell's face earlier had stunned her. How could he possibly be upset with her, when he hadn't really been interested in the first place? Why would he dare get worked up over Kevin when he'd hidden his own motives for days? The very thought of being used, of allowing Jerrell to touch her, kiss her, send her head to places it had never been… all of it had just been the setup for an ask.

He'd made her the fool. Somehow, her body managed to burn and freeze in her chest at the same time?

"I'm taking up for what's right. As I always have with all of you."

"And he wasn't right. So, why would I want to hear what he has to say?"

"Because you're jumping to conclusions, based on your past bad experiences. Listening to him is important. Both of you are haughty. But good people," he replied.

"Why didn't you just tell me you were paying him $35,000?"

"It was not for you. I was investing in what I believe in. I visited his father Charles's office one afternoon, to meet him for lunch in the city. While I was waiting, I caught the tail end of a terrible argument between them. I felt bad for Jerrell. I remember being the youngest in my household, first to go to college, breaking out on my own. Men in my family worked at the oil rigs. There were no dentists, and my uncles gave me flack for separating from the family's work. I found Jerrell later to see what business idea he had. There was nothing involving you at all."

"Then why didn't you two tell me about whatever product he needs from Brazil, from the beginning? Instead of embarrassing me and playing me for a fool. Especially after all the other bad screw-ups."

He shrugged. "There was never a right time. When you and he clashed, and were at each other's throats, it didn't surprise me. Both of you are strong-willed. So, I had to step back and let you two work it out. For a moment it seemed you would."

Maddy sighed. Her father had meant her no harm. But Jerrell... "He was going to play me."

Dr. Page's gaze softened. "No, baby girl, I don't think that's it. Not at all."

"He was acting interested, while he had a motive the whole time. What other conclusion can there be except what Lana said—he was using me?"

Her father stared at her for several seconds. "Ask. *Him.*"

Confused about that, and with Adella's disclosure still on her mind, Maddy eyed her dad.

"Did you cheat on Mama?"

Stunned, his Adam's apple moved up and down, his eyes blinking. "Yes."

She shuddered, her hand clamping her mouth as disappointment crushed her. It shattered all the images of kickball, basketball, ballet recitals, and Saturday morning pancakes.

"It was years ago, when y'all were young and I was going through a lot. I didn't love you guys any less, or your mother. But men go through periods where... where we... get off track."

"Off track?" she asked. "Did you marry Mama just to make her your trophy wife?"

He stiffened. "No! I'm crazy about that woman. But sometimes, affection is not enough for our fragile egos. Everybody has a weakness—some people gamble, some folks drink, do drugs, spend money. And yes, sexual curiosity. Your daily routine starts feeling too familiar, and then you itch for something different. But any good man will stick with his responsibility and the vows he took. Where is this coming from?"

Her eyes dropped to Kevin's necklace.

Was this the prize she'd wanted her entire life? To wed a guy whose love was questionable, and whose ego would never be satisfied? So she could ride the highest echelons of society? Like Chrissy said, was Maddy prepared to marry a front? And then, she would spend the rest of her life in marital jail—miserable like Chrissy, and as Del soon would be. The kind of shackles Maddy had worked so long to avoid.

Dr. Page nodded his understanding.

"Maddy Marie, I do believe Kevin loves you. But always

know that he'll love himself more. I got as much from talking with his folks."

"You've talked to his parents?"

"Of course they called. But I refused to get involved. Your mother will not insert herself either. This is all you. Just don't be blind. Decide with your eyes open. So you have no regrets later. And you'll be stronger and more prepared through it all. Come what may."

Maddy weighed his words. "I need to ask you one more thing. Charles Rouse's phone number. I'd like it."

AND IF I DON'T?

JERRELL

If the previous day hadn't qualified as the crappiest Christmas ever, Jerrell wasn't sure what did. One close competitor might have been when he was age ten, grounded on Christmas Day for setting his neighbor's rose bush on fire with a firecracker, and couldn't play with his new toys for two weeks. Instead, he'd spent playtime replanting flowers and doing yard work.

But not even that had cut as deep as being a struggling business owner who might have bitten off more than he could chew this time.

And for the grand slam, another dude appeared at the house of the girl he admittedly liked. Had stepped into the role he always played, and took the last minute three-point game-winning shot.

Never mind that dude's McLaren MSO X limited edition sitting on the street had twenty-inch rims and was a rare make of only five hundred ever produced. Or that dude's Swiss watch appeared in several Hollywood A-list movies. Or that when Maddy gazed at him, her face melted, and her tone fell to a respectful murmur. Far from the clipped disdain she displayed with Jerrell.

He'd known this damn girl all of a week, so why was he tripping? This distraction was what he'd wanted to avoid when he quit his job. Why was he wide open when he needed to focus most?

He and his grandmother had spent her New York Christmas holed up in his apartment video-calling relatives while they ate pastries from a pop-up. Dr. Page was also kind enough to give them to-go boxes. Gram had handled it like a champ, laughing and watching Jerrell's streaming services while he reviewed budgets and handled tasks on which he'd procrastinated.

To make matters worse, the traffic delayed his trip to the store that morning, as drivers waited for the city to clear snowed out streets. Afterward, he finally delivered Gram to his dad's.

Ears closed, guard up, Jerrell had refused to give his father an audience.

Arriving at his store, the sight of Kami's car parked in the back comforted him. Sure, he'd have to take a few jabs for Gram being stuck at Christmas, but the balm of her presence would soothe the ache in his chest.

Since the store was closed after the holiday, quiet awaited him.

"Eh, Kam, you came. Why didn't you cook breakfast?" He asked, wiping small crumbs off a counter.

No response.

"All right, fine. I'll make it. Let me guess. You don't like that my desk is still messy. I haven't been sitting around here twiddling my thumbs," he said, going through the mail.

He pulled out the contents for peanut butter and banana

French toast, plus the cheesy scrambled eggs she liked. To keep her from ratting out his worst offenses to Mom and Dad over the years, he'd learned to cook her favorite dishes, so she kept quiet. He fired up the stovetop and cooking pans.

"My office isn't that bad."

A terrifying thought flew through him. If his sister was rearranging his things, or had gotten rid of his old-school rotary telephone, there would be blood. He loathed people touching his stuff.

"Damn, girl," he said busting through the door separating the kitchen from the office, "If you moved my ph—"

He stopped mid-sentence upon seeing the vision behind his desk.

Wrapped in the fur-trimmed coat she wore the first day he met her, Maddy's eyes remained lowered, focused on the paperwork across the desk.

Frozen in his doorway, Jerrell forgot his last thought.

Face natural, lips glistening, hair puffy and unassuming, Maddy could have fallen from Heaven.

"I would like breakfast, thank you. And while you do that, I've set up three interviews for potential store managers to help you. Given your drivers their schedules for the next two weeks, arranged your pop-up times for Sag Harbor, and I replaced Myles."

"You replaced *who?*" Jerrell shrieked.

"Myles," she said, her face unflinching, still not looking at him. "He never wanted to work for you. He won't tell you, and he doesn't want to upset his grandparents. Hire a kid who needs the money and wants to make connections. My long-time friend's niece is into cuisine and could use the experi-ence. She'll be a good fit."

"I've gotten to know Myles. He's good at it, needs to learn something besides video games," Jerrell protested.

"I'm his former babysitter. I know him better. Myles makes a hundred thousand dollars a year as a gamer on the internet. His employment for you is cutting into his profits." Maddy's eyes finally rose to meet Jerrell's. "You would have known that if you had looked him up."

He hated how she did that know-it-all thing. Still, excitement pulsated through him that he resented. "Where's Kami? Why are you here? In my business? Going through my stuff?"

Her stare narrowed. "She took a walk. And honestly, I'm not sure. I would be lying if I said I was only reviewing my family's financial interests."

Jerrell ground his teeth.

She continued, "From the agreement I read, I have a right to inspect the books."

"Your *father* has a right. And only with twenty-four hours written notice, and a duly expressed specific concern," Jerrell responded.

"Noted. He has appointed me his proxy. Here's my documentation, with an express concern, but I do admit my review is early." She stood up, touching her father's letter she'd placed at the edge of the desk. "Though I don't think my work for you this morning has hurt you. You're welcome."

He swallowed, unsure of whether to ask her to leave or snatch her up. He glanced at the sparkle along her throat, just above the zipper of her jacket.

"I appreciate you. But where's your pretty boyfriend? Why aren't you out with him... jetting off to Europe on a private plane somewhere?"

"Why didn't you tell me about the brown sugar in Brazil?" she asked, her eyes tightening into slits as she moved to the edge of his desk. Three feet of distance separated them now. Close enough for him to see tears roll down her cheeks, and evaporate in the heat of a face that might have spewed fire. Her voice lowered to a shaky whisper. "Instead of pretending you had feelings."

"From the first moment we met, you hated me." Remembering her condescension irritated him all over again. "With you shitting on my business all the time, what was I supposed to say?"

She moved closer, confronting him. "Mm... Maybe, *I can't stand you but give me a meeting.* You could have put it in a note. Anything but try to play me."

"I didn't hate you. And I wasn't pretending."

"Liar." Her words were so low they barely came out. "You thought I was some snobby rich girl, who had everything handed to me. And you were going to play me and teach me a lesson."

"But who taught who, huh?" Jerrell muttered. "Because I learned a lot about you snobs when you left me standing at *Sharon's*, holding your flowers. With our night all planned out."

"He shocked me. Came from nowhere. Kevin was in the house when I got home. He had gathered all our old friends. It brought back memories I haven't dealt with in a long time."

Jerrell fumed, unsure whether to accept her tear-streaked effort. "Now who's lying? He's the one. Isn't he? The dude who hurt you. And you've been damaged ever since. He didn't shock you. No. You've been waiting for him your entire life. And that was more important to you than honoring your word. And showing up for a stupid dinner with some guy you don't know."

She wiped her face. "I don't lie. And you have no clue what I think is important."

"Yes, I do. Because you're no different than the rest of them," he snapped, staring down at her necklace.

"Don't talk to me that way," she muttered.

Jerrell continued, his voice rising. "He makes you feel like a princess."

"I don't need a man to make me feel like a princess."

"Wrong. You can be bought, and I wasn't throwing out enough money. That's why I didn't tell you about the sugar."

"No, you were simply planning to screw me for your product!"

Jerrell roared, "Why do you think I didn't touch you that night at the hotel, *Madison*? I was feeling you, and I needed your help. But I did *not* want it in your head that I was only sleeping with you to get something!" His eyes fell to the necklace again. "And like a dumbass, I held back for you to stand me up."

"I screwed up and made a *mistake*! I'm sorry!"

"You kissing him? A mistake? If that's all it was, then why can't you take that off?"

"He kissed me. I hadn't seen Kevin in over five years, and it caught me off guard. And I'm wearing this because I *earned* it. It's the least he could do for me after the hell I went through!"

"Maddy, if he's got you all wrapped in him, *why* are you here?"

"Because *you* make me feel like a princess!" she screamed. "Where am I right now? With him or you?"

"And where will you be tomorrow? I don't think you know, little girl," Jerrell snickered.

"I'm not your little *fucking* girl," she snapped, pushing him. Hot frustration shook her. "What you saw was Kevin finally making his move, after fifteen years. And I'm not having breakfast with him and his family, as they asked me to. I drove two hours here, at five in the morning, to make it up to you and tell you that. But you're right. This girl is so stupid for even trying with a complete *asshole!*"

Her cotton puff of hair turned from him, and she snatched up her purse and keys. "Sorry I wasted both of our time."

Jerrell still stood in the doorway, and as she approached to move by him, his arm shot out, blocking her exit.

"Move!"

He leaned down so his forehead bumped hers, pressing her backward. "And if I don't?"

His weight clashed against hers, as natural as magnetism attracted polar opposites. Maddy tried to kill him with her glare, and her chest heaved up and down as if preparing to explode.

But her anger ignited him.

She huffed against his skin, exhaling on his face, and Jerrell kept using his body to block her.

She attempted shoving him aside, and Jerrell flexed. His muscles didn't budge. That was enough of her believing she could push him. So Maddy pummeled him. He grabbed her wrists with one hand and pressed the door shut with the other. Jerrell's weight shoved her backward until she hit his desk. She shook against him, and a small sob crept from her throat. Jerrell wrapped his arm around her, pulling her to him and closing the space between them.

His other hand slid under her chin, tilting it up, so her furious eyes pounded his. With his thumb, he wiped her tears. Against him, he felt her caving. Her glare softened, and underneath him, the wrought-iron gates of her eyes opened.

He bit her lip, sucking it and staring into her, as she had

nowhere to escape. Her warm skin, her pulse so tender under his fingers, prodded him onward.

His tongue penetrated her mouth, and Maddy responded, kissing him back. Hot and wet, she surprised him, her tongue sliding through his lips like it was breaking out of a prison. Curious, exploring, intrigued, she sucked like she'd been waiting forever.

Her urgency was an electrical charge propelling his hand under her sweater. The flesh on her stomach was firm and smooth under his fingers. Lithe, with muscles reacting to his touch that confirmed she took her fitness seriously. He rubbed her back, loving its twisting muscles and how she arched at his touch, pressing her breasts against his chest. Kneading her skin, his fingers slid underneath her bra, to her tender breasts that melted into his hands, and hard nipples that beckoned to him. Lifting her sweater over her head, he shoved down her bra and helped himself to the erect tips, enjoying her moan that was a Christmas carol in his ear.

Jerrell kept expecting Maddy to stop him and listened for hesitation. But her nails scraped his chest while hunting under his sweater and T-shirt. While his teeth munched her breast, she bit his ear and lightly clawed his scalp, the sensations sending a train straight through him, to his dick.

With every opening of her clothes that Jerrell unzipped or unbuttoned, he waited for an objection. He removed her jeans, sucking her navel. The silk of her stomach…

"Goddamn," he muttered.

Licking her thighs, nuzzling his tongue inside her panties.

Maddy opened wider. Her legs were every bit as strong as they looked, wrapped around his neck. Jerrell slid his tongue inside her slit, tasting her folds and sucking up the pearly stream that dripped onto his desk.

"Aahh…" she whined, squeezing his head.

The Capitol Hill queen squirmed. Jerrell's hands clamped her thighs firmly against his face.

He wanted to hear more of her helplessness. Relished her vulnerability. Her head flexed back, mouth opened, the curve of her throat forming an arc.

Hungry for this woman he'd ached for since the first day he laid eyes on her, but wanting to torture her, Jerrell took his time.

"Mm," she half-moaned, half-pled as she tried to get away.

Tasting, sucking, taunting, as every one of her whimpers urged him to keep going. Until Maddy's hips raged, her legs pulling and stomach convulsing. Screaming, her entire body tensed as she came on his tongue. Jerrell kept licking, loving the last few aftershocks of ripples he felt through her midriff.

Then her arms shoved the papers and supplies off his desk, and she threw him into an abyss when she reached for his jeans and unzipped them. Circling her legs around his waist, her fingers shoved them down. Then her warm hands were palming his dick, rubbing him, inviting him. As he'd imagined so many times since he'd met her. Except this was real and her glorious ass really was there, panting in front of him.

Maddy's sexiness spun Jerrell's thoughts faster than a cake mixer spinning batter.

Still, through the exhilarated pounding of his heart, Jerrell stared at her, to make sure she was sure.

"Maddy," he murmured, gazing at her and nursing his own fears and questions. Especially about her father. His own company. This Middleton guy. Their very different backgrounds and lives. "We don't have to do this."

Maddy's fingertips stroked his stomach. Before meandering to his chest.

"Yes, we do." The deep diamond mines of her eyes sat open, as if waiting for Jerrell to come and mine her. "We've needed to do this since we met."

Her trembling lips hung open, displaying her wet tongue that glistened.

His wallet was in his jeans, and he reached for it then. Thankfully, a condom had been sitting inside waiting on some action for months. Jerrell handed it to her, and she slid it on him.

He pressed himself against her. "This isn't the best place to do this, and if you want to go back to my spot—"

"What's taking you so long?" Maddy arched, not having looked more confident in the short time he'd known her than she looked right then.

Shock struck Jerrell at how unwavering her gaze was. He gulped down the millions of tiny neuron explosions in his head.

With a last glance at her, checking for any sign of doubts or second-guessing, Jerrell thrusted forward. Soft, moist, her hot wetness had been waiting for him. She grimaced a bit at his size as she adjusted, but she held onto his desk and her toned legs clung to his waist.

Holding her head in place, his fingers entangled in her furry locks, he savored her eyes that dared him. Jerrell gripped her against him, not releasing her, while he thrust harder, faster.

"Mm," she moaned, her hands squeezing his ass, pulling him inside her.

Their hips moved in unison, matching each other, finding a perfect rhythm, and Maddy stared at him through eyes that didn't run.

Her little squeals, her tongue sliding across her top lip,

head falling to the side, fingers scraping his stomach and chest, hardened his manhood. And softened his heart. Every kiss, grip and thrust unleashed another level of delirium that pushed him harder, deeper into her.

A growl escaped his throat.

Maddy's body responded as if it thirsted for him the way he'd ached for her. Her walls turned hot, oozing all over him.

Groping for each other, she shrieked in his ear and convulsed.

"You're hot, baby." With every thrust, he relished her slick womanhood constricting on his shaft. He couldn't get enough, wanted to lay down and nap in her. Especially with her whines stroking his erection.

Gyrating her hips against his pelvis, her muscular legs still clutched him, and her titties still bounced against his chest. Her cream splashed with each of his dips inside her, the sound filling his office and hardening Jerrell more.

"*Shit*! Maddy."

Her energy, sensuality creeped into his vital organs. A grimace on her face, all her intensity clenching her teeth, her fierce spirit was becoming vital *to* his organs. Their rising ecstasy kept banging until their blizzard stormed his desk, in the collision of their mouths, and that final violent pound of their pelvises. Jerrell banged himself deep as he could, toward her head and came as she writhed out her orgasm underneath him.

Collapsing on top of her, he kissed her chest, chin, neck and jawline. His chest still dragging in air over hers, he checked in with her eyes again.

"Ms. Page, you straight?"

"Better than in a long time. You?" she asked, running a finger down his face. He kissed it.

A small chuckle left him. He thought of the last time his heart had been so open to a woman. The memory was sad. Yet it dissipated in Maddy's gaze.

"I'm doing pretty good," he murmured.

She smiled, from her eyes. Not the fake, tired grin she offered the neighbors at public events. Her lips whispered, "Good. Where's my breakfast?"

He kissed her stomach and smiled back. "Comin' right up."

When he peered outside for Kami's car, it was gone. Jerrell laughed to himself. He would definitely get his sister for agreeing to schemes behind his back.

Madison Page surprised Jerrell, unlocking a gate in him he thought would never open after Raychelle.

A Bermuda Triangle of passion was waiting for Jerrell in her ocean, and as he sailed into it, he had not been prepared.

By nightfall, he was still sailing through the waters of her. Pushing, pumping, navigating as she kept pulling, whirling and tossing him. As if she were a remote locale that had been waiting forever for him to sail her.

In the middle of the night, after several vigorous rounds, they hadn't let up.

COVER YOU IN DIAMONDS

MADDY

"Shit," Maddy whined.

Jerrell's nine inches of hard steel tortured her inside his stone shower. Growling in her ear, Jerrell held her firmly. She opened wider while he made her G spot purr.

Water cascading over them, he drove her to climax, his fingers pressing her clit, driving her crazy. Her fingers clinging to the stone paneling, she came all over him. Behind her, his hands clung to her as she took him over, pumping hard and deep.

The pressure of his hands on her skin, massaging her breasts, her stomach, she felt like gold he was palming.

"I see you're appreciating my goods a little more now," he said in her ear, biting it as he toweled her dry.

"Your grandmother's goods." She corrected him with a smirk.

It was the second shower they'd taken. After the first shower, they'd taste-tested some of his desserts, smearing each other's bodies with cake icing, creams and pastes, and all that action required them to wash off whatever they hadn't licked.

"It wasn't my grandmother who just had you begging though, was it?"

With one of his towels, she snapped him. "I wasn't begging!"

"The hell you weren't."

Unable to keep their hands off each other, they hit his couch. As she straddled him and rode his dick, he pulled her hair, staring *into* her and not *at* her. His erection thick and filling her to the hilt, Jerrell cupped her ass and slowed down his stroke, seeming to savor her. He pulled her to him, sliding his tongue through her lips and her tongue welcomed his sensual command of her. The stroke of their tongues matched the devastating motions of his shaft in her walls.

Surprising her, he stood from his sofa, still carrying her like she weighed nothing. Her legs strapped around his sculpted waist, his hands still cupping her ass, he carried her through his condo, never letting them disconnect. She loved the feel of his hardness filling her.

"Nice pussy," he murmured against her mouth.

Maddy licked Jerrell slow, from his muscled neck to the tip of his chin and up his bottom lip, which she grabbed with her teeth. Before letting it go. "Nice dick," she murmured back.

Still inside her, he lay her back against his bed, lifted her legs up over his shoulders. Towering over her, leaning against her, he rolled his hips forward. His full length drilled deeper, stretching her until he was massaging Maddy's heart, sending her head back into his pillows. "Aaah."

Jerrell continued, looking at her sensually, like he wanted more from her. "That the best you can do?"

His nice dick swerved, side to side, playing in her walls, small, intimate thrusts driving her crazy while he killed her G spot softly. She bit her lip, her gaze disappearing behind her closed eyelids. She'd never had it this good. "Mmm…"

"Open your eyes, baby girl. Because your pussy is throbbing and getting hot around my dick, like she wanna love me long time," he whispered against her forehead.

Maddy half-gasped, half-laughed. He chuckled with her.

His shaft splashing in her nectar was the sound effect to his ass rolling. His gaze locked her into him, and the twitches on his face told her he was feeling it too.

"Come here," his low voice commanded, before she lifted her head, and they shared an open-mouthed kiss.

Maddy felt her valley gushing, her walls clamping to him as he dug through her treasure.

"Sss" she hissed at the ecstasy in each tiny nerve-ending along her womb.

"Oh, damn, Maddy Cakes. Your pussy is cake. This hot, sweet ass pussy," he muttered, dipping his hips in and out.

His tiny strokes, wet tongue, filthy words were too much. Another orgasm overtook her, and she couldn't hold back her scream of immense pleasure.

"Look at me, baby, so you remember this dick."

Maddy forced her eyes open, staring at Jerrell while he pushed harder. She brought Jerrell over the glorious edge, and he growled.

Later, she damn near cried on his dining room table after they'd finished the pizza he ordered. He'd eaten her for dessert.

When she woke up from a nap, Jerrell took her on his living room floor sweeping aside documents and papers where he worked.

He'd tapped, pounded, and massaged an ache she never thought any man could truly reach.

Laughing, cracking jokes and trash-talking between romp rounds, they finally rubbed and kissed each other to sleep around 2 a.m.

Darkness still fell over Jerrell's condo when his alarm sounded at 6:15. He reached over and shut it off, before his arm slid back around Maddy.

"I can't sleep in. Store is open today. I've got a lot to do," he said into her hair.

His body still warmed hers, and she snuggled in his arms a little while longer. She closed her eyes and savored their last seconds. There wasn't a place on her that Jerrell hadn't put his tongue. No man had ever made love to her as if she was his last meal and he could eat her to the bone. He'd emblazoned his name on her, and she would now return to D.C. with a ferocious jones.

"The debutante ball is tonight," she mumbled.

She had no dress. Her hair was a chicken coop of a mess. And she still needed to fix her scuffed gel polish.

"Yes, we're working it." His hand kneaded her hip. "I don't want this to be the last time I see you."

"See me? Or get to know me?" she asked, grinning.

He turned her over in the dark, so she faced the outlines of his set jaw. "I already told you. But I'll answer again. Both. What are you doing for New Year's?"

A happy, sleepy grin oozed from her. "I guess I'm seeing you."

"Among other things you can do with me." He sucked her nipple. "Do to me." He licked her. "Do on me." Then he came to Kevin's diamond necklace around her neck and held it up. "I may not be your man, but seeing you with that dude pisses me off. If you and I are going to do this, what is Middleton to you?"

Maddy's chest quivered, eyes pressed tight as she touched the pendant again. What did she say? Was she ready to leave behind a world-class, potentially lucrative life? And settle for regular hobnobbing on a lower level?

Jerrell pulled from her. "What do you need to think about?"

"Where this is going. What we are doing. If we can work," she said, grabbing at him, but not before he jerked his arm away from her.

"You're lying. You need to weigh the money and power that dude could bring you. It won't come to you riding around in one of my cake vans."

"That's not fair. I've known him my entire life."

"What's unfair is you shopping your pussy to me, while keeping your options open with him. Don't game me, baby, I'm a master. What was in *your* head when you came to see me, Maddy? That you would screw the boy from Louisiana while the one from New York buys you matching his and hers Porsches? And you could have the best of both worlds?" He shot up and the bed linens fell from around his toned nakedness.

She sat up. "No. I didn't expect this to happen."

"Then what were you expecting?"

"I'm not sure. We needed to talk. You wouldn't hear my side, and there was no point in me calling. You wouldn't have answered. I was feeling you. I am... *am* feeling you." She scoured her brain—no, her heart—for the words.

In the dark, the silhouette of his muscles flexed as his arms aimed at her. "You enjoy torturing dudes! You get off on that shit. Makes you feel powerful, like some kind of slick Cleopatra."

"Don't insult me."

"Then don't lie to me." Anger whipped out of him. "Give me a straight answer. Maddy, be a damn woman and decide what you want."

"And you expect me to toss out the emotions I've had my entire life, all of a sudden? For a guy I met a week ago?"

"No. But I do expect you not to piss on *my* emotions." Jerrell's eyes flickered in the rising sun.

She breathed, her thoughts flailing everywhere. "I wore this necklace all day yesterday. It wasn't a secret. And now you're complaining?"

His eyes flared. "I was hoping you would take it off. But I was the damn fool."

"Give me some time, Jerrell. Please."

At that, he flinched. "I wish you had taken your time before you dragged me into your mess. But now, I'll grant you plenty. Let me make it simple for you. This goes nowhere. I'm sorry I brought you into my home, into my bed," he said, turning his back on her and heading toward the shower. "You can see yourself out." With that, he slammed his bathroom door so loud she jumped.

Watching him walk away stung, and to her surprise, it hit her as hard as Kevin's grade school pranks. But more this time.

Maddy started to go to Jerrell and express how much she wanted him. But she needed to be sure.

The relentless cold bit into her after she threw off the covers and got dressed. On the drive back across Long Island in her rental car, she cursed herself. Last night had been one of the best of her life. A connection like that was tough to find. And for the first time, she hadn't needed to work for it or overthink it. Her making love to Jerrell was as natural and random and unforced as an unpredicted rain shower in the middle of the day.

What was she so scared of?

She stopped by the dressmaker's boutique and picked up a gorgeous dress with a $4,200.00 price tag. She could wear it tonight and recycle twice before putting it away for a few years.

"And will you be needing anything for Mrs. Emma's memorial tomorrow?" the dressmaker asked.

The news was a brick busting up Maddy's sulking. *"Memorial?"*

"Oh, yes, dear. On Christmas Eve, her hip went out. She fell and suffered a stroke, went into a coma. Died on Christmas Day. Her children want to have a service while many of her friends are in town, so people don't have to come back."

Mrs. Emma and Maddy's grandmother had been thick as thieves, cornerstones in the Sag Harbor community, protecting its integrity and legacy. Mrs. Emma's ancestors had also been among the first to settle Sag Harbor. They'd swapped recipes, helped each other with cooking, watching each other's children and grandchildren, started professional women's societies, investment and travel clubs.

Maddy suspected it was Emma who'd guided her and Jerrell together, with her low-key scheming. She never got to thank the woman. And in one of their last conversations, she'd asked Maddy to take over some of her grandmother's former community responsibilities.

Now what would happen to Sag Harbor, with the old guard passing away? What would become of Emma's house?

Long gone were the days when Blacks had few vacation options and stuck together in Southampton. A generation was dying out, and Sag Harbor had just gotten a little dimmer.

When she returned home, her family was in shock, chatting with neighbors and discussing the same questions on Maddy's mind.

"People have started saying Black Hamptons is dead," her mother worried aloud. "And it's all about Houston, Atlanta, and Miami now."

"That's not true. We are very much still here," Maddy insisted.

Her mother tossed back a scotch. "We can't allow Miss Emma's property to go to outsiders, I'm sorry."

"But you don't come here that often anymore. We're not even sure how long we'll keep this house," Dr. Page replied. "We've been paying taxes on land we haven't used in years. Time to let it go."

"Oh, God, it's too much to think about right now. Let's just get through tomorrow, and then talk to the other neighbors," Mrs. Page said.

On her bed, a large box awaited Maddy. She read the note tucked inside, from Kevin:

Would love to see your gorgeous body in this. Pick you up at 5:45?

He didn't bother explaining himself, after all Lana had said on Christmas Eve. Out of curiosity, she opened the present, pulling out an incredible, strapless Jason Wu in deep green velvet.

Reet waited in the doorway, whistling. "So?" One look at Maddy's heavy shoulders, and Reet sucked her teeth. "That's not good."

They headed to get their nails done, to prepare for the ball that evening.

"What will you do?" Reet asked, sipping non-alcoholic cider.

Maddy drank champagne. "He's amazing, Reet. I was not expecting Jerrell, not at all. My partners have always been meh," she lowered her head. "Average. I had no idea that kind of feel-good was possible." Jerrell's strokes and positions had arrested her thoughts, making her twitch even where she sat. He'd flipped her expertly. No fumbling or uncertainty. Lifting her legs, twisting her, hoisting her up for hours, he had pulled reactions out of Maddy she didn't realize she possessed.

But the real drug was the way he'd looked at her, like she was already his.

Reet smiled, giggling. "Oh, girl, when they're throwing you in the air and tossing you and putting it in spots you didn't know you had... then it hurts real good... ooweee!"

They both laughed while Maddy closed her eyes and sucked her bottom lip. "Yeah, so much that."

Reet's head cocked as she got serious again. "But Kevin is the dream. That man is trying to become the Black Bill Gates. If he never does to you what Jerrell does, you can go cry about it at your house in Switzerland. And even if Kevin gives it to you like that..."

"... He'll probably give it to other women too," Maddy finished.

"You heard that Kevin asked someone else to marry him, so he gets the second phase of his grandfather's inheritance?" She took another sip of cider.

Maddy sat stricken in her chair. "What?"

"You heard me. Inheritance. The requirement in Kevin's

trust fund that says he doesn't receive the next ten million, plus the mansion in Malibu, until he has a family."

So that was why Kevin had popped up at her door, out of nowhere. "He proposed to someone else?"

"Mmhm, almost three months ago. And she said yes, until Kevin's mama started laying down the law. She would always have a key to their house, her own quarters, and would watch his accounts like a hawk. Tehe," Reet chuckled.

"And you weren't planning to tell me?"

"Would it have mattered?" Reet replied. "Your nose has been wide open for Kevin since we were little. That man could murder somebody, and you'd still marry him."

A HOPEFUL MADDY entered the *Oasis Cove Hotel* lobby with her parents. On her figure, she donned the dress she'd bought herself earlier that day.

Their fellow Black families cloaked in furs and diamonds greeted them, but Maddy's eyes darted around the room with expectation.

A debonair Jerrell made the most delicious dish as he oversaw tables of his starter pastries. His gaze met hers, and he cut his eyes away. She'd expected that, but Maddy continued scanning, stretching her neck even, for a group of people in particular. It had been some years since she'd seen them, but they had not appeared. Her hope sank a bit as she trudged behind her parents to mingle.

Alongside Jerrell was his grandmother, laughing and throwing her head back with her boisterous energy. Her laugh infectious, and bold as a shot of strong tequila, Maddy could see now why he left behind his career and staked it all on her. Of course, the older woman's greeting with Maddy was stiff, and she supposed she could understand why. She would also be hot if a woman was yanking her brother William's chain.

Not far, in the next social circle stood Kevin, his own laughter booming as he held court with debutantes' parents. They sought him out for his advice and insights on which companies and programs to send their children for the best opportunities in tech. And the debutantes' still-single older siblings took turns fawning over him, asking superficial questions to keep his attention. He reveled in it.

Maddy's parents exchanged greetings with Jerrell and his grandmother, before Jerrell gave Maddy a curt head nod and moved on to another group. The muscles across her chest tightened, as if to catch her falling feelings.

Her father noticed the cold shoulder. He kissed her forehead. "I swear, between the two of you, I can't tell if it's hot or cold. Whatever it is, give him time to blow off steam. Because it's pretty clear how he feels about you. I'll see you inside."

She had to go meet the other judges but waited a moment so Jerrell could wrap up his other conversation. While she waited, she kept perusing the lobby area as it grew thin with attendees filtering into the ballroom.

A distant Jerrell spun toward her. "What?"

She whispered, "If me seeing Kevin is so important to you, why did you...?"

The irises of his eyes danced around the room. "Because I wanted you."

"And I wanted you. Neither one of us was thinking. So how can you be angry when," she paused for someone to pass and say hello, "you didn't think about it either? I enjoy spending time with you. Don't treat me like a she-wolf who devours men at night, just because I don't have all the answers you want, off the jump."

He leaned closer, and she inhaled pastries, sugar and chocolate for which she resisted the urge to bite him.

"I don't look at you like an animal. I see you as way more." As he spoke, his eyes narrowed with his attraction to her. "Yesterday was… I haven't experienced anybody that way in… a long time. And all right, I felt it more than I thought I would. But I have a business to run. It takes up all my time. Any other point in my life, you dabbling between him and me… might not have been an issue. Maybe I wouldn't have cared. But not now. I can't have you messing with my head. No doubt, you can understand that."

His eyes dimmed as if a snake approached behind them.

"Hey, Maddy, uh, I don't mean to interrupt," Kevin said, walking up to them, "but it's about showtime, and I figured we should get in there." He turned to Jerrell. "Good evening, brother. You arrrrre… so sorry, I forgot."

"No worries. It's irrelevant to you, man. Besides," Jerrell said, glaring at Maddy, "it's showtime for you two. Knock 'em dead." He walked off.

Kevin held out his arm, and Maddy slid hers through, before they entered the ballroom where she and Jerrell had danced an electrifying waltz less than a week before.

Her entrance alongside Kevin now felt so much different, emotionless, as if she entered a refrigerator. In fact, staring around at the beautiful table linens, brass candelabras on the tables, expensive champagne bottles, and rose petals, the ambiance was all more of the same. Another dull and predictable party that she attended to uphold her family name.

When Kevin entered with Maddy on his arm, their longtime neighbors and friends who'd watched them grow up in Black Sag Harbor, began clapping and whistling. He escorted her to the judges' table and leaned over to kiss her lips. Their well-wishers went wild. At seeing his necklace on her neck, Kevin grinned, licking his lips.

"I knew you would love the diamonds. You always did like sparkle. And I promise, there'll be more sparkle coming. I'm going to cover you in diamonds, baby."

Just as he walked off, Maddy's eyes met Del's. She sat at the first table as her family was the highest-paying sponsor of the gala. Next to her stood Desmond, standing back on his heels and also clapping for Maddy.

Her childhood playmate raised her wine glass to Maddy, bowing her head, her steely eyes a prescient warning.

As the Master of Ceremonies for the show, Kevin proceeded to the stage, grabbed the microphone and began what Kevin did best—woo his admirers.

To Maddy's left, at another table, sat a preoccupied Chrissy trying to get her children to eat.

From the back of the room started the procession of beautiful debutantes who walked in on the arm of their fathers and curtsied with grace, as Maddy had taught them. Hair, necks and wrists bedecked in jewels, they beamed under the stunning chandeliers, candlelight from the tables bouncing off their skin. Out of respect for the occasion, no one whooped or hollered, but gave proud looks and smiles. Kevin read the biography of each, inserting the well-timed wisecrack to keep things interesting.

Maddy tried to focus on her scoring duties as a judge, observing their grace, poise, and depth of curtsy, remembering how special all this had been to her thirteen years earlier. Dreams of sororities, trips, job interviews, internships, and prestigious accolades had danced in their heads, and kept their desk lamps burning at night.

All so that, in a few years, would come the social clubs, parent circles, fundraisers, and meaningless titles.

And that was likely why she hadn't married. Why her two fiancés had bounced on her. Because after marriage, everything became predictable. The same people and circles. The same settings. And predictability often killed possibility.

A sinkhole opened up in Maddy's stomach, and she feared falling into it.

Maddy struggled to stay awake, let alone pay attention.

On the stage, Kevin's eyes moved to the back again, as he named another debutante, and again the room turned to see the young lady present herself.

Maddy's head turned with the others, but looking beyond the girl, her artery almost jumped from her throat.

Her invited guests had arrived!

They stood at the entrance. But they looked confused while searching for their table. She twisted more, toward her mother, and tried getting her attention. Del helped, flagging Maddy's mother. Maddy motioned toward the door, and Mrs. Page recognized them, rising to cross the dark room and greet them.

Jerrell's entire family had come to support him.

One of the other judges nudged her to pay attention, and she mouthed an apology. But swiveling in her seat, rare giddiness overtook her that made her heart skip again. She could no longer deny the reason. Her nerves rattled as she tried to keep her focus.

After the gala ended with a new debutante queen crowned and ecstatic, Maddy couldn't unchain herself from the table fast enough.

On the stage, adoring parents and friends swarmed Kevin, and some of them called Maddy over. Kevin waved for her to join them.

Maddy glanced at her parents' table where they visited with the Rouse family, and once again, she had to decide.

Terrified it might be the wrong decision, she moved toward Kevin.

WHO ELSE COULD HAVE

JERRELL

*J*errell's day couldn't get any worse.

Another gala attendee, one of Jerrell's top customers, strutted into the *Oasis Cove Hotel* lobby. And walked right by his pastry table.

He turned to his grandmother. "Gram, I'm so sorry."

"Boy, don't you dare apologize to me. You gave this your best. Hold your head up high. God will make a way," she said, giving him a firm squeeze with her sturdy arms.

He stopped himself from punching the long display table, still full of treats. Instead, he grabbed his phone again and searched for Poppin' Pauletta's in the search engines. He wouldn't sleep tonight while figuring out how to fix this.

First review: *I don't know what happened, but the Poppin' Apple Pie took a real dive from the last time I ate them. They taste okay but missing something now. Plus, the delivery's been late twice. It may be the holidays, but get it together. Three stars out of five.*

Second review: *Not impressed. I tried these after my family talked them up and they're pretty good. But not the best on Earth, like everyone says. I don't understand the hype.*

Rather than holing up with Maddy for two days this week, he should have been addressing this brown sugar situation. His priority was to ask her about the tariff wars in Brazil holding up his product. But no, stupid had found him and tied him up.

With the use of white cane sugar over the last couple of days, his grandmother's pastries were now so-so. He'd already sent emails to sugar distributors and sweetener companies to send samples so they could experiment with alternatives.

Hope shot through his veins each time someone approached his table, and picked up a pastry. Jerrell moved to a corner of the room, watched for a while as they bit into it. Gone was their wide-eyed delirium. Now present was the satisfied face, followed by them carrying it from conversation to conversation, and then tossing about half in the trash. By the end of the night, the wall had to prop him up. His pastries may as well have been smelly fish.

Then he had to watch the beautiful woman he didn't want to adore, prancing around with some jerk. Heavenly in her floor-length, off-shoulder, body hugging gown, Maddy's breasts had poured over the top bodice and waved for Jerrell's attention. She'd swept her vanilla-scented ass around him, making him want to take her to the nearest available, semi-private enclave and bang out his irritation at her, until her hot walls creamed all over his wood again. He longed to break into those gorgeous, steely eyes, and watch them roll into her head a few more times. And then hold her in his arms and stroke her velvet skin while she slept.

But his business…

Should he swallow his pride and go to Maddy? He needn't date her, to still ask for her help with the brown sugar delivery. Back and forth he questioned himself in his head. As he cursed under his breath, he missed the footsteps that approached behind him.

"Glad to see you don't just do it with me." That deep, authoritative voice froze him in his tracks, as it had his entire life.

A brief flash of fear raced through Jerrell's nerves before he whipped around. He could have cried a river through the hotel.

Dressed to the nines in a tuxedo, his father stood before him.

"Dad?" Half-chuckling, half-panicked, he asked. "Do what with you?"

"Curse and mumble under your breath."

But why was the man standing here? Something had to be wrong for Charles Rouse to have used his Saturday night after Christmas for "some girlie affair." Jerrell's heart tanked.

"E-everything okay with Mom?"

Not seeing her, he gripped the table. They had not spent time together since Thanksgiving and now, what had happened? No, that made no sense. He had dressed for the occasion.

"Your mother's fine, roaming around here somewhere, while Mrs. Page introduces her to folks. She'll be back in a minute." His father's eyes inspected the three tables of delicacies. "So, this is what you've been up to these last few weeks?"

Jerrell longed to spread everything out, all over again, so his dad would get the full, elaborate layout, complete with layers, silver and crystal, all arranged like floral displays. "It looked better than this before. I was about to—"

"I know. Saw it when I came in and you were in the bathroom," his father said, picking up Pauletta's Pecan Fire, a bourbon-filled cream treat with a pecan crust. He took a big bite and closed his eyes. "Hmph, I remember Mama making these for cards night when I was a boy. Her friends would come over for dominoes, or spades, or gin rummy, but they were especially coming to eat these here." Mouth moving around, crumbs collecting under his mustache, the reminiscent smile was worth a thousand of Jerrell's late nights. "It's even better now than forty years ago."

"Yeah, people were going crazy over them for a minute," Jerrell replied, shoving his hands in his pockets, not bringing up the rest of the situation. He would not give the patriarch something to criticize.

"They were? Why aren't they still?"

Well, so much for keeping things light. "I ran into an issue with ingredients. I'm working it out."

"Hmph." Mr. Rouse smacked. "You don't say. An issue you might have avoided if you'd planned it better, huh?"

Damn.

So, this was why he'd driven across Long Island—to throw Jerrell's failure in his face. Jerrell had hoped at least the man would keep his venom in his own house and not trash Jerrell in public.

"Dad, why did you even bother to—"

"Hey, what's all this?" his brother Sheldon popped up, surprising Jerrell. "You don't have dancers out here or something, offering us samples? You're slipping."

Jerrell laughed, glad to see his second oldest sibling. "Man, stop with that. *You're* the dancing girl, homey. Get over here and put this plate on top of your head."

Then came the rest of Jerrell's siblings. In disbelief, he embraced each one like he hadn't seen them in years. He turned to Kami when she appeared.

"Thanks, sis, for bringing everybody out. You don't realize

what this means," he said, his heart full enough to burst after all the headaches that day.

Kami snapped her neck back. "I didn't."

Puzzled now, Jerrell thought he misunderstood. "What do you mean, not you? Who else could have--"

Kami motioned behind him, and Jerrell pivoted.

Maddy approached, wearing that hideous necklace. She stretched out her hands toward his dad. Wasn't she the smooth operator?

"Madison! Smart girl who thinks she can crush me in political debates. It's been a while," Mr. Rouse crowed, throwing open his arms. Jerrell's mouth almost fell to watch Maddy go into them with ease.

"Correction. I *can* crush you in debates. And I hope the years we haven't seen each other gave you enough time to practice," Maddy replied.

They laughed as if they'd talked many times.

"So, let me get this straight," Jerrell asked. "You guys met down in Virginia Beach?"

"Yes, we did. You kids had left home, so your mama and I could finally start traveling. We met the Pages on a cruise, and when they'd host us down there, we'd run into Maddy. From what I hear, you ran into her too. Literally," Jerrell's dad retorted.

Maddy's eyes dropped as she stifled her laughter.

Jerrell sucked his teeth.

Great.

So, they were double-teaming him.

"You mean… you two have been talking?" Jerrell asked.

His father nodded. "Oh, yes. And Madison here tells me the people of Sag Harbor have fallen in love with my mama's cooking." He stroked his chin, continuing, "That you've been working day and night to get her exposure and a loyal customer base, and that it means more than anything to you."

A warm rush flooded Jerrell's insides. He wondered how to feel about his father listening to someone else over his own son. "I could've told you that, Dad," Jerrell muttered.

"Yeah, but it's hard to know if you're serious or only blowing off steam. How many times have you hauled off over the years and either quit, or almost did?"

"Dad, drop it. You came to support him, so do that," Sheldon replied, intervening and giving Jerrell's shoulder a squeeze.

"I should go," Maddy said. She exchanged a weird eye contact with Mr. Rouse in which Maddy seemed to give the old man a playful warning. "It was nice seeing you again, Mr. Rouse."

"You're right. My bad." His father stepped forward, closing the distance with Jerrell. "I was proud of the things Maddy, Kami, and Sheldon have told me. That you are indeed putting your back into this—walking people's dogs, delivering to their homes, and they are seeing you as one of them. If this is what you want, I hope you stick with it and prove me wrong."

Jerrell couldn't resist attacking this point. "So, you don't believe I'm capable?"

"Damn. Come on, J. The man came. Why do you have to throw gasoline?" Kami pleaded.

"Of course, I think you can. I'm just not sure you're committed. There's a difference," his father replied. "You can prove I'm wrong."

"For my entire life, my commitment has been to pleasing you. Sorry if it's taking me a minute to figure out committing to myself." Jerrell's hushed tone was still forceful.

"Well, you're grown. You've talked your shit. Now back it

up," the senior Rouse challenged. "So far, seems it's going well. Congratulations. And I mean that."

Both father and his youngest son stood at the same height of six foot two, studying each other. Jerrell supposed this was the best he would get from the old man for now. Until he had something to show for his efforts, his father would withhold respect.

In the meantime, Jerrell would at least appreciate this moment. "I'm glad you came, Dad. It means a lot." His father's presence had lit up his night, even with their differences.

"Are you gentlemen playing nice? Why can't I leave for just five minutes?" his mother asked, appearing in a beautiful gold gown, and her white hair swept up. "The Pages invited us here. Let's not embarrass them with our two resident juveniles. Where's that gorgeous Maddy? I want to see this dress everybody's talking about." Jerrell felt his mother squeeze his waist while scanning the lobby.

"You just missed her," Mr. Rouse said. "Over there. Seems we're not the only juveniles here after all."

Across the room, Maddy mediated yet another conflict between her friend Chrissy and the estranged husband.

"Mrs. Mason," Sheldon noted, his eyes shimmering like stars in the night. He nudged Jerrell. "You know her?"

"Who?"

"Mrs. Mason. That woman over there with the kids," Sheldon responded with a lusty smile, and licked his lips. "I want to talk to her. Can you have Maddy arrange it?"

Across the room, in a tight-fitting dress, displaying thick curves, stomping when she walked, was a very determined Chrissy Mason.

Jerrell's face scrunched. "Man, yeah, she and Maddy are friends, but she's got kids. And a husband."

"Looks to me like she has a headache. And needs a real man who can help her get rid of it," Sheldon replied, his eyes dropping to Chrissy's tightly wrapped rear end, and rising again to the fullness of her breasts.

Jerrell rolled his eyes, which then fell on Maddy, who had returned to networking on the other side of the room. She looked like a character out of a fairytale, as always—elegant, polished, cool and in control as she nodded, smiled and laughed on cue. But in his memory banks, less than twenty-four hours before, he'd opened up a different Maddy. Wild, hungry, rough and ready, taking all his strokes while her thick poof of kinky hair bounced on her head. That hair had brushed his neck and face for a few precious hours as they slept together through the night.

"Man," Sheldon said, observing Jerrell, "take your ass over there and say something to her."

Jerrell's heart was performing a feat it hadn't in a long while—it was feeling again. This terrified him. Especially since Maddy was feeling someone else. He had successfully avoided being stupid over any woman since Raychelle. There was no way he would start now.

But still, Jerrell was seeing his family for the first time in weeks. It stunned him that Maddy was the one who'd made it happen.

Despite the large weight dragging his chest inward, he moved toward her. He would at least thank her for being so thoughtful when she didn't have to.

He started walking toward her, admiring how her ass filled in that dress, how firm it was. Even though she'd worked his nerves, he wondered if he could discreetly grab it.

But before he reached her, Kevin appeared at her side.

He touched her collarbone, where the necklace lay, sparkling under the light.

Jerrell's chest caved, swirling around and around in the Bermuda Triangle until it disappeared in an ocean of upset. He pivoted toward the exit.

That was a wrap.

JAIL

MADDY

A hand slid around Maddy's waist, and its touch shot her heart out of her ribs.

A holiday smile already spreading across her face, she turned expecting to see Jerrell. He had changed his mind after learning how she'd gotten his family here, and come to speak to her.

But her gaze ran into Kevin's. She met the same arrogant smirk on his lips, his same audacious invasion of her space, the thoughtless way he expected her to melt at his looks and bling. No tenderness or consideration stared back at her. And she'd literally spent a lifetime waiting for it.

Maddy's eagerness plummeted. That was her answer.

She could no longer cling to a fantasy.

Kevin's eyes crinkled. "I've been searching for you. Some of us are headed for drinks after this." He walked her out, grabbing her coat from the coat check and helping her into it.

"Actually, some of us are concerned about this situation of Mrs. Emma's home. It's up for sale, and we don't know what will happen to it. Chrissy, Del, Mama and I were plan-

242

ning on having a call with Emma's children and husband after this."

Kevin scoffed. "Girl, who cares about that old house? Someone else should come in and give this place a facelift. It needs new people with fresh energy."

Maddy chafed. "Any newcomers must appreciate the history of those who came before us. Our traditions and values are worth preserving."

He shrugged. "I suppose. So why can't you have somebody bring you up to speed on the call tomorrow? You and I haven't been on a proper date yet." His fingers stroked her hand. "And I'm eager to get things rolling between you and me."

Again, the words may as well have been bulldozers driving a gulf through them. Maddy opened her mouth to question if his real intention was to roll onto the next phase of his inheritance, but she held her tongue. She didn't care. And maybe down the road, if she maintained positive relations with him, she could use Kevin as an ally.

At the thought, she smiled. She supposed Jerrell was right. Maddy was always strategizing her future moves before she spoke.

"I see that smile on you," Kevin noted. "You're as curious as I am. I'm glad."

"Kevin, I'm happy you've changed. And that you're a better man today. Wiser and kinder than you once were. I hope you stay that way."

She reached behind her neck, and unclasped the necklace, as his eyes shuttered with bewilderment.

In doing so, Maddy seemed to unchain herself from a bigger burden. One that had hung over her a very long time.

She placed it in his hand. "I hope the next person you give

this to, is someone you will value and cherish, just as much as I know you cherish me."

Moving away from Kevin, she went to search for Jerrell.

Outside, Jerrell's family helped him load his van, and he continued to avoid eye contact with her.

But his brother broke away to run toward her. Surprised, she anticipated some encouragement about Jerrell. What else did she and his brother have in common? They'd never spoken.

"Hey, Maddy, I'm Sheldon, J's brother. Um, your friend, Mrs. Mason, I think her name is Chriselle?"

Confused, Maddy looked around them, at Chrissy coolly engaging with other event sponsors and organizers, shaking the hands of guests, running her hand over her hair (and Maddy was certain she was doing it to avoid knocking the hell out of Blake's girlfriend who'd come inside for the kids). "Yes? What about her?"

"Do you think you might, uh," Sheldon gulped, his gaze traveling up and down Chrissy's fishtail dress, "introduce us?"

Wow. "Um, as her friend, I must say, now may not be the time. And I don't want to get my friend card pulled. Lord knows I've already got enough people ready to stone me in the street." She rolled her eyes at Jerrell and started to rejoin her parents.

"I'll tell you what then. If you put in a word with Chrissy, I'll do the same for you with Jerrell. All you gotta do is set me up, and I can do the rest." This older man, sporting a swath of gray hair in his beard, flashed a tantalizing grin. Sheldon's charm game was far tougher than his younger brother's.

"All right," Maddy laughed. "But if Chrissy throws me in friend jail, I'm taking you with me."

EMPTINESS CREPT into Maddy while walking away from Mrs. Emma's memorial service. The old guard was leaving, one by one. And who would be left to protect Black Sag Harbor's future? As well as its distinctive past.

During the call the night before, Emma's adult children had complained of nobody they knew wanting to buy the property. "Everybody's in Atlanta now. Houston. The Carolinas. We don't want to change the character of the community, but we're getting some fantastic offers from outsiders and would be fools to turn them down," Mrs. Emma's daughter had said.

That left Mrs. Page with the issue of what they would do with GeeGee's home.

Also, it was finally time to clear out GeeGee's things. Maddy had a breakdown while going through her grandmother's church dresses, and she wasn't able to finish. Maddy, her mother, and sister all agreed they'd return in a few weeks. Maybe cleaning house on the very first trip back was doing too much.

"So, did Jerrell get around to talking with you about his sugar issue?" her father asked as she packed.

"No," she answered, not wanting to hear his name.

It was bad enough she couldn't stop thinking of his long, thick manhood stirring up a storm in every nook and cranny of her, how he'd taken his time rocking her body, and battering her like she was his dessert.

But at the gala, and at the memorial, Jerrell had treated her as a stranger who'd robbed him. She tried to make sense of his attitude.

I don't look at you like some animal. In fact, I see you as way more. Last night was good, and all right, I felt it more than I thought I would. But I have a business to run.

Jerrell's company was everything to him—life or death—and it would literally build him up in the eyes of his father, or destroy him. And despite his fierce devotion to his dream, he *still* hadn't asked Maddy for what he'd wanted all along.

Her siblings shared sympathetic looks with her. Even Marguerite.

"It's okay. I'm a big girl. I'll be fine," she mumbled at her family crowding inside her room.

But through tearful eyes, her laptop bag also caught her attention.

The memo!

She had recommended to the senator that he hold a hearing on South American trade. That decision could be favorable for Jerrell—a man she was sleeping with.

Realization was a nuclear warhead hitting Maddy and sinking her.

With her father's investment in Jerrell's company, Maddy's family stood to benefit financially from brown sugar coming out of South America. If Maddy tried to influence the outcome of an international dispute, it would look like she was using her Senate position for personal gain.

She had a conflict of interest. Almost certainly, she could have sworn she heard a splatter against the wood floor—the sound of her career crashing.

She would have to email the legislative director and chief of staff right away and declare the conflict. The Legislative Director would take her off the South America proceedings after New Year's. She'd miss her opportunity to showcase her talent and be front and center to audition for White House Domestic Policy Council.

At her father, she hissed, "Daddy, if you were buying into something that might involve my work in the Senate, you should have told me. Since the deal involves my family, this means I can't touch the South America trade issue now."

Dr. Page fell stricken. "How was I supposed to know the ethics rules of the Senate?"

"Which is why you should've talked to me," she replied, nursing her disappointment.

She closed her suitcase, and kissed him on his cheek, reassuring him it would be okay. Other opportunities sat on the burner, and Maddy knew she was talented and determined enough that she wouldn't have to wait long for her next shot.

As soon as she got in the car for William to drive her to Grand Central Station, she flipped open her laptop and constructed the email to her bosses. Fingers shaking, she hit "Send."

Not one word her brother uttered on the way to the train station entered her ears. Her thoughts all over the place, they vacillated between Jerrell's legs entangled inside his Egyptian cotton sheets and him giving her his whole behind to kiss her earlier that day at Emma's memorial service.

Whatever Jerrell's brother, Sheldon, mentioned to him, it hadn't worked. She peeked at her phone every few minutes to check for a text, or outside her window for a van. Her eyes had even roamed down the street a few times to see if he was making deliveries in the area today. At Grand Central Station that evening, Maddy's heart could have dragged the railway platform.

While waiting for her train, she still swung her head around, peeking for anyone she noticed that might have been searching for her. After several scans of the platform, she realized no one was coming. *He* wasn't coming. Not that she should care. Maddy was leaving Sag Harbor just as she'd arrived—single, with no attachments.

It's what she'd wanted.

Right?

All the way back to Washington, she checked her emails repeatedly. The Foreign Relations Committee staff always worked weekends, rarely ever letting a day go by without checking their inbox. But she received no reply about her declaring a conflict.

Back in D.C., she entered her Georgetown brownstone, dropping her things and tipping the driver who'd helped with luggage. Her shoes tumbled across her wooden floor after she kicked them off and fell against the vestibule.

How many times had she walked into this house after arriving from out of town, thrilled to be back every time? She could always count on her honey-scented candles, plush throw rugs, and smooth leather to cushion her from life's ups and downs. She'd decorated her home so that, at the end of the day, it was always her slice of heaven.

Now all that stared back at her was a well-furnished empty space.

JERRELL

"Gram, it's eleven o'clock! Pills!" Jerrell called when he received a vibration from his new digital watch he'd purchased just to keep up with his grandma's medical schedule. "You're wearing the same watch as me. I know you got the notification too."

The kitchen moved at full steam that morning. All hands were on deck, and Jerrell was in the back, baking right along-side his grandmother and great aunt.

Two weeks after the bad write-ups online, one of Jerrell's bank buddies had put in a big order. Plus a few frat brothers scattered around the city had placed orders that helped him out. Jerrell needed to rebuild his word of mouth and pump up the momentum again.

And miraculously, Brazilian brown sugar had shown up at his door that morning. He had been at the office, calculating losses and how much longer he could stay in the shop before his condo became his new store. All the back-ordered supplies from phone calls and emails he'd sent came rolling into the store at six a.m.

He'd gotten so damn happy he accidentally spilled a bag of it all over the counter. At some point, he planned to call Dr. Page and thank him. And Maddy.

She hadn't needed to do this, especially after the way he'd treated her.

Perhaps he was a little harsh. And Jerrell had expected her to write him off and move on, off to Paris or the Swiss Alps with whatshisface. Whatever moves she'd pulled on her Senate committee to do this, Jerrell would thank her for it.

But he had not changed his mind. That amazing day with her—in his bed, on his kitchen counter, on the couch, kissing and sucking and feeding each other—was seared into his brain. He hadn't known her long, but he may as well admit to himself that her pricey boots had marched straight into his head. And maybe even his heart. Now Jerrell's feelings about Maddy were at least deep enough that he could not stomach sharing her with somebody else. Especially not a guy that she'd clearly been jonesing for since she was a teenager. Hell, no.

That scenario had a big "L" all over it.

He shook the thoughts from his head and moved to find his grandmother. For now, they had to deliver. They needed to recover the ground they'd lost. His new store manager's only assigned task for that day was finding pop-ups and events for them to hit. Carnivals, festivals, book fairs, folk dancing, it didn't matter.

"Gram!"

"I heard you the first time. Good Lord, don't make me drop these biscuits on the floor. It only took us an hour to get the filling in," she crowed.

"Fine then, I'll bring the pills to you. Where are they?"

"Under the counter in the front," she replied, sliding the biscuits in the oven and almost tipping over while doing so.

He rushed to help her. "We ought to have somebody else do the heavy lifting. And you just oversee things."

"And I ought to oversee my foot into your you-know-what. Boy, if you don't go on," she snapped back, paying him no mind and moving on to the next set.

Chuckling, he burst through the double doors to search for her pills, when he stopped at the sight of a tall, sweeping figure in the line of patrons.

The dapper gentleman looked uncomfortably familiar, standing above most of the other customers. Heat traveled up Jerrell's flesh.

"Mr. Rouse, how are you today?" the man asked in an almost taunting tone.

Jerrell's eyes narrowed, grateful the high display case separated the two of them. "Oh, wow, you remember my name now? Funny, I don't recall yours."

"It's all good, man. Kevin. We met in Sag Harbor. I'm, uh, Maddy's longtime friend."

Jerrell seethed underneath his casual Hemsley shirt. He slid off his apron and gloves, briefly wishing for the days when he wore a suit also, just so this dude wouldn't underestimate his value.

"Ah, yeah, that's right. Maddy. How is she, by the way? Last time I saw you two, you were taking Black Sag Harbor by storm. The little debutantes were falling all over themselves." He inserted the obligatory fake laugh. "Y'all made quite the pair that night. Gorgeous necklace she was wearing."

In through the nose, out through the mouth.

But Jerrell's fists curled behind the counter.

Kevin walked up to the register now that it was his turn to

order. "Hmph, thanks." Pretty Boy thumbed his chin, scanning the dessert display. "I've heard a lot about these desserts you have. Wanted to come through and check it out. I was in the neighborhood, thought I'd pick up some goods and impress the lady friend."

"Oh, I think I know what Maddy likes." Especially since Jerrell had spent an entire afternoon smearing her naked body with jellied crescents and creams of every consistency and flavor. Licking filling from between her legs. Blindfolding her while she sat on his kitchen counter, feeding her different desserts while she decided which was her favorite.

Fuming, remembering, Jerrell shook the curves of her naked breasts from his head. He examined the counter at the man whose necklace she had worn. Which Jerrell had hoped she would remove.

"Maddy enjoys the pecan cream delights, so let me grab you a box and I'll just get—"

"It's not for Maddy, man," Kevin said, peering through the glass case for what he wanted.

Jerrell might have had steam shooting from his ears. This dude was playing her? "Oh, my bad."

"No problem. I'll take some of these. And those. They look pretty good. While I'm here, I might also get some for my moms. The queen, you know?" Kevin smiled.

"Yes, with my two sisters, I definitely know about queens." Jerrell brushed aside the store clerk so he could stare Kevin directly in the eye, man to man. When he finished ringing up the sale, he handed the two boxes across the counter in a bag.

Kevin reached to grab it, but Jerrell's fingers clenched tighter, not letting go. The exchange—or *lack* of one—forced the tech mogul to look up at Jerrell.

"I hope you treat Maddy like the *queen* she is. Give her my regards, will you?"

Kevin applied a little more force and snatched the bag from Jerrell.

"Give them to her yourself. Maddy would be a queen, if she was with me. But she's not, so she isn't. She gave my necklace back that night."

At hearing this news, Jerrell's insides sputtered. Maddy returned it the night of the debutante ball? But Jerrell had seen her wearing it. Why didn't she tell him?

Kevin continued, "Pro tip, man: If you're going to do business in Sag Harbor, get you an insider who'll keep you in the loop, and instruct you on which motherfuckers you should not piss on." Kevin looked around the store before sliding on his Ray Ban's. "Poppin' Pauletta's sure would look good on my ownership portfolio. And then Miss Pauletta can stand on the street and perform for *me*."

Jerrell's basketball legs jumped through the opening between glass cases, over the counter, easily clearing the cash register.

Kevin held his ground, daring him.

Fists balled, nails cutting into his skin, alarms went off in Jerrell's head. In a different time of his life—high school, fresh out of The Boot, with a chip on his shoulder—he would have pulverized that man's face.

In a different time.

He had one hit on his juvenile criminal record, which was now sealed. It was the reason his father had to press harder for Jerrell than all his other siblings to admit him into Brown —not because of his intellect, but his temper. He was not a juvenile anymore. Now a grown man, Jerrell had too much to lose.

"Get out," Jerrell muttered.

Once Kevin had gone, Jerrell gripped the counter to keep himself from changing his mind and following the guy to the sidewalk. He waited for his heart rate to stop busting holes in his ribs.

A hand slid around his shoulders. "Proud of you, little brother." He had been so irate he hadn't seen Kami walk in. "So, are you going to get her or what?"

"No. I can see why no woman would want to spend a lifetime dealing with that. Maddy probably dropped him because of him, not because of me. Still, he was her first choice. I'm not moving in for sloppy seconds."

"That's unfair, J. You and her kicked it for just one week. She asked you for time to deal with her past, and you weren't having it. Maybe since the two of them have history, she needed to clear the air with him and make sure they were good before she moved on. That's not the same as putting you second." His sister threw him a chastising side-eye. "You know how you can be with your cowboy attitude—Mr. 'Shoot First and Ask Questions Later.' You didn't give her space to choose you."

Kami pulled her phone from her purse, scrolled through it, and pushed it into his hand.

Jerrell stared at a photo on her screen, of Maddy and Kevin making their grand entrance at the debutante ball.

"I don't want to see this shit." He pushed her phone at her.

His older sister shoved it back. "But you need to. Check her face. No smile at all. She looks like she's headed to prison." Kami's fingers then scrolled to the photo of Maddy with Jerrell.

As they low-key argued each other down that morning, Maddy's eyes came to life, effervescent and amused while she gave him hell. Her pompous, oversized head drew Jerrell's heartstrings into a smile even now.

But on the outside, he tried to brush it off. "So, it's like I said. She enjoys torturing men."

Kami finished. "Looks to me like she enjoys torturing *you*."

That night, before he headed back to Sag Harbor in the morning, he was doing some clean-up at his condo in the city. He'd let go of the house cleaner that was coming every two weeks, since he was rarely ever home now. And when he was home, he brought take-out or survived with the food essentials requiring little to no time—cereal, PB&J, bologna—so he didn't have much to clean.

As he emptied out his trash can, one of the used condoms from his and Maddy's day together fell to the floor.

As he picked it up to transfer it to the main trash, his jaw fell.

Shit.

EVERY OTHER FOOL

MADDY

Maddy rolled her travel bags to the door of her D.C. brownstone.

Once again, she would hit the road to Sag Harbor. No boozy train ride this time, but a fast plane straight to JFK. Chrissy was flying in from L.A., and with the kids, they would all ride together across Long Island.

This weekend would be no vacation.

Several weeks before, within hours of Maddy leaving, chaos had erupted in the Hamptons. She'd gotten panicked phone calls from Chrissy that their old stomping ground was under siege.

The Turner family was putting up the historic *Ivory* for sale. And a bidding war had broken out for who would purchase it. Offers and prospective business-owners were rolling in from all over the country, bringing chaos to the Black establishment.

But of all Chrissy had informed her, what surprised Maddy most was hearing the name Lana Gilley.

Lana had enjoyed Sag Harbor so much she now refused to

leave, and along with her mother, had submitted a proposal to purchase the *Ivory*. Maddy was still figuring out how Lana possessed eleven million dollars to buy the *Ivory* in the first place.

Then Maddy's mother wanted to clean out GeeGee's house, and their family's most precious memories.

But before all that, Maddy's first order of business was taking a pregnancy test.

Her period was several days late. Fatigue had her dragging, putting her to sleep early all week.

She hoped the symptoms were no more than stress. Her reassignment from the South America hearing might have upset her more than she expected. Her co-worker Collin had received it and had spent the week of the hearing prancing around the Senate Committee office, acting as if they had promoted him. She was sick of the number of trips he made to the Legislative Director's office, asking their colleagues what they'd thought about him on C-SPAN. Maddy told herself the next opportunity was not far, but she hated losing.

And now she was possibly pregnant. A baby.

No. Jerrell had worn a condom. She'd watched him strap one on each time.

This weekend, she would likely see him. No matter how she tried, thoughts of him refused to leave her mind. His thighs, his arms, his back, his intensity, his tongue...

What would he say if she carried his child? He believed she was in love with Kevin. And he would certainly question paternity. Humiliation she neither wanted nor deserved.

The test shook so much in her hands she feared she would drop it. As she set it on the bathroom counter, she recalled every unfulfilled dream that still lay ahead for her. How would she achieve them all now, if she had a burden that weakened her? The women's movement in America was going hard, but the truth was that pregnancy was *still* low-key viewed in the workplace as weakness.

The doorbell rang, and she greeted her normal driver.

"Hey, Stanley, I missed you at Christmas. I hope you had a good one," she said, padding through the house in stockinged feet.

"Miss Maddy! I went back home to my family in Alabama. Didn't know you were going anywhere for Christmas, or I would have stayed here just to drive you. Haha!" he laughed, grabbing the bag and rolling it out. "You know I'm lying. Where are we off to today?" he asked, taking care with her things as she preferred.

"Back to Sag Harbor," she said.

"Oh, wow, I haven't heard you say that in some years."

"Yes, but I can't put off family business forever. Just a couple minutes, if you don't mind, and I'll be right out."

"Take your time. I'm on your dime. Ha!" he chuckled, to which Maddy shook her head in amusement. She had missed his saucy humor on the rides to leave town.

But at this moment, she needed confirmation that she had no worries. That her life would remain her own, unentangled, and free for her political ascension. Heading back to the restroom, she peeked at the test.

THAT NIGHT, Maddy and Chrissy sat stoic in Chrissy's back yard, snuggled inside blankets in front of the fire pit.

Once Chrissy's children went to bed, Maddy broke her news.

Chrissy also broke hers. She'd begun a secret affair with Sheldon Rouse, Jerrell's older brother.

"You didn't tell Jerrell you're in town?" Chrissy asked.

"We're not speaking." Maddy stared into the flames.

"What do you think Jerrell will say? When do you plan to tell him?" Chrissy asked.

"Probably never. Jerrell thinks I'm in love with Kevin, and he wants nothing to do with me. He would likely demand a DNA test. Why would I put myself through somebody questioning me like that?" Maddy's eyes flickered, at the thought of a man besmirching her character.

"Damn Kevin Middleton," Chrissy murmured. "I wish there was a way we could get rid of him."

"Now why would you want to do that?" A third voice interrupted from the side of the house.

They both turned to see Kevin entering Chrissy's backyard.

"Sweetheart, did I hear you correctly that you are pregnant by a man you've only known a month? Little Miss Perfect Maddy?"

Maddy's fury burned so hot she couldn't recall what happened after she threw her cider across the fire, onto Kevin's expensive coat and shoes. She had grown sick of the fake civilities. In her livid state, a stream of words exploded from her mouth that might have awakened Chrissy's children. This was indeed the old Kevin. He hadn't changed.

"Chrissy?"

They all turned to see Jerrell's older brother Sheldon, who'd come to check on all the yelling.

At his side stood Lana.

"What is she doing here?" Maddy asked.

Lana grinned with glee as she entered Chrissy's yard. "I'm

meeting with my business partner to discuss my purchase of the *Ivory*." Lana's eyes danced over the flames. "And that partnership includes Jerrell."

Maddy reeled at that news.

If Jerrell was working with Lana to take over her neighborhood, the arrangement would make her baby's father only one thing to Maddy now—a rival.

A chess game was unfolding. There was only one way Maddy dealt with rivals.

"Yes, thank you, that's exactly what I need. I'll be waiting," Maddy said before hanging up the call with a private investigation agency she'd hired.

Maddy and Chrissy made phone calls, did research, and read through proposals and reports. That coming Tuesday, after Martin Luther King, Jr., Day, they faced the Sag Harbor Village Council to defend their bid proposals. The process would last for months, but Maddy had committed for the long haul. It would require numerous trips between D.C. and New York for a while.

"We need to know how Lana has money to participate in this deal. I don't see it. She's never mentioned wealth, but then again, we've never gotten super personal." Maddy scanned the information on Lana, Jerrell and others that she already acquired.

"Good question, and why does she want to come here to Sag Harbor when she's from Texas?" Chrissy searched also.

"Her mother has other children. We should also take a look at them, see how they earn their coins, what they have."

Maddy peered at Chrissy.

"What is that look?" her friend asked.

"Forgive me if this is too nosy, but how are you sleeping with Sheldon while he's trying to destroy our community?"

Chrissy smirked, lowering her voice and checking that her kids still slept. "Simple. We like each other. Business is separate. I intend to shut him down, and he knows it. The rivalry makes the sex more interesting." With that, she tucked away a satisfied smile.

As Maddy readied another question, she leaped from the floor and bolted to the bathroom. Nausea had hit. The biscuits, eggs and bacon Chrissy prepared all came up.

Damn.

When she looked up from the toilet, her friend stood holding crackers and Sprite, with a knowing smile. "You should tell him."

Maddy shook her head, remembering the disgust on Jerrell's face the last time she saw him. She pressed her eyes shut from more than the foul taste of vomit in her mouth.

"I haven't decided if I'm keeping it."

"You are. I see it all over you."

"What?"

Chrissy stared at her through the mirror. "You and Jerrell almost started a new Cold War at the debutante ball. The whole time, Kevin kept competing for your attention, but you and Jerrell were the electricity keeping all the lights on. And he wasn't even talking to you. When you two were Santa and Mrs. Claus, you almost melted the fake snow at Christmas Town. How many times did he touch you per minute?"

Maddy swallowed, now hugging the bathroom sink. "Not right now. Let's stay focused and get this Village Council meeting behind us first."

That night was a red-carpet Open House at the *Ivory*, a beginning of farewell events the Turners were hosting. Maddy guessed they were trying to draw more high-dollar bids and whip up more buzz. A Black-tie affair, the exclusive event was already filled to capacity, with celebrities and big names flying from up and down the Eastern seaboard. All set to pay their respects to the historic *Ivory* restaurant.

Maddy had turned down six invitations from potential buyers requesting for her to arrive in their car, and to make her entrance with them. They sought the validation of her grandmother's Ellis lineage, as a public stamp of approval on their pursuits. She'd declined and had called her extended relatives to caution them to do likewise.

Tonight would not be a social call for her; it was a work night. As a representative of the old Sag Harbor, she would stay cautious and cognizant of whom she acknowledged, and whom she did not. For her to fire on all cylinders that night, she needed to maintain her stamina, ensuring her food stayed down, and that she did not faint during her step and repeat. A light soup and crackers was her only meal early in the day, and she put her credit card on file with the *Ivory* so she could jet right away if illness caught her by surprise.

"You don't look well, girl. Maybe you should stay here and rest tonight, while I go handle the Open House," Chrissy suggested.

"No. Outsiders need to see all the old guard out in force, so they know this will not be a slam dunk for them. Especially Sheldon Rouse." Maddy inhaled, staring at Chrissy and recalling the night before. "We cannot allow personal business to distract us from this."

"Of course not. I'm the one who called you to come work, remember? How will you feel when you see Jerrell?"

"The same as when I see every other fool who's trying to cross me."

Then there was Kevin. She had also rejected his fresh invitation to arrive at the *Ivory* together. The man had no shame, but she didn't begrudge his ambition. His offer was tempting. But Maddy didn't think his idea of a children's technological playroom was strong enough. And also, she suspected he was giving Chrissy a hard time. So, Maddy planned to support another idea, from Mrs. Emma's granddaughter, to rent out high fashion dresses that would later go up for sale. Their clashing ideas would now place her and Kevin at odds. Together, they would have made an unstoppable force, but instead, each of them would work tonight's event separately, as opponents.

Hours later, after a full Saturday of work, phone calls and visits with neighbors, Maddy left the house. As she prayed to keep her nerves and nausea under control, she got into the chauffeured Cadillac Escalade that arrived to pick her up.

This evening, for anybody who questioned if the old Sag Harbor was still alive, she would send a message. For her grandmother Estaire Ellis, Mrs. Emma Vincent, and all the other ancestors who'd built this.

When she arrived, the event ushers opened her door, and Madison Page stepped out.

THE NUMBER ONE WEAPON

JERRELL

No purse.
Sans makeup.
No date or escort.
Red-bottom Christian Louboutin heels.
Not even some girlie gown.
No diamonds or pearls.

When she appeared at the threshold of the *Ivory*, the dining room held its collective breath.

A thousand cameras must have snapped for a full minute, while she stood and surveyed the entire ballroom with a cavalier, "boss lady" scowl, hands in her pockets, in a stance that might rival Clint Eastwood.

When her hand finally moved, it was to adjust the bowtie atop her $3,700.00 Tom Ford satin-trim tuxedo.

On the sidelines, the elder women of Black Sag Harbor brightened. At the sight of her, they pumped their fists, and clasped their hands together. Their mouths fell open, as their aged necks stretched to get a full, doting glance. They seemed to celebrate this young version of them as if she was their defender.

With a flick of her head, her team fell in line. All men.

Then Madison Page—granddaughter of Estaire Ellis McGee, great-granddaughter of Mayberry Ellis, and great-great granddaughter of Preston Ellis—strutted forward.

A clear wire curled over her ear, she stared straight ahead as her toned physique marched to the center staircase. She ascended without shaking hands, making eye contact with no one.

Behind her marched an army of young women, all in tuxedos. She had corralled all of the Black Hamptons.

Chrissy, her cousins Cher and Neera, and the other residents of the community, held up their chins with proud defiance. They had discharged their number one weapon. And fired a warning shot across the bow:

The Black Hamptons was still very much alive.

On the second-floor open balcony, they took position at their reserved area, where she went to work.

The debutante had indeed shown up tonight as if she was nobody's little fucking girl.

Even teenage Myles scurried along behind her, jumping every time Maddy pointed a well-manicured finger.

"Stop slobbering and start hustling." Sheldon slapped Jerrell back to life with a hard knock against his ribs.

But he couldn't. Instead, he stared at the other side of the balcony, where Kevin Middleton stood, already sizing up Jerrell.

Sheldon had told him about the fight in Chrissy's yard the night before. There was tension between Middleton and Maddy now. So neither man held the advantage.

She was Cleopatra standing between Marc Antony and Caesar.

Only one unanswered question remained.

Kevin winked.

THE REAL REASON I'M HERE

MADDY

"Every face. Don't miss a single name that's spoken. Not one. I want to know who's talking to who, where they came from, who they represent, how much they're worth, and *especially* who won't disclose their client," Maddy commanded.

"Yes, Maddy," the young high school and college students murmured, surrounding her in hopes of her blessing them with Capitol Hill internships, law school recommendation letters and other high-profile opportunities.

Her bone-straight ponytail whipped away from the crowds below, and she leaned against the balcony railing. Grateful she'd eaten hours before, there was nothing inside for her to throw up.

Maddy's eyes met Chrissy's. "How was that?"

Her longtime friend smiled. "Perfection. Now come take a seat before you give up the ghost."

Maddy shook her head. "No. I can't show any signs of weakness."

"Resting is not weak, love."

One hand in her pocket, another holding a glass of Sprite, she remained on her feet. "Yes, it is."

Adella couldn't make the trip, having to return to her job as a surgeon in Boston, among her other responsibilities she needed to manage leading up to her spring wedding. Maddy's father had not traveled from Virginia Beach for the event, but her mother circled the building and made rounds, along with other New York-based relatives from her grandmother's Ellis bloodline.

She returned to her position, from which Maddy's eagle eye zoomed in on Lana. She raised her wristwatch to her mouth and paged Myles. "Who is Lana talking to?"

"Jeremiah Briscoe. He owns a chain of spa installment companies. She's offering participation shares to bring people in."

"Excellent. Stay on her."

She turned to find Kevin approaching her.

"Kevin, I'm busy."

"So I see. Can we take a walk?" He eyed Chrissy, who didn't budge.

"What is it? Anything you have to say, you can do it in front of her."

He faced both of them. "All right, fine. Marry me."

"What?" Both Maddy and Chrissy spat at the same time.

"That's right. I want to be the father of your baby." There was no hint of humor on his face.

Pissed, Maddy closed the distance to confront him. "Let's get one thing straight. My business is none of yours." Her nail rose between them. "You know nothing. You will say nothing. To no one. And if you do, I will make sure everyone learns how you *really* got into Harvard."

"Maddy," he whispered. "Stop this. Did you see how the

room fell down, ready to worship you, the moment you walked through the door? You are a legacy, a scion, of the Hamptons, going back over a hundred years."

"You don't think I know that?"

Middleton's eyes flared like he was going to war. "Apparently not. You sure as hell didn't think about it before you slept with Rouse. If you have a baby by some... cake man who has no name, nothing to offer you—out of wedlock, no doubt! —you lose that prestige. We all know it."

"First, he's more than a cake man. He attended Brown, comes from a reputable family who's rising on Wall Street, and his business is gaining steam. It's a wonderful idea. Don't knock it just because he's only starting out. And not so fast about my stature. I've built up my own rep these last few years, aside from my family lineage."

He turned to Chrissy. "Will you please tell her, as her friend?"

Chrissy shook her head. "Have you ever known Maddy to step wrong?"

He snickered. "That's why it concerns me, what you're about to do. Mad Dog," he started again, with the name he'd used to taunt her as kids, "you might judge me as a lot of things, and fine, I probably am. But I do care about you and what happens to you. Don't throw so much away. Let me father your child, and be your husband, and we combine everything we are, to retake Sag Harbor together."

Maddy could only recall Adella, and the misery on her face the night before Christmas, of being pressured into a marriage for wealth.

She shook her head. "I see right through you. It's become a pissing match for you. Territorial. This would always give you something to hang over Jerrell's head."

"And his brother Sheldon, who you obviously hate," Chrissy added.

Maddy stroked her chin as she weighed his suggestion. "You also forget that, because I'm a legacy, if I marry him, that elevates his stature. You said so yourself the other day—time for new blood in Sag Harbor."

"But you shouldn't have to do somebody else's heavy lifting. I'm the better man, and that should be my baby you're carrying," Kevin insisted.

"You've had a decade to realize that." As she spoke the words, a liberated part of her said goodbye to her childhood, and the girlish fantasies that had fueled her foolishness in falling for the wrong guys.

Mr. Middleton's green eyes appeared gold under the warm chandelier lights. "I realize it now."

"Too late. Five years ago, maybe even one year, or six months, I might have jumped. Not now. And I won't let you hurt Jerrell." Regardless of Jerrell not speaking to her, and his crappy attitude toward her, that was between the two of them. She would not use Kevin as her proxy to attack him.

They all turned at the sound of a throat clearing.

At the edge of the balcony, Jerrell stood, his gaze pinpointing Maddy. Tall and gorgeous, the sight of him slowed the air flowing through her airways until it caught in the hollow of her throat. Warm lighting around them could have been from a Wolf Moon, its pale yellow light cresting his chocolate face. They may as well have been the only two souls alive. She did her best to quell the backflips of her heart.

Kevin's back stiffened, and he tossed Jerrell a condescending stare, as if expecting him to scram. "This is a private conversation, man."

"Which is over," Maddy concluded. She wondered how much of the exchange Jerrell had caught.

Kevin fumed, his eyes grilling her, his head swinging from side to side as would the pendulum on a grandfather clock. A silent and final warning. He might have cared for Maddy, a once-in-a-lifetime girl on which his time had finally run out.

Chrissy got up after Kevin's departure. "Good evening, Mr. Rouse."

"Chriselle." Jerrell stretched out his arms to hug her. "You look lovely in that gown."

After their embrace, she held onto his hands. "I never got to thank you for helping with my son at the Christmas town last month. People told me how you supported him. Now that I know your true talents, I may send him to you in the future." She smiled, and Maddy picked up on her friend's genuine respect and appreciation for the man.

Jerrell laughed. "It's my pleasure. I have a soft spot for tough little dudes, so if you ever have issues, I'm a phone call away."

Chrissy turned to Maddy and squeezed her arm. "I'll go make some rounds and come check on you in a few."

Jerrell shot her a playful grin. "Don't you mean my brother is waiting for you at the bar?"

Chrissy's own girlish joy burst through her lips. All of their eyes roamed downstairs to the bar, where Sheldon Rouse was indeed staring at her and waiting for her to come down. Biting her bottom lip, she gave Jerrell a little shove.

"Remember, Maddy, you've got eyes on you." Chrissy raised an eyebrow at Jerrell. "No touching. She's on my clock right now."

His eyes were already hugging Maddy. "No matter how bad I want to throw her over that rail?"

"No throwing..." Chrissy cast them both a stern eye, "... or anything else."

His head dropped, and he chuckled. "Yes, ma'am."

With that, Chrissy was off. To her own exploits with Sheldon. Maddy had never seen her friend beam so much in all their lives, even through all the school crushes and dates. And she couldn't have been happier for her girl, because after all Chrissy had been through, she certainly deserved it.

Maddy turned her attention to all of Jerrell's handsomeness. "Wow. I'm worthy of being in your presence now."

"How else will I learn how Middleton can hurt me?" He shoved his hands in his pockets, casting the net of his penetrating eyes on her. Leaning back on his heels, he waited for her answer.

Fighting not to let his presence unnerve her, she sucked in a sharp breath. "It's not important."

Jerrell moved closer, until they stood a foot apart, his gaze continuing to pick at Maddy.

"So, you're doing that thing where you strategize your moves before you give me the truth."

A smile crept onto her lips, hating the way he could read her. "I'm saying, for now, it's irrelevant—an issue for another time."

"Why don't you let me decide that?"

Maddy snickered, allowing her inner smartass out for a romp. "Because, according to some people, I enjoy devouring men's hearts during a full moon. *I love torturing you all. Makes me feel powerful.*"

He chuckled. "So, yeah, I might have said something like that."

"You *did* say it. Why are you here?" she asked, changing the subject. Her face turned serious again, and she tried to ignore how yummy his skin looked pouring out of his suit. "And by that, I mean, participating in this farce, where you and your brother think you'll take a piece of history and trash it with some backwoods beauty salon?"

Jerrell's shoulders lifted as if it were no big deal. "It's a business opportunity Shel invited me into, and I jumped on it. As would anybody."

Now Maddy was worked up. "My father brought you into Sag Harbor, set you up, and helped you make connections. As did Mrs. Emma, a bastion of this community. And this is how you repay them? By betraying its legacy and siding with outsiders against us? Is that the only reason you opened a shop here, to bring in your brother so all of you can invade our space? Have you spoken to my parents about your involvement in this and explained yourself?"

Now it was him on the ropes. "I ran across your mother, and like I told her, it's getting my company some exposure. That's it. Besides, I'm the one who's talking down Sheldon and his friends from going overboard, telling them they need to reach out to locals. If I wasn't pulling his collar, it might be worse."

Maddy clicked her teeth. "It may definitely get worse. For him. You should know that. As a courtesy, I'm warning you."

Jerrell stepped forward until she was inches from his mouth. "Consider me warned." His gaze poured over Maddy like torrential rain. "I've missed you."

There was no escaping the rain. Not this time. For one moment—just this one—she would yield. And expose her true mind to a man. "And I crave you."

Her words ignited the irises of Jerrell's eyes. Their breaths mingled in a two-step. Hands remained in their pockets, feeling the other's heat.

Tonight was a work night. Maddy recollected herself.

"Did your brother send you to distract me, while he works the room?"

"Both you and him are ridiculous," Jerrell murmured, his breath brushing her forehead. "I came to apologize. For how I treated you the last time I saw you."

She shrugged. "You wanted what you wanted. I'm kind of glad you pressured me. Had you not been around to hold up a mirror, I might be on the wrong path right now. With the wrong man."

"But I was a jerk, and I could have been more patient and understanding."

"You could have." Maddy reflected on what he said. "Or it's possible something greater was working for my good, and your impatience was part of it."

Jerrell's hands remained shoved in his pockets, as if jailing them so he didn't violate Chrissy's rule.

"Which brings us back to the real reason I'm here."

He scanned the area to ensure no one lingered, and then Jerrell's eyes became spotlights that searched her body from her toes to her scalp.

"I want to fuck you tonight."

His revelation did a swan dive down her chest, and splashed giddiness all over her.

And then uncontrollable laughter escaped Maddy's throat. The suddenness and spontaneity had come from left field.

Jerrell sucked his bottom lip, lowering his head, so their heads touched. His mouth brushed her ear. The warmth of his breaths heated all five feet and seven inches of her, until it touched her nipples and kindled a throb in her panties. The mix of forest and pastries in his scent was already screwing her nostrils.

"I want to fuck you." His lips kept teasing her ear. "And by that, I don't mean make love, or have sex, or cuddle. I mean fuck."

She was pretty sure she was too dark to blush, but whatever her blood was doing in her face right then, *no* man had ever done it before. And that wasn't the only part of her body flush with bodily fluid right then.

But most of all, she couldn't believe he was finally standing in front of her. And that she no longer had to lie in bed wishing him up.

Still, she had to shut it down and concentrate. "Stop it."

"Do you think I'm playing?"

"No." Was she really standing here... *giggling?* Still, Madison Page needed to get her head back in the game. "But you're the enemy tonight, and you are trying to distract me. I won't let you." She returned her attention to the dining room floor, still chuckling as she refocused. Even as his magnetism screwed with her imagination. "Have a good evening, Mr. Rouse."

His concentration on her intensified. "And what if I give up this business opportunity with Lana and Sheldon? Would you still view me as the enemy?"

Maddy stiffened, unable to believe what he'd just posed. "You would do that? Abandon your brother?"

"It's not abandonment. Sheldon is a big boy. He finds these investment ventures all the time. He will be fine, with or without me. But I won't be fine without you."

There was not an ounce of humor in his stare that handcuffed her.

"Let's walk."

Both of them strutted with their hands in their pockets, trying their best to look all business. The moment they found a discreet corner, he pinned her against the wall, placing his hands on both sides of her head.

Jerrell's tongue instantly slid across Maddy's lips. She opened up and pushed hers in his mouth, until they were swirling and sucking their way to a truce.

"Mm," she let out a tiny whine at the flavor of his liquor on her taste buds. A drunken ecstasy shot fire from her lips to her breasts and then crept to her navel. The volcanic heat formed a pool between her legs. Fearing the floor might cave underneath her now, she made sure her back hugged the brick wall.

They finally pulled away, their foreheads touching.

"You're kidding," she murmured.

"I'm not. These past few weeks have been hell, thinking I'd lost you to that dude." Massaging her neck, his fingers soothed her. He moved his thumb over her mouth. Maddy kissed it. The fireplace in his eyes warmed her through his thick eyelashes. "You need to know there's no beef between you and me. And I do respect your father, and Miss Emma's memory, and all this community means. Most important, I want there to be trust between us. So, if I have to show you how serious I am, yes, I'll do it."

She hadn't prepared for this.

"I can't let you do that. Your business needs this. And Mr. Rouse would never forgive you for letting a woman come between you and your brother."

"He's likely to forgive me if he knows that woman is you." His eyes twinkled. "I think dude has a crush on you."

Maddy laughed. "That's not true. He appreciates another sharp mind."

"No, Dad *likes* you. He doesn't look at Roland's wife, or Sheldon's ex-wife, that way. But the old man can kick rocks.

Because the only thing I give a damn about, is you being underneath me tonight."

The smoothness of his voice—God, how she'd missed it—was velvet sliding over her heart… and between her thighs.

"Underneath you?"

"Fine. If you want to be on top, that's cool too. As long as I wake up with that poofy hair in my face, that ass against me, and those feet rubbing on mine."

She stroked his jaw, skin, and that luscious mouth, which he opened, his tongue gliding across her fingers. The depths of his eyes might have been more vast than the night sky.

Jerrell's features turned serious. "Madison Marie Page, I love you."

He may as well have placed all the burning stars inside her. The core of her shook and Maddy's fortress crumbled. Though she'd heard it from men before, this was the first time she'd actually felt it too. Living and beating in her, and not an emotion she had to question or force.

Tears crowded her eyes, and she tried to beat them back, so they didn't ruin her makeup.

His lips kissed her cheek. "What's wrong? Why are you crying? Am I saying it too soon? It's okay if you're not there yet. I'm just telling you how I feel. I've been thinking about this for weeks. What I should have said, what I should have done, and the last time I felt this way…"

Maddy placed her finger over his lips.

Her fear, of being vulnerable to a man rattled against her ribs like a bad engine. But she made up in her mind that this was happening. Tonight, he would get the truth.

"I didn't think love was possible for me. I'm a bossy brat and I know it doesn't go over well with most guys." They both broke into joint laughs. "It was lonely, and painful. If I ever got married, I thought I would have to settle. For somebody who could tolerate me. Never was I expecting you."

Jerrell kissed her cheeks again. Then the tip of her nose. Then her forehead. His lips then moved back to hers, sucking and nibbling.

"You're my bossy brat," he whispered.

"I love you, Jerrell Isaac Rouse."

Then, Jerrell slid his hand underneath her jacket, to rest on Maddy's abdomen. "My love includes both of you."

Maddy's shock sent her eyelids fluttering faster than a hummingbird's wings. Her mouth fell. "How did you—"

He kissed her temple, his lips moving against her ear, his fingers stroking her hair.

"Maddy Cakes, you act tougher when you feel weak. The whole sidewalk incident, when you fell, you got up with this chip on your shoulder. And at the debutante dance practice, after I asked who hurt you, you came at me harder. Our fight that day in my office, you started pushing and screaming when you felt rejection. A tough exterior keeps people from seeing you're vulnerable. So, a few minutes ago, I asked myself, why would she show up here, in front of all these people, acting like an asshole and dressed as a man?" He pulled away to stare at her. "So no one will guess she's in the most vulnerable womanly state."

Maddy averted her eyes, both loving and hating how much he paid attention to her. A tear tripped down her cheek, meeting Jerrell's lips that kissed it.

He continued, "Then I watched you. You didn't think I would notice how you haven't drunk liquor tonight, or eaten a thing? You're trying to avoid throwing up."

"How would you know what was in my drink?" she pressed.

He grinned. "I gave your server a nice tip to keep me informed."

Maddy's mouth dropped.

Jerrell continued. "And you're clinging to that balcony rail like you're on the *Titanic*. The whole time, Chrissy looks nervous and won't leave your side, with her arm out to catch you. And there was no way in hell I was letting Kevin Middleton act a fool, especially not with my child inside you."

Maddy pursed her lips. "So what if I haven't eaten?"

"Girl, whenever you go out, you eat. You might be skinny, but you don't miss a meal." His eyes rolled into his head. "And, I found a broken condom in my trash back at my condo." He smiled. "I might have gotten a little carried away that one round."

"You kept that to yourself?" She scoffed.

"Just like you, I thought it was *an issue for another time*." Jerrell's eyes widened as he used Maddy's earlier words against her. "Why stress over what hadn't happened yet? I had a lot on my plate, and so did you. I figured if something had gone down, Dr. Page wouldn't let that slip."

Her upset with him evaporated in the blanket of his arms, his hand stroking her stomach, his mouth brushing her temple. Jerrell's lips calmed every one of Maddy's frayed nerves as she melted against him.

"I'm glad you're here," she said.

"Baby, I'm sorry for turning my back on you. But you and I were vibing when that guy came from nowhere, expecting people to worship him. Expecting *you* to drop everything and worship him. And for a moment, you did. I wanted to be that dude. Not because he's worth squat, but because he had your attention."

"Jerrell, I dropped everything to say goodbye to a little girl.

And the little girl fantasies that led me to be a fool for guys like him." She suppressed her nerves, not moving her eyes from his. "But my foolishness… betrayed how I really felt about you. I needed to work through that. I'm sorry I caused you to spend even a moment questioning how I felt."

A whole other world inside her panties pulsated for him when his mouth claimed hers.

"It's good we went through this, now rather than later. But I don't want to go through it again."

Maddy nodded, both her hands holding his face. They moved toward one another, their tongues swirling so that Maddy had to hold onto Jerrell for life.

Until she remembered where she was.

"I need to go. And pulverize your brother."

Jerrell's smirk was her answer. "I don't care what you and Sheldon do to each other in business. As long as when you get home, you pulverize me."

Right then, Myles paged her on her watch. "Maddy, a couple of Fortune 500 CEOs would like to meet you."

Jerrell grimaced at hearing his former employee. "So, you stole him from me, and he works for you now?"

She burst out laughing. "No, he doesn't work for me. This is a community effort, and we're all working together to take you Wall Street guys down. He volunteers at his convenience."

He sucked her lips a final time. "I'll let you get back to torching every obstacle in your path then."

She grinned. "To a crisp."

"By the way," he said, "thanks for the brown sugar. I owe you."

Maddy remembered and shook her head. "Not me. I had to give up the assignment because of your little arrangement with my dad. It's an ethics conflict. So… thanks a lot."

Jerrell's eyebrows lifted in confusion. "If not you, then who?"

"I did what you should've done. I called your dad."

He snickered. "I wish you wouldn't have. I'll never hear the end of it."

"But it saved your butt though," she shot back.

"I forgive you." As he walked backward, mischief crossed his face, and he threw her two thumbs up with a hopeful expression. "So… tonight. Fucking? Yes, no, maybe?"

Despite the smile he put on her lips—both sets of lips, up top *and* between her thighs, Maddy rolled her eyes. "Bye, Mr. Rouse."

"That means yes?"

"It means I'll think about it," she replied, unable to hide her tiny grin that gave him the real answer.

Of course, she intended to screw all the deliciousness out of him. As soon as she demolished Lana and Sheldon.

And got something to eat.

Maddy resumed her position atop the balcony.

From the floor, her co-worker Lana's eyes met hers. They traded silent threats across the room.

"How in the hell does Lana have money to play in the Hamptons?" Chrissy asked. "She's nobody down in Texas."

"I don't know," Maddy replied. "That's what I plan to find out."

A FEW HOURS LATER, at 1:30 a.m., Maddy finished plotting and comparing notes with Myles, Chrissy, Adella, and the other Hamptons residents.

Her chauffeured Escalade pulled away from the event. Unable to keep her eyes open once she stepped in the truck, her exhausted head tipped over, and Jerrell held her as she fell asleep.

The last moments of the night, he carried her through her family's doorway. Her mother pulled back Maddy's bed linens while he lay her in her bed. Before exhaustion closed her eyes again, his lips were her last vision.

"Goodnight, Maddy Cakes."

THE NEXT NIGHT...

Stumbling over each other on the way into Jerrell's Sag Harbor digs, he gripped Maddy's hair, wrapping his fingers in it, and lifting it up while sucking her neck.

Flipping her to face the door, he lifted her dress and unzipped his pants.

But she shocked him. And dropped to her knees. Turning back around, she finished the job of whipping out his dick. Maddy's eyes stared up his chest, and into his eyes, as she put his length in her mouth. She enjoyed the stunned expression on his face, while she gathered spit and started to suck.

Jerrell's jaw fell, and eyes rolled back. She inserted him until his long shaft was hitting the back of her throat, her tongue slid along his meat, and the sound gurgled in her throat.

Her man pulled out of her. "Hell, nah, Cakes. I can't take that shit right now. Get up."

He pulled her from the floor, panting like he couldn't get

inside her fast enough. He threw her face forward against the wall to finish what he'd started. She arched in time for him to thrust. Deep, hard, fearless. No fumbling or hesitation.

"Ah!" she moaned, biting her lip.

"Sorry. Are you okay?" he asked between heavy breaths, assuming he was hurting her.

"Stop babying me," she whispered. "I thought you didn't apologize."

Her heart beat so fast it begged to leave her ribcage. Her feet left the floor as he picked her up. Never in her life could Maddy have imagined a man holding her as fiercely as Jerrell held her. As if the same pent-up river of desire inside her also flowed through him.

He pushed harder. "Definitely not apologizing for what I'm about to do."

NOTHING LESS THAN A BLESSING

JERRELL

"I'm terrified," Maddy whispered.

"Don't be," Jerrell murmured back.

The heat inside Jerrell's truck curled around them, warming their bodies from the frosty, spring evening. Winter in New York City had only barely eased the freezing temperatures.

As the sun abandoned the east, dipping beneath the skyline behind them and spraying orange hues from the west, they faced Prospect Park. Where Maddy's grandmother took her, her siblings and cousins to ice skate and play.

The LeFrak ice skating rink lay ahead, where couples and families still skated. With her pregnancy now, Maddy couldn't chance going out on the ice, but skating or not, her restless mind sought the solace of this place.

He'd brought her here on the anniversary of her grand-mother's passing.

As she relived her memories, Jerrell massaged her hand, kissing it occasionally. His touch then slid to her stomach, where her baby bump was starting to tell on her.

"What will people say when I can't hide this anymore? Madison Page, granddaughter of the Ellis bloodline, got pregnant out of wedlock. What am I doing to my family's legacy?" Her lips shivered as she shared her fear. "After I've worked so hard for people to respect me."

He turned her face toward his. "Baby, your value is in who you are. No disrespect to your lineage, but you are way more than that. You shine because you're a powerhouse who works hard. The whole birthright thing is extra."

He thought of all that attracted him to her.

"When you walk into a room, and you're pregnant, own it. Your womanhood is your superpower. Wield it. The same way you've owned every other challenge that's come at you. And you've turned it into your She-ro cape."

She shifted in the seat, as if her brain was switching gears, as if she was anticipating all the ways her life might fall apart. Jerrell could almost feel the weight of her doubts.

"And what us about us?" she asked. "Me living in D.C. and you in New York? With a new business? I'm not giving up my dreams, and neither should you. How will we raise a child that way?"

Potential plans bounced in his mind, as they had for weeks.

"I was thinking you could have the baby in Sag Harbor while you take a few months of maternity leave, and I can be closer. Our mothers can help us. Then, after you go back to D.C., once the baby's here, I'll spend half a week here and half there for a while."

"Jerrell, that's crazy. It's expensive and would be so much pressure on you." Maddy's nervous eyes darted around them, and worry was etched all over her.

He squeezed her hand, bringing it to his lips. "You're worth it."

"I don't want to put you through that."

Despite all the concerns she tossed at him, Jerrell remained unfazed. "Why are you stressing?"

Maddy's gaze stretched toward the trees that were only barely in bloom. "Because we're moving fast. We haven't spent genuine time together, learning each other's faults and flaws, and all the things that could trip us up later."

Inside him, Jerrell's heart softened at seeing her so vulnerable. Madison Page, for once, didn't have all the answers. And he could comfort her, and be a pillar of strength. Finally. "Baby, tell me what's really going on."

Her eyes dipped to her lap.

Jerrell kissed her hand again. "Yes?"

"This seismic shift is about to happen. My life has always been about me. I don't know the first thing about what somebody else needs. Especially not this small, helpless little boy inside me. What if I screw it up? If I lay him down wrong? Or if I'm so exhausted from work I don't hear him crying? What if I can't pull myself out of being Maddy Page?"

He smiled. "Maddy Page doesn't screw up. Even when she screws up, she doesn't screw up. We all know that."

Both of them laughed, and he soaked up every one of her chuckles.

Still, another exhale escaped from her lips. "And in a long-distance relationship, you could be tempted. When I'm not there. Me having a child makes me... a tired mom, with less energy. And not so attractive anymore."

She sucked in a couple of big, nervous breaths, and continued, "Then you'll cheat, the way Chrissy's husband did, and my father did. Especially when you have all these young workers around you. We'll be at each other's throats, like Chrissy and Blake…"

"No." Leaning over the center console, Jerrell's head met hers, and as he tilted his to the side, he buried his face in her hair. "You became more attractive to me when I realized you were carrying my baby. I wanted you even more. I'm honored to be the man whose baby you carry. I don't take lightly what we've created. And I'm going to do everything I can to make sure I hold you up and not pull you down."

Her skepticism tripped from her chest in uneven breaths. "J, you say that now, but in a year, two years when we have a screaming toddler and we can't agree. And we're both too frustrated to hear each other…"

Jerrell collected his strength. And gathered his emotions for the reason he brought her here, on the anniversary of her grandmother's death. At this park, in this spot, Maddy had let her guard down completely with him, for the first time, at the place here she was comfortable, and she remembers her grandmother's love.

And this would be the place where Jerrell would share his whole heart with her.

But it wouldn't be easy.

"Maddy Cakes, when I was in college, and I was busy with my fraternity and school," he began, "I was playing the field. Left and right. I could have any woman I wanted because I was a young Black man at an Ivy League school. White girls, Asian, filthy rich, you name it."

He cleared a years-long lump that had gathered dust in his throat.

"But in my heart, I loved Raychelle. More than anyth—"
Maybe he shouldn't be doing this.
Could he?

The visions of Ray came back so clearly. Of her agony when she caught him in a lie… more than once. The way Ray's face had twisted like a discarded doll that he no longer loved or wanted. He very much wanted her. It was just that…

"She was an angel. Funny and sweet." Unable to sniff away his sorrow, it swelled up in his chest. The memories became reality again, fresh and present and visceral. "She got pregnant. We never told anybody. I convinced her to terminate it. I was scared of Dad…"

Now it was Maddy who leaned over and squeezed his hand with both hers.

As if it were only yesterday, he could still see the torment on Ray's face as they sat at the abortion clinic. "I told Ray we'd have plenty of time for marriage and kids. That we should just focus on graduating." The flashbacks rolled down his face in tears. "I wasn't ready for fatherhood. And I was still on some hoe mess. A few months later, Ray wasn't feeling well for a few days. We thought it was just a bug and it would pass. But out of nowhere…"

Sobs returned to him that he'd already cried when he stood at Raychelle's bedside, as she was hooked up to life support.

"Her friends took her to the hospital while I was with my boys at a game. It took me forever to get there, going through all the cars, people and traffic… The next time I saw her, she was in a coma." Anguish shook Jerrell's shoulders.

Maddy's hands gripped him as best as she could. But he could barely view her through his blurred vision.

"I couldn't talk to her. Couldn't hold her. I'd never get to apologize… tell her how sorry I was for cheating and making her cry. I swear I loved her, thought she would always be there… that I had plenty of time to straighten up and do right by her."

His body convulsed, and Maddy squeezed his upper body. Her arms clinging to him, fingers massaging his neck and face, and bringing Jerrell back.

"I didn't want to feel that ever again. This black hole she left in me, eating up everything. She loved me, and I broke her heart."

"No," Maddy whispered to him.

"I did. If anybody should be here right now, it's her and not me."

"Don't say that."

"It's true." Jerrell sniffed. "She was the best of us. So pure. I was her first. I was planning to marry her, once we graduated and got jobs, settled into life. But I took her for granted."

"You were young. I'm sure she knew you loved her."

He wiped his face. "For years, I've done a good job of not loving anybody else. Not letting any woman have that part of me. Casual dates mostly, never more than three."

His tearful gaze turned to Maddy, and he swept his fingers across her chin.

"And then I walked into Dr. Page's house, and you came down those stairs."

Through his tears, he laughed, capturing her hand and lacing his fingers through hers.

He dragged in a big breath. "With this halo of hair on your head. You had a smart mouth, but I didn't hear a word. All I saw was your heart. It was crazy, how the lights shined on you perfectly, like Raychelle was inside you. And she was forgiving me, telling me it's okay. She was saying to me, *this is her. She's the one.* It was so clear to me. The more time you and I spent, the black hole started to disappear. Ray was releasing me."

Suddenly, he opened his truck door, and got out.

"Baby, what are you--"

Jerrell came around to her side.

Opening the passenger door for a confused Maddy, sniffling back his angst, he held out his hand.

Though she had no clue why he had gotten out, without question, she took it and followed him.

Jerrell continued, "I prayed. Not a day went by while you and I were mad, that I didn't pray."

He placed her gloved hand between his, as he walked her toward the ice-skating rink.

"When you showed up at the *Ivory*, after I found that condom in my trashcan, I knew you were pregnant. In my soul, I just knew it was Ray forgiving me. And blessing us. I'll never think anything different."

Jerrell shook his head, staring down at Maddy. "No, sweetheart, I don't believe my love for you is a hardship. Or that our baby is a burden or an inconvenience. He's a blessing. One that I will never, *ever* take for granted."

He kissed her hair, and Maddy melted against him. Their arms clung to one another, as they kept walking in the area where they shared their second kiss. Where her grandmother had encouraged her to stay focused and keep her balance.

"You're right," Jerrell said. "We haven't known each other for years, or dated for long, but I have this sense that everything in my life right now is coming together at the right time, as it should. With my business, and you, and now our child. And I'll fight like hell for all of it, with everything I have in me."

They hugged one another tight as they arrived at the rink.

But Maddy still had concerns. "That's the most precious thing anybody's ever said to me. I'm almost afraid to love you.

This might be too good to be true. Jerrell, baby, you and I haven't really talked much."

He grinned in response. "That's probably the best part."

Turning her toward him underneath a chilly, tangerine evening sky, he kissed her forehead.

"You weren't telling me the truth anyway, or even being truthful with yourself. You were protecting your heart with this mental wall you built to keep guys out. The same wall I've had. Instead of listening to you, I paid attention. To all the little ways you react under pressure, to the real Madison Page, the good, the bad, and the ugly."

A chuckle escaped Jerrell, and Maddy joined in.

He continued, "And let's not forget the crab boil. *Would that be your tacit admission?*" He said, mocking her. "Girl, I wanted to strangle your ass."

Maddy now erupted with her amusement, before they quieted down and she pulled his face toward her. Her tongue licked his until Jerrell's rib cage seemed about to burst with fullness.

She inhaled, and her eyes seemed to search for her truth now. "You were right. I wanted you to be a bad person, so I could have an excuse not to fall and to go on being untouchable. You're a special man. Stubborn, but special." She exhaled and her lips shook while she spoke. "How awesome you are… scared me. The way you see through me… scares me. You're all the man I've ever wanted, and that scares me."

Jerrell heard the fear in her voice that trembled like a candle. "Strangely enough, you help me see more clearly. I'm rarely so certain about anything as I am about us."

"But will you say that when I'm busy and preoccupied on the Hill, and life gets crazy?" she pressed.

"Girl, I'll be cheering you from the rooftops. Louder than

your grandmother did! *Look at my baby on t.v.* And if I only see you once a year, that one time will be worth waiting for. There is nobody else walking this Earth I'd rather endure crazy with."

He circled his nose around hers, his gloves cupping her neck, before his lips rained kisses on her cheek, jaw, neck and back to her temples, covering his Maddy Cakes with his heart.

He watched her close her eyes, as if she still processed her whole soon-to-be-mommy list of worries.

Her hands stroked his chest over his sweater, lighting up his desire for her.

"You've opened me up, Jerrell Isaac Rouse. I'm all yours and my heart is in your hands. Please don't drop it."

Laying his lips against her hair, he whispered, "Do you trust me?"

She shook like a newborn foal, and the tear sliding down her face may as well have been rolling over him.

"I'm so scared. I don't want us to hurt each other."

"Do you trust me?" he asked her again.

Maddy nodded.

"You swear?"

Maddy nodded again, her eyes pressed tight, as more tears seeped through them. "Yes. I trust you."

"You are my queen. And I would like you to be my crown jewel. If you'll have me."

Her eyes were still closed, and confusion swept Maddy's face. "What?"

An earthquake of emotion rocked Jerrell, shaking his next words. "I'm asking you to be my wife. To marry me, Madison Marie Page. And give me the honor of making you Madison Rouse."

When Maddy opened her eyes again, Jerrell watched the astonishment freeze her face.

The lights had gone out in the skating rink. A single spotlight shined on the two of them. Candles began coming toward them. Held by their families, friends, and her grandmother's close friends.

Jerrell lowered himself to his knee, and shook as he pulled out the large yellow Harry Winston diamond ring. His father had helped him get it.

Maddy's hands covered her mouth. "Oh…"

"I know how important this night is for you. And how much your grandmother shaped you, gave you your fondest memories right here. So, I would be remiss if I didn't have her with us when I acknowledge all that you are."

He took her hand.

"Baby, you're not alone. You weren't alone then, and you're not alone now. I'm here. If you want to be alone, I'll respect that and it'll hurt me. But I would much rather be with you." He swallowed. "And for us to be partners, and conquer the world together."

He watched Maddy gaze at the people she loved—her parents, Chrissy, her siblings, and a few of her grandmother's friends from Sag Harbor—and he could have sworn she was swaying with the emotion.

"My dad's not pressuring you?"

He chuckled. As did everyone around them. "First, nobody can pressure me. And second, *I* had to convince *him* that I've got this, and this is right for us. You are indeed his child." He kissed her hand. "But no matter what, you're mine now. And I will not drop you." His eyes caressed hers. "So are you going to make me ask a thousand times?"

Maddy's mouth fell open. "I love you a thousand times.

You're my king. And it would be my honor to become your wife."

Jerrell slid the ring on her finger, stood up and pulled his true diamond into his arms. The black hole that had been eating at him for a decade, closed.

SHENANIGANS

FOR FUNSIES

EPILOGUE

Maddy and Jerrell entered the *Little Italy* restaurant, linked hand in hand, and he searched for their families. Tonight, they would tell their folks about the baby.

"They must not be here yet," she said. "Let's go ahead to the table. We're still a little early, so I'm sure they'll be here any moment."

He didn't notice the calculating grin creep across Maddy's face.

"We should probably be patient and wait for them."

"No, it's fine. I'm hungry," she said, pulling him to the table she'd reserved.

"You're always hungry."

"And now it's time for you to feed me." They sat down, and the waiter arrived to take their drink and appetizer orders.

Kami was the first to arrive, and with her came Maddy's friends, Chrissy and Adella.

He stood up to greet them, but Maddy remained seated, sipping her water and trying not to laugh.

His sister gave him a big hug. "Hey, little brother, you don't have to stand. Tonight's your special night. Sit down."

Confused, Jerrell sat. Kami wrapped her arms around him, from behind, squeezing him and pulling his arms backward. Chrissy hurried next to her with rope, and flung it over him, while Adella gripped his wrists and tied them together.

Realization dawned on him, as to what was happening. He squinted at Maddy, while she sipped her drink.

"Kam, I can't believe you're participating in this," he said, rolling his eyes. "Okay, maybe I can."

Kam squeezed his shoulder. "This is way better than Beyoncé   tickets."

Maddy brought her seat closer, so she faced him. In her hand, she held a bowl of buttery lobster drenched in garlic sauce. The same dish he'd eaten that snowy night at the hotel.

"Jerrell Isaac Rouse, graduate of Brown University with a BS degree in… well BS, really. Since that's all you guys do over there—tweak numbers and cookbooks." She swiped his cheek with the lobster. "MBA from Columbia. Treasurer and Step Master in Alpha Beta Kappa fraternity." She swiped his lips. Jerrell licked them with a smile. "Top Forty Under Forty Young Business Leaders in New York." Her elegant, unblemished fingers rubbed his chest. "ASG President at Brown. Martin Luther King Scholarship Recipient. Summa Cum Laude graduate."

She held the lobster to his lips. "Open up."

Tickled, his eyes twinkling and heart full, Jerrell did as he was told.

Maddy swiped his jaw.

"You're hotheaded. And often act without thinking first or

planning accordingly." She intentionally brushed his chin and jaw with more food. "You're the baby in your family and often get frustrated that you live in your older siblings' shadows. And your father's."

She leaned toward him and sucked his cheek. As she leaned over Jerrell, her dress bodice displayed her growing breasts and the baby bump that made her even more provocative to him.

"So you take it out on the world." She moved to the other cheek. "You don't want to be perceived as weak or inadequate. That's why you rarely apologize." Her tongue licked his chin, setting him on fire. "You lost your only love a long time ago. To lupus." Her soft lips touched the exposed skin over his turtleneck, shooting an electric charge through him. He needed to get out of these ropes. "And in your eyes, no woman could ever fill her shoes. So you played them all." Maddy rose again so they were face to face, and Jerrell could look nowhere else but into her endless sienna eyes.

"And nevertheless, I love you."

Jerrell's insides shuddered every time he heard her say it.

Maddy sucked his lips, her finger stroking his jaw, and he kissed her back with an ocean of love swelling inside him for her.

"I love you too, baby," he murmured.

"I know," she said with a devious smile. "And I look forward to all the ways you'll show me."

With that, she grabbed her purse and walked away from the table, leaving him tied to his chair.

He wiggled around, helpless and unable to move.

"Maddy?" He jerked around. "Kam?"

He chuckled, leaning back in the seat, realizing none of them would free him. And his parents were not coming.

This wasn't the real baby announcement.

It was payback. The entire restaurant had cleared out.

"Y'all are going to pay for this. Maddy!"

* * *

Reactions to the baby announcement

Maddy's father

He froze, staring at Jerrell. "I thought you were only talking to her about sugar."

Squirming, Jerrell replied, "Well, sir, the conversation went a little deeper than we expected."

Long side-eye. "Clearly. Way deeper."

Jerrell blinked, shaking his head as he realized what her father really meant. "Oh, no, sir. It didn't get *that* deep though."

"But my daughter is pregnant. So it must have. Gone deep."

Jerrell rubbed his face.

Jerrell's father

At the dining room table, he looked past his son. And turned to one of his favorite people in the world, Madison Page. "I thought you were smarter than this."

Maddy hung her head. "I know, sir. I thought I was too."

At that statement, Jerrell glared at her, pushing her under the table.

Mr. Rouse held out his arms. "Awe, sweetheart, I'm so sorry. We all make mistakes. Come here."

Jerrell shook his head. His hand pushed Maddy back in her seat. "No, Dad, that's okay. She doesn't need anymore hugs."

"But she's carrying my progeny inside her," Mr. Rouse insisted.

"No. She's carrying *mine*."

Maddy's sister Reet

"Tehe. You little whore. You spent all those years being perfect, just so you could get knocked up."

Sherman, Maddy's casual sex partner in D.C.

"So… does this mean you and I won't be… hooking up anymore?"

EXCERPT FROM BOOK 2— HOT CHOCOLATE THIS WINTER

CHRISSY & SHELDON

CHRISSY

"*E*xcuse me?" Chrissy asked the person on the other side of the counter. She suppressed her growing irritation. She would not give her audience the pleasure of hearing her voice elevate one decibel. Besides, Chrissy could easily convey her point with a raised eyebrow.

The bank officer in heavy makeup spread her strawberry red lips into a fixed smile. "I said, Mrs. Mason, I regret to inform you that your ability to use the account has been frozen."

"I'm sure that's not what you intended to say," Chrissy replied, letting her thumb glide across her sharp nails in a veiled message. "What you meant to say was, now that you've seen my ID, you will give me access to my account immediately, before I call my close friend, who is the Regional Vice President. In case you're not aware of your bank's structural hierarchy, that would be your boss's boss."

The bank officer appeared as if she had sucked on vinegar. The woman did not back down.

"I'm afraid the only way you can regain this account is with an order from a judge, or with special authorization from our regional office. My boss would tell you the same thing."

Ugh! That damn Blake. He had frozen her out. Chrissy and Blake had agreed they would not touch the children's account, as a condition of keeping their marital differences out of court. How had he done this? Without a judge?

"I never received lawful notice of this freeze on my funds. You all should have informed me. Therefore, statutory notice compliance is lacking. I request you respect my legal rights. And because you have not, I'd like an explanation from your regional Vice President." Chrissy seethed.

Where did Blake get off? Her estranged husband's domination and control tactics rivaled those of any zookeeper. Of course Blake was not answering the phone.

Two minutes later, the associate returned with the branch manager, for whom Chrissy had no time.

"Mrs. Mason, we apologize for the inconvenience today," the branch manager with a bad comb-over said. "Unfortunately, we have spent quite some time looking into the situation, and this is a unique hold on the account. We have no say in the matter. I believe you are going to need an attorney. You should have received some papers."

"But I received nothing."

"You are correct. You should call the regional office. Here is the number, as it involves higher authorizations we do not have access to."

She ignored the piece of paper. Enough heat and electricity might have boiled in her eyes that they could bolt out lightning.

When she turned around in her Carolina Herrera burgundy suit and pink pearls, a small waiting area of other high-income account holders sipped their complimentary coffee and wore sympathetic fake smiles.

Ensuring that she glided and did not stomp, Chrissy began her humiliating exit several long yards to the door. Already, she wondered how the conversation with Blake would play out, and which version of her husband she would get this time — the relentless devil, or charming liar. How much longer would she let this go on, before she finally went before a judge?

"Excuse me," a male voice said behind her. "Hold up. Wait."

Great. The deep baritone indicated an ambitious brother, perhaps overly confident in himself. This was all she needed right now, a dude who thought he would shoot his shot simply because he had a black credit card. She kept strutting.

"Mrs. Mason, is that her name?" the male voice asked in a low tone, as if speaking to someone else, and then to her. "Ma'am, have you changed your mind about your account?"

Chrissy stopped in her tracks. Her Prada shoes pivoted to face a dapper pair of Berluti Scrittos, underneath a crisply lined Ermenegildo Zegna wool mohair suit, topped with a silk square tucked in his breast jacket pocket. A set of teeth smiled at her that could light up the Times Square ball on New Year's, not to mention a bald head, shaved clean enough for fingers to skate across. But he must have been some years older than her, with flecks of salt-and-pepper whiskers winking at her from his goatee.

"Um..." she started, taken aback to find this steaming cup of hot chocolate appear from nowhere.

"Your account?" he repeated. "I can probably help you with that. Come on. Let's open it up."

Open it up?

This gentleman's long legs took off, brushing past the astonished branch manager and the branch officer.

The manager objected "But sir, no one may gain access to—"

"I'm well aware of the rules, Martin. Thank you very much," the Christmas dessert declared in an unbothered tone that gently chided them to fuck off. As they proceeded, her eyes dropped to the sculpted ass strolling toward the largest corner office in the bank. Once inside, photos on the desk displayed a smiling, picturesque family belonging to the same Martin that had just shaded her. Mr. Christmas Delight closed the door to Martin's office. "Coffee?"

"No, thank you. I'm trying to quit," she confessed, nearly forgetting why she was there. *Blake who?*

Within moments, this handsome stranger was inside Chrissy's account. "Oh, you share this account with someone. Maybe your parent? But then, you are quite confident, so I'm guessing not a parent. Your spouse."

She linked her hands together, trying not to let his velvet voice wrap around her. Chrissy remembered to focus. "Wow, you have apparently done this a few times before."

"Not really," he replied with an easy smile. "I build the bank's technology. So I'm aware of procedures for freezing an account. I overheard you say that you never received notice. One should have automatically gone out," he noted as he continued to type.

Christy watched aghast at the big red letters crossing the screen, with blocked access and blurred lines that prevented her from seeing the status of her and Blake's joint funds. His fingers moved deftly, as if he did this in his sleep.

"I'm sorry, sir, but who are you? And why couldn't the branch manager do all this?" she asked.

"Because the branch manager's job is to run the branch, and my job is to know the bank system's infrastructure," he answered with yet another Times Square-illuminated ball drop of a smile. "My name is Sheldon Rouse."

She breathed a quiet sigh of relief. "I appreciate you coming by when you did, Mr. Rouse. Wherever you came from."

"I see what your problem might be. This is strange. I'll need to investigate it. Seems we sent you a letter to a 43586 Bedford Avenue, Los Angeles. Ah! Ladera Heights. Black Beverly Hills," he laughed. "I've got a few friends in that area."

The heat of potential humiliation rose from Chrissy's chest and crawled up her neck and face. She prayed her expression did not betray her fear of more gossip.

Mr. Rouse stopped laughing soon as his eyes met hers.

Damn. So much for keeping a good poker face.

He cleared his throat. But rather than returning to the screen in an awkward moment, his gaze deepened. "Not to worry. Our clients' circumstances remain confidential. However," he said as he turned his attention back to her account, "there may be an issue of who in our bank approved this. I will dig around some more to see if there's a court order somewhere. If not, this action was unauthorized, and I'll be happy to restore your access to the account."

Chrissy reeled. "Unauthorized freeze? So if there was no court order, how could this have happened?"

"That's what I plan to find out. In the meantime, I am going to recommend someone back in L.A., whom you might want to contact." With that, his elegant, well-moisturized fingers scribbled out a name and a phone number. "One of my good college classmates out there takes care of bullies with her eyes closed."

The thick, ivory parchment paper had bad handwriting on it, drawing a snort from Chrissy at the man's chicken scratch. "I'm guessing your degree was clearly not writing."

Laughter flowed easily from deep in his gut, and she imagined what that gut must've looked like.

His relaxing smile returned. "And now my technology salary makes up for the handwriting fail." He got up to open the door for her. "Either I or someone from our team will be in touch with you. I was just on my way out. Let me get you my card."

They headed back toward the front of the branch. The original bank officer's eyes escaped everywhere they could to avoid Chrissy's glare.

Not that Chrissy was interested to stare any place than Mr. Rouse's fetching derriere, anyway.

After grabbing his briefcase, he whipped out another fine, parchment business card with beautiful raised lettering.

Sheldon Rouse

Chief Technology Officer

Executive Management

It listed three different phone numbers, including his cell and direct line.

"I will try to contact you in twenty-four hours. But don't hesitate to use it if I don't get back to you before then," he said, waving goodbye to the bank employees and then holding open the exclusive backdoor entrance for her.

Chrissy almost hated to leave. On the way out, she caught

a whiff of woodsy, rich cologne that placed her inside a cabin in the mountains.

"Thank you. I appreciate your being there today," she replied, concentrating on her step so she didn't lose it.

"And likewise. Not too often I see our people walking through that door. Glad I happened to be in the building when I was."

When she turned to wish him a Merry Christmas, she noticed his eyes leap up from her hips. A self-conscious grin spread across his lips in a subtle acknowledgment she had caught him. Somewhere inside her heart, and perhaps between her legs, a gush of warmth lightened her mood. She still had it.

Chrissy managed to hold in her appreciative snort this time. "You enjoy a Merry Christmas, Mr. Rouse."

"And you try to also, Mrs. Mason, despite the circumstances."

They went their separate ways as she headed to the guest parking and he toward the employee spots.

She wondered if it was safe to peek at him one more time, but her phone vibrated in her purse.

Her mother. "I know you said you wouldn't go, but come to the debutante ball with me this weekend. I don't want Neddy Watkins yapping all night."

Chrissy winced, irritated at her last shot of Mr. Rouse being interrupted.

"Mom, there's a lot going on right now." She rattled off every excuse, any excuse, so *she* wouldn't suffer three hours of boring upper class diamond-flinging, fur-swinging, and car-parading.

"Chrissy, please. You've been absent from Sag Harbor for years. People want to see you."

"No, Mom, you are showing off your daughter who was recently in the *Wall Street Chronicle*." Her mother would not pull any fast ones on her.

"And? Can you blame me for being proud? You're finally making something of yourself after all these years of letting Blake do the heavy lifting," the old goose clucked from her end.

Ouch. The words stung. But the woman was not wrong. Now, more than ever, though she longed to hide out in remote shopping boutiques and nail bars, Chrissy needed to be front and center. Strong and vibrant, rather than cowering to Blake in fear of drama he might bring.

"Alright. Find me a dress and I'll pick it up?" Chrissy asked.

As she drove through the bustling streets of her beloved New York City she missed so much, her thoughts drifted back to the tall chocolate bar she'd just met. A tiny twinge of disappointment twisted her chest. Like most corporate types at big companies, he'd probably never call her again.

SHELDON

Sheldon let out a tense breath as he settled behind the wheel of his Maybach.

Before starting his car, he took a moment to shake off the memory of a womanly waist enclosed in a single-breasted pantsuit that flared out at the hips, teasing a very voluptuous posterior.

Poised, well put together, and calm, Chriselle Mason had almost snuck by him.

But standing in the exclusive section of the branch reserved for high-net worth clients, her stiff-armed stance showed she was reaching a boiling point. At which damn near every Black woman prepared to go off, without the poor person in front of them having a clue. He'd initially jumped in to rescue the branch officers. But once Sheldon sat down with Mrs. Mason, her tense smile screamed she needed saving herself.

Even the most successful bank clients rarely got his attention, regardless of what country they visited from, what job they did, or which celebrity they hosted at their homes. Sheldon had done and seen it all the last fifteen years, from the White House, to The Met Museum, the Kodak Theatre, Buckingham Palace and the Taj Mahal.

And yet, here in the plain old bank waiting room, a precious ruby had snagged his eye.

His phone vibrated with a text message from his younger sister, Kamilah.

Kamilah: *This Saturday night. We're going to support Jerrell. Oasis Cove, Sag Harbor, @ 7 p.m.*

Irritated, Sheldon texted her back. *Busy. It's the weekend after Xmas. Why? What is that?*

He got a final response.

Kamilah: *Cancel. Debutante ball. Family table.*

Sheldon sighed. Same eye-watering social functions, different day. He was happy for his little brother starting his own business, but he wanted to relax after all the Christmas engagements.

While he had the phone in his hand, he called up his ten-year-old son in Chicago. Though Hadar spent most of the year with his mother, they still alternated holidays and Eugenia got Christmas this year. He should have been at his grandmother's house playing video games. The phone rang continuously. Sheldon tried two more times.

"Hello?" a deep male voice finally answered, stunning Sheldon.

"Um, yeah, I am Hadar Rouse's father. With whom am I speaking?" he asked, suppressing his fury.

"Don't matter who I am, man. Hadar's not here right now. I'll tell Genie you called."

"Well, where is my s—"

Click.

Sheldon had a mind to get on a plane and go see for himself what that woman was doing in his son's presence. But if he did so, she'd jump at the chance to haul him before the judge court and request a modification of visitation. He was too close to going for shared custody next year, and didn't want to give Genie a confrontation she could use to strengthen her hand. Hadar was getting older, and within a couple of years, Sheldon expected his son to soon tell the court for himself that he wanted to return home to New York.

Steaming, Sheldon headed to the next branch on his list of visits that afternoon. Another surprise check-in. Pressing more flesh. Meeting new starry-eyed tech boys who had taken the bank job with fantasies of Silicon Valley. More bank tellers batting their eyes, "accidentally" showing off their cleavage, and leaving their numbers and social media handles inside their printed reports.

The second-oldest of Charles and Verona Rouse's children had literally. Seen. It. All.

As he wondered which houses he'd hit up for Christmas, the phone rang again. Looking at the name, he hesitated to answer.

"Hey," he said, hoping he sounded as upbeat as he intended.

"Hey yourself," his girlfriend's voice greeted him from the other end. "I don't hear you outside among ocean waves, near seagulls, or in the dead quiet with snow somewhere. So you're still here in town."

He cringed. "Yeah, yeah, but I'm doing a lot with family. On my way to pick up my nieces from school and I'll take them to buy a few things for Christmas. And then I'll kick it with fam for the next few days." So it was partially true. He wasn't due to get the girls until tomorrow. But after hearing another man's voice on his phone, tonight he wanted to stew alone.

"You sure have been busy lately. Anything I should worry about?" she asked. "My bath tub has missed you these past few weeks."

"You know how crazy things get during the holidays, with employees leaving town and I have to cover. Then the family gets super needy."

His parents could have cared less where he was. Sheldon wasn't their first son, with all the responsibility and the perfect family setup. And he wasn't the last son that pissed everyone off. Sandwiched in the middle, Sheldon was more the forgettable, call-at-the-last minute child.

"Well, just don't forget that certain other people need you too. Speaking of family, mine would like to meet you. Annnnd," she paused, and Sheldon braced himself, "I was wondering when you would introduce me to yours."

He sighed, swallowing, staring out the window and the humming downtown traffic before he squeezed into it. How did he lie his way out of this one?

"Hmph," she scoffed after several seconds of discomfort. "That certainly is not a good sign. Sheldon, if there is something you have to say to me, I really wish you would just tell me."

As she said the words, he entered the grid-locked New York City traffic that seemed to represent his life. "I thought I already did, Darian. You know how I feel."

"Actually, I don't. We've been together almost a year. You said at first that you didn't want your ex-wife to find out about significant others. Then, you told me you weren't over the divorce and losing your son, and it's hard for you to trust. Now the job is taking a lot out of you. Let me grab a pen so I can mark on my calendar when you'll be ready to move us to the next level. What day will it be, Sheldon? You tell me."

He swallowed. "Baby, I cannot lie to you." Sheldon considered Darian more of a little sister or a close friend than wife material. Sweet, loyal, and hopeful. Like a pet. Someone to keep him company, until the person came along who would… he wasn't sure.

A small, muffled cry vibrated across his car speakers via the Bluetooth. Why did so many women take a man saying he was unsure to mean they could change him?

"I have to go," she said. "I have a family of my own that needs me for Christmas."

But laced within her words was the wishful tone, hoping he would stop her.

"You have yourself a good Christmas if we don't talk, baby, okay?" Sheldon wouldn't string her along for the convenient sex. She deserved better. Especially at thirty-four. Up to this point, she'd chosen to stay. But over the last couple of months, her demands had grown from a whisper to a roar. If she stayed now, he would be reduced to telling her lies. And he couldn't. Even if her leaving came with a little lonesomeness.

Another shriek, this time not so muffled.

Click.

A tiny pain shot through his heart. But if a woman was with him, he held out no false promises. She would likely text him next week.

That left one final call to make. A conversation he'd longed for all day.

"Mr. Rouse, you're still working two days before Christmas," his secretary greeted him.

"I live on the clock, Lela. You know that. Could you be a dear and patch me through to that one client, Chriselle Mason? That'll be my last business of the day. Standard drill. Answering service is to call me if any issues pop up. Thank you and your Christmas gift should arrive in the morning."

Lela patched him through. The delay that afternoon hadn't been necessary. Sheldon could have resolved Mrs. Mason's issue easily that morning.

But he'd chosen not to.

"Hello, this is Chrissy," a nonplussed voice answered on the other end. He could hear the tired, motherly drag in her tone, as if she expected bad news.

"Yes, Mrs. Mason. Mr. Rouse here. Bank of New England calling you back."

"Oh," came a new energy. It sounded as if she was shuffling, maybe getting up.

"I hope I don't have poor timing."

"Of course not."

"So, I spent more time wrapping my head around your issue. And I've straightened out your account status."

"You did?" Her tone perked up more.

"Yes, although I'm afraid you'll have to watch the account, in case this person you're dealing with asks to change the code on it again. I placed a note in the system that no one should touch this. But your co-holder may try this again later," he posed. Why did he kind of feel heroic at the moment?

"Oh, my goodness. Thank you so much. But do you know why the bank is restricting my access without a judge?"

Sheldon bit his bottom lip. He definitely had a theory, but wanted to deal with that part himself. "I'm not sure. There could be a ton of reasons that banks authorize a freeze. And it's unclear what the employee conducting the transaction may have known. It's what I plan to investigate. But for now, I hope getting your access back helps some."

"Absolutely it will. I really appreciate your assistance." She paused, as if having more to say. "And I'll also connect with this divorce attorney you've provided."

Sheldon hadn't told her it was a divorce attorney, so Mrs. Mason must have already looked her up. "No problem." Intrigue sat on the tip of his brain, imagining those luscious thighs on the other end, what she was wearing over them. Where were they sitting? Or lying. "You have yourself a nice Christmas… Mrs. Mason."

A pause, as if she didn't want to hang up.

Sheldon smiled, recalling her suck her bottom lip, as she had sat on the edge of her chair nervously at the bank.

"You too, Mr. Rouse," her voice said, having dropped to a sultry murmur that warmed his flesh.

He sat back in his seat.

As he did, a text from Darian came through his phone. Make that several texts of angry pleading and vitriol, intermittent, one after the other, all for which Sheldon had gotten too old.

Stopping himself from redialing Chriselle Mason,

ignoring Darian's incoming calls, Sheldon headed to his next destination—an empty house.

When he arrived, at the end of the litany of texts from Darian, was a lone text.

From Mrs. Mason: *Can't tell you how helpful that was. You didn't have to. Don't know where you came from, but you're the guardian angel before Christmas. Thanks again.*

Christmas sweetness melted through Sheldon's chest. She was thinking of him too.

WHO MAKES THE NEXT MOVE? Chriselle or Sheldon?

THANKS FROM LULA

Thank you for reading *Sag Harbor Black Romances*! If you enjoyed this story, please leave a review at your favorite retailer.

If you were feeling the Rouse family and the characters in Sag Harbor, here's how you can stay connected.

Web site: www.lulawhitebooks.com

Email: lula@lulawhitebooks.com

Join Lula's Luxe Suite Reading Group:

www.facebook.com/lulawhitelounge

Read the stories before they go on sale:

www.patreon.com/lulawhite

Lula's stories are available weeks to months in advance as she writes them on her Patreon.

Books In The *Sag Harbor Black Romances*

Brown Sugar This Christmas - Maddy & Jerrell

Hot Chocolate This Winter - Chrissy & Sheldon Part 1

Flinging All Spring - Adella & Desmond

Overheated for Summer - Chrissy & Sheldon Part 2

Rouse Family Christmas - All Couples

Books in the Sag Harbor spin-off series *Explore Men of the Hamptons*

Explore You - Kevin & Cher

One Tasty Night - Solomon & Chaitra

Taste You - Solomon & Chaitra

Drink You - Lion & Kamila

See Through You - Keenan & Eugenia

Find You - Roland & Neeraja